# A Stem Full of Thorns

### *The Unicorns*

Lord' Williams

# To Some Very Special People

This novel has been a long time in the making, and I know so many of my readers thought this sequel would never see the light of day, and for that, I apologize, and I feel a short explanation is due. Just before the publishing of *Shadows of the Heart*, I was diagnosed with Type 2 Diabetes, suffering with carpal tunnel syndrome, and awaiting surgery on my hand.

Between the publishing of the two books, I have undergone many surgeries, been hospitalized a number of times, developed sleep apnea, and uncovered a hypothyroid condition, but, you—my readers—kept me writing even when it was painful to do, and re-do because my mind could not focus long enough to produce a page. It was you who pushed me, and kept me treading to the completion of this novel, and I would like to say, thank you!

First, all the glory goes to my Heavenly Father, Eilohem, and much love and thanks to my wife.

To Anita Burns who will always be special because she was the very first person, who purchased my novel, *Shadows of the Heart*, and my short stories.

To Teresa Benton and Karen Talbert, as well as Teresa's daughters, Shawn and Shay, who I would have to classify as No.1 Fans, because between them they sold hundreds of copies of *Shadows of the Heart*, just because they thought the book was that damn good.

To Ms. Charles, Ms. Lane, Mr. Johnson, and Ms. Starks who would ask, at least once a week, for the last four plus years, "Have you finished the book yet?"

To Ms. Cherry, Ms. James, their daughters, Josephine Cherry and Mandy James, who stayed on my behind, and made me grow a tale!

To all my co-workers for their love and support like Ms. Kecia S. and Ms. K. Cosby, and no Ms. Jordan, no one got pregnant.

To Valerie Ragin-Daniels who threatened me harm if a certain character died.

Last, but certainly not the least, to my son-in-law, Reggie Lorde-Gray, for his inspiration and for selling hundreds of copies of *Shadows of the Heart*.

Much thanks and gratitude goes out to Debra Owsley of Simply Said Reading Accessories, Ella Curry of EDC Creations, and to Author/Publisher Jessica Tilles. I know I didn't call, I missed many events, and all sorts of gatherings, please forgive me, and know that you are in my heart, and that you are meaningful to me.

To Mrs. Pricilla Roach, my co-worker, my editor, my friend. I miss you. We miss you every day. May your earthly remains R.I.P. May your spirit shine bright and continue on.


Of One.

# Rock Wit U

*P*ointing and stretching her toes, she molded herself deeper into his large frame. She always felt secure wrapped in his arms. Squeezing and kissing the back of her neck, she arches her back to push her large ass against his crotch. The evening was beautiful, they ate, she talked about her day, and he apologized over, and over again. They lay on the couch watching the last two episodes of *The Matrix Trilogy* on DVD. They haven't spoken a word about him. It helped a lot not to mention his name, as she wasn't in the mood to deal with his insecurities.

Rubbing her stomach and playing with her belly button, his hand slowly massaged its way down a little further, further, and further. She licked her lips, and rubbed his thigh with greater intensity. He could feel her body heat rise, signaling to him that she was ready for him. She desired him. She wanted it. It had been a while since their last union; long enough to have him masturbate several times during her absence. His manhood came to life, and she used her large, round ass to massage it into a fully erect organ. He pushed his left index finger between her lips, and she sucked it, then another and she accommodated it. Her tongue teased his fingers, while her soft slurps and short moans whispered obscenities to his erection with the bobbing of her head and gentle suckle.

Only wanting to please him, she wanted to assure him of her love for him, so he would know that her past was far behind her and with no regrets. She never wanted her man to worry about another man, especially where it would cause him to become fickle, insecure, or unsure about her. Her free hand found its way down into his jeans, into his boxers, and around his member while she sucked on his fingers, as he sucked her left earlobe.

Their breathing was labored, the heat was hot, their humidity climbed to a hair wrecking point and she just got this perm put in a day ago. She turned around, grabbing his face with both hands, and kissed his mouth. "Baby, rock me. I want you to rock my boat from the bowel to the stern, and then water my deck all over."

He jumped up from the couch and walked over to the entertainment center. The CD changer was prepared and programmed earlier with her favorite tunes. He pressed play. R. Kelly's *TP-2.com*, "Strip for You," filled the dark living room. He lit the large, Jasmine-scented candle on the end table next to the sofa's right side, before lighting the cherry blossom-scented candle on the end table next to the sofa's left side.

Standing before her, he twisted his body rhythmically from side to side, and slowly raised his T-shirt over his head to let the flickering light from the candles dance upon his brown, caramel-colored skin. The motion from the ripples of his abs, and the bulge from his chest caused her ocean to stir. She removed her blouse, as he started to unveil his lower half. She had no patience, as she pounced to the floor, and reared up on her knees; it had been too long since she drew on his pipe. He began to sing a tune, which caused her to wonder, who would be putting out whose fire? The thought intensified her blaze. Pushing him, she swept at his feet, he fell backward, she lifted her skirt to her waist, pulled her thong to the side, placed her hands around his thick neck, applied pressure, and straddle him.

Big, wide, and round, her behind started to descend, circling around the tip of his head; she dazzled him.

"Round and around your pole-ly, is my pocket feelin' cozy? Talk to me, Kevin. How do I feel, baby? Is it wet, baby? Am I wet enough for you? Is it tight enough, baby? Do I fit like a glove? Oh, Kevin. Baby? Oh. Damn, baby, handle it. That's it. That's it, baby. Oh, my lover. Handle it, baby."

Never hearing Kevin's replies, Dana was in her own groove, for this session he was an end to her means. Her rhythm was steady, her thrust was medium, her stride was fueled by the sound of Ashanti's "Rock with Me" until the sound of her coochie smacking against Kevin caused an Atlanta burning in her groove zone.

The last few weeks had been trying. Her company was undergoing some tribulations—unforeseen problems with no warnings of any kind—ranging from electrical failures to break downs of the machinery to losing nearly one-fourth of her trucking fleet. She understood every business suffered through some kind of a bad spell, but this was too much, too fast. Hell, she grew her company from the ground up. Great sacrifices of blood, sweat, sex, tears, family, friends, and her God were offered, holding as collateral upon her success. The blood came from internal bleeding, which came from a physical altercation between her and Clayton, her lover for two years.

Breakfast Pastries & Love, her baby. Her baby that carried the blessings of the entire congregation of Christ Jesus Eastern Field Holy Church, and fifteen thousand of their dollars they invested in her talent. The others—who invested in that belief—prayed nights, days and weekends for her to succeed in this major venture. She knew the odds were against her, and she knew the weight of her family, her friends, cash advances on credit cards, and a bank loan was riding heavily on her shoulders.

Everyone, but Clayton, knew and understood the stress and the burdens Dana carried with her day in and night out. He didn't like the neglect he was receiving from Dana spending all of her time with her newfound baby. Dana was leaving her home, her bed, and her man early every morning, seven days a week to catch two trains for a forty-minute ride to Soho to open *her baby* and like with a lot of dogs, Clayton found someone else to scratch behind his ear.

She saw the signs. He stopped calling. He wasn't home when she dragged herself through the door in the late evenings. He stopped going to Christ Jesus Eastern Field Holy Church, and took membership elsewhere. When she questioned him about his recent activities, he told her he was a grown man and he had the right to choose any church he found fit to worship in. He told her he was only at that church to be united with her. When she asked him if he was still united with her, he didn't answer. He turned his back on her and left the apartment. That was the night before she met William.

Needless to mention, she didn't sleep that night. She was up crying, leaving messages in the voicemail of his cell phone, trying to find some understanding, trying to make sense of her man's actions. She was having a hard time keeping up with the orders that morning. Thank God for her assistant. The morning rush was over, and she was preparing for the afternoon and evening rush when William called. She felt something when she heard him speak. She didn't know what it was, but the feelings— strong, magnetic, intoxicating, and forbidden—were like none other she'd felt before. However, despite the urges and nudging impulses to learn more about William, his arrogant behavior reinforced her thoughts that all men were *assholes*.

It took William's knowledge of women, his charm, and a couple of hundred dollars to restore a little faith in Dana's eyes in regards to his species. William had to purchase two sets of diamond earrings, one each for the waitresses he pissed off, a week after it was two dozen of roses for three straight days, and a surprise visit to the hospital to see her at her lowest point in her life. The flowers made her smile even though she thought she would never smile again. He made her laugh during his visits, even though she didn't think she would ever laugh again. She didn't think she would ever be able to push that most tragic night out of her mind.

She came home late in the evening, as she had been doing since opening *her baby* and Clayton was packing his cloths into a suitcase. He thought he would be out of there before she got home, but he didn't realize just how much of him had moved in with Dana.

"Clayton, is it something I've done wrong? What it is with you? Why won't you talk to me? What have I done?"

He didn't say a word. He tried to push past her, but she wasn't a little woman, she was almost as big as he was. She reached out to him.

He pushed her outreached arms aside. "Don't touch me, just move and be a woman about it." He stepped around her.

She looked toward the ceiling. *Oh Lord, Jesus this cannot be happening.* She turned and gave chase after her man who was half way down the flight of stairs. "Clayton, Clayton! Look, I'll come home earlier. Please, Clayton, stop! I'll hire a night manager. I'll pay someone to close up for me. Clayton, you can't do this!"

"I can't do this? You did this. You had to chase this fuckin' dream of yours and become the big, fat Aunt Jemima of SoHo, instead of being a woman to me. For three months, I watched you push me out of your life. For three months, we didn't fuck, and or three weeks, you didn't cook one damn meal for me. When I come home from work, I wanna eat…"

"But you weren't eating the meals I left for you. You haven't been home. I can start back cooking for you—"

"Excuses are all the fuck you have for me. For over two years, all I've been asking was for us to start a family. That's all I asked for…a simple life, but your barren ass couldn't produce the one thing I asked—"

"That's not my fault! I've been to all the doctors and they've said I was fine. They've said there was no reason why I couldn't conceive, but you refuse to go get checked out. Besides, how are we to start a family when you haven't asked me to marry you? You know we need to be married before—"

"Fuck that. I told you marriage ain't for me. Later, I got someone waiting for me." He stepped out the front door.

Dana gave pursuit.

Clayton stepped off the curve, and his Range Rover pulled up in front of him. "Open the back, babe," he said to a woman behind the stirring wheel. As he closed the back door, he heard a woman's scream. He looked around the vehicle to witness Dana trying to pull the woman out the truck, via the window. He ran to her aid and punched Dana in the side of her face. Dana turned and focused her rage on him, while the woman climbed out of the truck, snuck up on her from behind and commenced to beating her down with a heavy object. As Dana crawled to the sidewalk, the duo stomped and kicked her until she reached the steps of her building, and onlookers and neighbors came to her aid, chasing Clayton and his partner to his truck and away.

Dana understood sacrifices quite well for she did not only lose her man, but she also lost her unborn child that night, along with any future possibility of having any other, which is why she called Breakfast, Pastries & Love her baby. Therefore, when it came down to strange events of loss, Dana was sure the devil was hard at work, trying to steal everything she had been enjoying for over four years. However, she had lost nearly two hundred thousand dollars in three weeks, and was on the verge of losing some major clients.

Dana was one of those big-boned, thick, man-size sisters. Meaning, she was bootylicious, curvaceous, and voluptuous all rolled into one. She stood about five-ten, solid, thick meat through and through, and large but firm in the waist. Mocha-colored skin, a good length of thick, black hair that stopped just above her shoulders and an ass that operated on ball bearings; her walk made men shout, "Damn!" She was a sister that had to be matched with a man who was taller, larger framed, solid, firm, distinguished, bold, but not overshadowing. She had been described as classy, intelligent, and spiritually grounded.

Although she has been losing money over the last few weeks, her greatest stress came from her lover, Kevin, who has been tripping over her former lover, William.

William knew about Kevin's insecurities, and he understood the riff in Dana's relationship, so he chose to keep a distance and not infringe upon Kevin's time, even though he didn't' like it. William didn't think it was right that he should have to limit his friendship to Dana for the sake of someone else's ego, or for his inability to deal with his emotions and trust issues. Yet, he wanted Dana to be happy and to live a decent life with a man she could love and call her own.

She sat straight up, taking in all of him. Kevin thought he was in new territory, which caused him to wonder if he grew some. She slid her pelvis slowly back and forth upon him, raised her arms, and placed her hands behind her head. Slowly she increased her rhythm, and his breathing shortened with each change in her frequency. It wasn't long before she pressed her hands on his chest, and arched her big ass. It was her bone to his bone. Her thrust had the force to snap him like a pencil, and it wasn't long before she snapped him.

"Ooooo, shit!" he cried, sitting up and grabbing her.

She held his sweaty, shaved head while he gasped for air, trying to absorb the pain from his member. She was pleased that she broke him first, but she was just getting started and needed him to recover like yesterday. She climbed off him. Forcing him to lay down again, with his throbbing cock in hand, she kissed the head. The taste of her sweet nectar excited her and she engulfed the entire head to permit her tongue to twirl around, and around, and around, squeezing his shaft tighter and tighter. She spat at his cock and lubed it with both hands, then swallowed him whole, and again, and again, and Kevin grunted each time she reached bottom. As Keyshia Cole's "Heaven Sent" filled her head, she drew on him faster and harder until he erupted.

# Not This Time

**10:48 p.m.**

"*B*ingo!" shouted the senior citizen in the back, on the right side of the large room. Mrs. Garcia wasn't too thrilled, as this was the fourth game and not one red cent came back from her investment on game boards, specials, nothing. She turned to her daughter, Joann, and asked her to purchase eight boards, four specials, and a cheeseburger deluxe. Joann was pissed that her money was dwindling. She left her apartment with three hundred dollars, and a token of some kind left behind by William, although she cannot imagine what it was. She tried to break him off a little something, but he rejected her advances. She never thought the day would come where she couldn't give away a piece of ass, especially to William. In her mind, William and she were identical in almost every way except gender. She rationalized William left her money because he felt badly about rejecting her. Or, could the reason be that he knew he was going to tear at the fabric of her soul before he boarded the elevator, leaving her soaked in tears?

Whatever the reason, hours later, those funds were down to one hundred and seventy. She purchased about forty dollars' worth of groceries, gave her mother forty, paid for a ten ride metro card, and damn near spent thirty dollars at the bingo hall. She was planning to put a hundred to the side for utilities, put a little food up in the house so her son could come home for a spell, and color her hair, but eight boards, four specials, and a damn cheeseburger deluxe was too much. Hell, she gave her mother the forty dollars to go play bingo when she'd asked for a "few bucks." Why the hell did she let this woman talk her into coming along, and then foot the damn bill, too? All she wanted to do was color her hair, watch some television, or read a book, and relax. However, her mother insisted that she come along. Mrs. Garcia hardly ever left her oldest daughter, Joann, alone in her apartment. It was as if she didn't trust her daughter, and Joann had pondered that thought a few times.

"Ma, I'll buy you a cheeseburger, but I'm not buyin' no more games. We got enough here. Let's just play what we got," Joann said, with her top lip turned up.

Mrs. Garcia didn't appreciate Joann's tone of voice, or her disobedience. If she weren't in public, she would definitely have let one loose across her face. Dare she speak back to her like that? She could use that tone with her hooker friends, but not with her.

Joann was tired. Her body was still hurting . She'd rolled her eyes back into her head, tilted her head backward, and massaged the back of her neck with a silent wish that she was pressed up against William's warm body like last night, wrapped in his arms.

Mrs. Garcia cut her eyes toward Joann. Joann caught sight, but could care less how her mother felt. Usually, she would give into her, but not tonight. She had too many things on her mind to deal with her mother's bullshit, too.

"I'll go get the cheeseburger. Play my boards for me," Joann said, as she stood.

The five-eight, butterscotch-flavored Joann wondered if there was some truth to Jay Dee's claim. "You see that motherfucker one fuckin' time and now you on a high horse." She didn't know if William's visit brought her back to reality, but what she did know was that he brought her life to some dangerous crossroads. She had the weight of the world upon her chest, because everything she loved hung in the balance with the decisions she would be faced with sooner or later. William had stopped by to repair her computer, and left her in the midst of an emotional whirlwind. It wasn't just for the ass beating she received from her now ex-boyfriend, Jay Dee, but it was first by William who told her she only has three years to live. William emotionally raped her by telling her about her entire past she'd tried so hard to forget; things she never told a soul, about her God, and about their sins, then he left her a wreck. Once again, he abandoned her. Her man, Jay Dee, came home to find her in tears, naked underneath her robe, and her ex-lover, William, had just left.

Joann waited her turn to reach the counter where she placed an order for two cheeseburgers with lettuce, tomatoes, onions, ketchup, and fries.

"You want something to drink with that order?" asked the counter person.

"Yeah, let me get two large lemonades."

She wrapped her arms around the lower half of her ribcage and held herself in an attempt to fight against the pain. *Damn!* She cursed the thought of not making love to him when they lay on her sofa, but his heat felt so good, his body offered protection, and the fact that he returned to aid her spoke volumes. Besides all this, she felt his warmth healing her body and spirit. However, being true to her nature, she tried to advance upon him in the shower that following morning. He rejected her advances, and left her, once again, with mixed feelings and confusion. He always left her with more questions than answers, but she figured he must've been in love with his wife that month or something. They always fell back in love with their wives, occasionally.

Joann shared a life with William years back. To the world, unknowingly to them, her neighbors and local merchants had mistaken William and her for a married couple with a son. For over four years, she considered herself the second wife and was happy with that, but she stood ready to assume the role of first wife if he ever cleared his head and opened his eyes to see where a greater true love awaited him.

For a long time, everything was going so well before she noticed his visits getting shorter and shorter, and every day became every other day, then the day after that, until he just stopped coming all together. They were never really the same couple after that night up in the Bronx, when a drug buy went bad. She had to pick up two keys of snow, and William felt the need to tag along, and with good reasons. Joann was set up from the moment she'd placed the order. The plan was if she came with four or more escorts, it would be business as usual, but any number less and the double cross was on. Joann and William went in a dark lot, on a secluded block, with three men. Ten minutes later, Joann and William drove out with the coke and money, leaving three dead bodies behind.

*Could that have been his reason for abandoning me, and our child?* she thought, reminiscing on that frightful night. *No. Not, William. It probably was that fat, black bitch-ass wife of his. Hell no, I can't believe I slept on that bitch. She had something to do with that shit. I feel it all the way to my bones. He probably felt guilty and all, and probably confessed everything that night to his ugly wife, that stink, cop bitch. She took him away from his little, outside family. I should have killed the bitch that first day we tangled on the phone.* Standing at the counter, waiting on her order, she turned up her lips and sunk into deep thought. *I paged my man, there was no answer, so I figured he would call back in a few after he checked his beeper, like he always did, and to my surprise this bitch returned my call. I tried to play it off and act like I dialed the wrong number and all. I didn't want to get my man into any trouble, you know. Keep his secret life on lock, so we have peace and harmony, but she wasn't having it. She read right through that shit. So my nature got the best of me and I had to fuck with her for the hell of it. But damn did she turn it around and get me pissed. Then the bitch had the nerve to hang up on me. I was like, "Yo, no the hell she didn't. Fuck!" It was on. I called that black heifer back and, like I said, it was on.*

"*I think you have the wrong number, or something, your man ain't here. But I do suggest you get some skills if you want to keep him home.*"

"*Bitch, I will fuck you up!*" Yvonne, William's wife, screamed.

"*No, bitch, you better fuck your man up. A'ight? 'Cause this way he won't be sniffing around other women crotches.*"

"*Yeah, talk that shit over the phone…*" Yvonne said.

"*What! You wanna step to this, bitch?*"

"*Yeah, where you at? Ain't no fear in my heart, bitch. I got some skills for that ass, a'ight.*" "*You wanna know where I'm at? You better ask somebody.*"

"*Yeah, well, just for you to know, when you go down on him tonight, keep this in mind: I just got off of it, you nasty, tricky ass, ho!*"

*A piercing thud was the sound of the phone in Joann's ear before the silence.*

"*Oh no! Oh fuck no. She didn't call me a ho. I'll kill her. I'd pull the hairs off her pussy, and shove my baby's bottle up her ass…*" *Then it hit her.* "*Oh, I got some payback for you,* bitch. Oh, you just got off it, huh? I'm gonna see you never get on it again." She'd dialed star-six-nine. The phone rang twice. "Come on pick up, bitch. Come get some of this—"

"What you want, ho," Yvonne answered.

"The name is Holly, so get used to it, 'cause it's going to be a household name 'round there..."

"No, your name is low life, bitch. What you call for, this shit is tired?"

"Fuck you, I don't need this, where is my baby's daddy, is he home?"

"You fuckin' ho bitch, don't fuck with me..."

"I ain't fuck you, and don't see how he can, but my son needs some Pampers, and milk..."

"You want Pampers and milk? Meet me at the Lindenwood Diner on Linden Boulevard, bitch, and bring that bastard baby with you," Yvonne demanded.

"You see, you gotta be a rude bitch, so now you get nothing but baby's mama drama from here on—"

"Be there in an hour."

"Oh, I'll be there, but I'm not in any condition to kick yo' ass, 'cause I gotta 'nother bun in da oven..."

"Be there."

Silence.

Yeah I was there, waitin' for her when she showed up. I didn't know it was her when she first road up. But when I saw this short, mean lookin', football player, wearing this extra shade of black on her, I knew it had to be her. Lookin like she sucked on a mothball or somethin' sour. I was like, what the hell does he see in her? That short, black, reject heifer ain't have shit on me. Please. She passed by my car, and I was so fuckin' tempted to run her ass over. I hit the gas, the car leaped out at her, but I hit the brakes, 'cause I knew if I had hit that bitch, William would *have gotten pissed, and he would be stuck at house watchin' those kids all by himself. Meaning, I wasn't going to get any time.*

*I looked at her and smiled. "Oh, I'm sorry, I ain't see you there." I was smilin' cause I was like yeah, bitch, you should thank me 'cause I just let yo ass live.*

Joann's cell phone started to ring, which brought her back to the present. She looked at the caller ID, but didn't recognize the number.

"Hello?"

"I just want you to know I'm still alive, bitch." The man's voice was queasy. He was having problems breathing.

"Who's this? This you, Jay Dee?"

"Yeah it's me, bitch. And I just want you to know your friends got me good, but I'm still here and your ass is dead." He strained to speak.

"Whatcha talkin' about? Whatcha sayin'?"

"You know what I'm talkin' about. I'm tellin' you now, watch your back Jo-Jo, 'cause I'm taken you out…"

"Yo, son, don't call me with this mess. You know what, Jay Dee? Bring it. I told you before if you put your hands on me again, it's a bloodshed feud for life," Joann declared.

"Yeah, well it's on, you stank ho."

"Who you callin' a 'ho'? You short, three-inch motherfucker, wishin' you had three more so you can hang just a little—"

"Fuck you, Jo-Jo. Watch your back, yo. Watch your fuckin' back, bitch."

"Play pussy and you'll get fucked, Jay Dee. I'm not like your wife. You being a man don't scare me. I'm not weak. I'm not weak at all. Come at me. Mark my words. I will end you. I don't fear you, little man—"

He disconnected the call.

*Punk bitch. You ain't puttin' no fear in my heart. I ain't ever lettin' any man put his hands on me, and let that shit go. I told you that, I told you Jay Dee. Hell no. It ain't happenin'. No way, no how, no more. So it's on, huh? A'ight, let me think how I'm gon' do this. I'm gon' take care of his ass first, then that black, Color Purple, Whoopi Goldberg-lookin' bitch.*

"That's fifteen dollars, even," said the woman with Joann's order.

*Fifteen dollars? Damn, Ma. That's it for your ass, too. Damn, this was a mistake, comin' over here. I got this dickless motherfucker wantin' to kill me, my momma bleeding me like I was a chicken head, and I'm in pain. Fifteen damn dollars.*

"Bingo!" Mrs. Garcia shouted.

"We hit, Ma? We hit?" Joann questioned, with a broad smile, feeling a spark of happiness and long-awaited joy in her life.

"We? What do you mean 'we'?" Mrs. Garcia lips turned up ugly.

Joann looked at her mother's face. She couldn't believe this woman just turned on her t. Just like that, her happiness soured and it was replaced with the feeling of exasperation. She looked closely at the winning board and sided with her mother, because it was her special that won the seven-hundred-dollar prize, and it was her board, which she left for her to play when she left the table.

"You're right, Ma. It was my game board that won, since I paid for it. Here take your burger while I go claim my prize money."

Joann picked up her winning board and made her way to the collection booth, while receiving claps, whistles, and cheers along her journey. She felt good about herself once again, and declared under her breath, "I ain't lettin' no one get over, not this time and no more from now on. Fuck all y'all."

# I Thought

**10:52 p.m.**

She wondered how he could be so thick. She couldn't believe he would do some shit like that to her. He must take her for a fool. Boy, she must've had "*idiot*" written on her forehead and back. He just sat there with his mouth open, looking stupid. She felt she had to put an end to this bumbling attempt to win her affection. If she didn't speak up now, if she let this shit go unchecked, she would be the stupid one. But the sight of him disgusted her more than all else. She just had to get away from him. She didn't feel a bang-bang on the head would help, so why bother?

*Lord, please forgive my language. How could he? I trusted him, dang it. With all the shit we've gone through over the last two years. I've stopped going out with my friends, stopped talkin' on the phone, and stopped dressing to tease. I'm not a tease, but this big, curvy ass that's holding on tight to my arching hips and huggable waist...ssshhh, even make me look forward to have moments with myself, and I won't speak of the rest of me. So why is Kevin hatin'? This man got everything—my mind, my body, my soul, my time, my money.*

She helped him when they were going to lock his behind up for being a deadbeat father. Not that he was by choice. He didn't know the former Mrs. Walker took his behind to court for child support, even though he was paying her something every two weeks, as they first agreed. She reneged. She went to family court and claimed she didn't know where he was, but that he'd been gone for years; he only stopped by occasionally to see the kids, and then she dropped the digits to his social security number. It was hard for them to track him down, at first, being that he was a private contractor, working with satellite installation.

A year after she planted the seed, he filed his taxes and the State of New York kept every cent, froze his bank accounts, and the City of New York locked him up. They took her man away from her for being a deadbeat dad, and for being twenty-six thousand dollars in arrears. Dana paid off his debts and placed him back on his feet. He'd been a good man for the most part.

He never yelled at her, he always supported her with things she wanted to do, and he was a good lover, for the most part. But this B.S. with William wasn't like him. She had been keeping William at a distance just to keep the peace between Kevin and the relationship. She didn't understand Kevin's insecurities. William and she hadn't done anything sexually since they parted over three, four years ago. She no longer saw him in that light, so fucking him would definitely feel like incest. It bothered her to think about all the times they had, although it was all good.

Dana felt she was not getting the same respect in which she gave to him. She didn't flip when that thing he was once married to would call. He had two beautiful daughters—eight and nine—that he would die for, and she respected him for that, and would never dream of coming between them, but she would love to give him a son. To give him something that wretched ex-wife, he was tortured by, could not give him. But, oh boy, did she give him drama. The way Kevin would tell the story, his ex-wife was so open, the mailmen actually delivered her packages, and no pickup slips were left in her mailbox.

Could that be the reason why he was so freaked by William's present? He came home and caught the ex-wife in bed with one of her long-time exes, who really wasn't an ex, if you think about it. But she was not Dana. She would never hurt him. She was constantly feeling hurt when she thought, *How could he even begin to compare me with that?*

He got his nerve. How could he?

*After I let all my love run down his shaft, around his nuts, and seep between the crack of his ass and onto carpet, I led him into his bedroom. The living room was nice for starters, but I wanted to make up for lost time, you know, but I could not deal with carpet burns. Yes, I wanted that type of party pleasure, you feelin' me? But when I entered his bedroom, I stopped dead in my tracks, and just thought, No he didn't, no he didn't. But I was looking at it, and yes he did. He's such a dick!*

*This man went out there and purchased a fine looking computer system. My eyes went wide, mouth dropped open and he was grinning like he did good. I don't know if his wife was a bimbo, or if the ones he used to mess with were, but I'm above the B.S. games, and ain't too keen on drama. I just stared at him.*

"Kevin, what is that?" She pointed at the boxes.

"Oh. That's your new system I got you. It cost me damn near thirty-five hundred, but it's the newest and the latest, the biggest and the best. Flat, touch screen monitor, it burns Blu-ray, HD DVD, CD, and has a complete HD video package. You can program your cell phone, sync all of your MP4s, wireless speakers, Blue-Tooth technology, and you can sync your address book to your Jeep. I mean, it has everything, baby…"

She placed her hands on her hips. "Why?"

"Why? Why, what?" He got stupid.

"Why did you buy it? Why was it so important for you to buy it now, Kevin?"

"That old one is always breaking down on you. The damn thing is so old; you can't even upgrade the operating system, it's time."

She shook her head and walked past him. She couldn't believe he had done that and then gave her that tired excuse.

"Where are my panties?" She spoke between the rapid pulses of her heartbeat.

"What? What's wrong, baby?" He trailed behind her. "Dana, speak to me."

"You know, maybe if you would have done this a month ago or some other time, it might not be so bad, but why now? What is this about?" She paused. She tilted her head and cracked a half smile. "It's about William. That is why you purchased all of this, isn't it?" She was fighting back the tears.

Kevin hung his head. "I don't trust the guy. I don't know. It's something about him I don't like."

Fuck the panties, she pulled up her leather skirt and threw on the matching jacket, grabbed her blouse, bra, and bag, and she was out. She turned around and gave him the nastiest look she could muster, and said, "No, Kevin. It's not him who you don't trust, it's me. I thought you were above this. I thought you seen something in me you didn't see in your ex-wife like trust, honesty, and sincerity, but you close your eyes to my heart, to my soul, to my character. You don't see me, Kevin, and I'm too much of a woman not to be seen."

"Boo—"

"No. No. I'll call you in a day or two. I still love ya, baby, but you fucked up. You're on punishment."

"Yeah, well, you better think hard for those couple of days, because when you come back you better have your head together. 'Cause it's one or the other…him or me. Your life, your world with me, he no longer exist."

*I closed his door with my good hand, and tried to figure out what just took place. Did I check him, or did he check me? I could not think straight at that moment I started thinking about the argument we just had, and cried all the way home. I felt so drained from thinking about all the shit that just happen. I just wanted to get in my apartment to take a bath and sleep, but that wasn't going to happen because a knuckle on my bad hand was killing me, no thanks to the dead pigeon I found nailed to my door. I just lost it, and started beating the dead bird with a rage that scared even me. I don't know how many times I hit the damned thing; I didn't stop until the blood squirted from its chest onto my face, my bare chest, and a small bone lodged between my middle knuckles of my injured hand.*

*Then I saw her. She was big as life, and ugly as ever. At first I didn't recognize her, but when the blood from the bone of the pigeon mixed with mine, I seen her clear as daylight. She stood over a wok, burning something inside, then, and then she held up my lipstick. I've been looking for my lipstick for weeks, I couldn't imagine where it had gone. I must have left it in Kevin's car, or at his apartment.*

*That Bitch was chanting over my lipstick. She was placing a spell on me. I couldn't make out what it was she was saying, but the image said it all.*

*I wanted to smash the head of the pigeon into pieces, but my injured hand wouldn't let me, regardless of the amount of rage that was running through me. It was like the pain I was feeling gave my hand a mind of its own. Then I'd remembered the conversation I had with William a couple of days ago, before Kevin started tripping:*

♦ ♦ ♦

"Why didn't you call me and tell me I was going to do this?" I said.

"What happen? What did you do?" He had a slight slur in his voice as if he been drinking

"You don't know?" I asked.

"No. My head is a little bad right now. I'm not receiving anything."

"I stabbed my hand. Twice!" I felt so stupid telling him that.

"Bad?" He asked with what sound like great concern.

"Well, at first I thought it was. I just got the bleeding to stop. I think I'll be alright."

"You want me to take you to the hospital or something?" He did care, I thought.

"No. I can take myself to the hospital if it gets to be that bad. I just wanted to know why you didn't warn me?" Hell I knew he lived in New Rochelle, how sweet of him to have asked.

"I didn't see it." He replied once again. Then I was sure he was drinking…Well not that it mattered anyway, but that would explain why he was not able to see me mutilate myself.

"I did. Just before I did it." I confessed.

"Well it was for a reason." That I knew, but why?

"Yeah, I know that, but what? Tell me."

"Don't know. It's to prevent you from doing something."

"Like what?"

"Don't know, but you will find out, soon."

"How soon?" I asked.

"Before the cut heals. And again, you may not find out at all. But it's to prevent you from doing something with that hand."

◆ ◆ ◆

Did she damn near cut off her hand, just not to beat on a dead bird! She couldn't believe this shit. She could not understand it, logical thinking, it made no sense, then an echo, "How deep is deep?" bounced around in her head. That was something William would always ask. She thought she knew the answer, but with this she had not a clue, and in the mist of all this with the little voices inside of her pleaded with her to call him. With little thought, she dared not call the man who was at the very root of her problems between her lover and she.

She ripped the bird from her door, stepped into her domain and looked about finding nothing out of place. She no longer felt safe. She could not imagine how, but somehow this person or persons had managed getting pass two locked doors and a nosey ass tenant up the stairs to harass her. She threw her coat onto her couch, walked into the kitchen soaked a dishcloth with a dishwasher liquid, and exited the kitchen grabbing a bottle of 409. She washed all of the blood and strange markings from her door and fled back into her sanctuary for an hot bath.

She laid in her hot tub for what seemed like hours, contemplating the evening's events. But her escape was a short run, her cell phone started to sound off an alert. She listened to the ringer, her response was in slow motion, the ringing had a different texture to it, as where it sounded more as if it was an alarm rather than a phone. It was hard getting her big behind out the tub, the water just seem to weight her down. She was tired and drained but she managed to drudged herself out safely and give a not so quick sprint to the phone. It was Kevin, somehow she already knew it was him. She felt as if she was expecting him to call. He was frantic, he barely made any sense at all, but then she caught the jest of it, when he demanded she come back to his wife's apartment to watch his daughters, because his wife ex-wife was rushed to the emergency room that seem to had an heart attack.

She hung up the phone in a dazed. She was about to learn just how deep, deep was? She knew she had something to do with that woman injury. Shit, she was trying to kill her. But she did not believe she had those powers to do so. William told her many times that she did, but William had been hit in the head a few times, she believed also. Was this stuff real, she wondered to herself? *My God, what had I done? I felt the energy through my rage. This is too much for me to bear. I needed a drink, those kids have to wait until I get numb.*

# Wanna Do You Right

The wife he exiled four weeks ago stood before him, waiting for him to speak, to say something, make a sound, something. But he was speechless; he had no words, only emotions. He didn't know what to say, or what his actions should be. He knew he'd missed her deeply. He knew the one thing he wanted most was to make love to her. He wanted to vow her anything her heart desired, but he didn't know where her head was. He wasn't sure where her heart was, and to whom her love was to be given.

Hell, Mrs. Yvonne Green just spent a week in the Bahamas with her boss, and getting sexed was a daily ritual. William knew she was back with her decision, with her sitting under the roof of their home telling him the odds were good, and for the moment that was his one and only concern, to know if she came back to live with him and their four children, or to agree upon a settlement and keep her back toward the wind. She knew he would fight her on hands and knees to keep his children with him. He would spare no cost, except death. And the price of death wasn't on the table, as he knew there were a million and one ways to kick ass, and win without having to kill your opponent, or get killed in the process.

When he looked upon her, he turned away from her, and instantly his head received a jolt, which felt as if he had been zapped by a stun gun. An electrical stock surged throughout the nerves of his brain, causing pain to burst and tingle in his temples. He closed his eyes to absorb the current, swallowed hard, balled his hands into two tight fists, gritted his teeth, and forced the current through his quivering body. It burned; he became warm from the heat, beads of sweat formed on his forehead. He turned and looked at her. She had a strong glow radiating from her translucent state.

She stared back at him, both waiting for the other to speak, and then, *My, this is a new look,* Mr. William R. Green thought to himself.

*You can see the difference?* Yvonne asked.

*Yes, I can. Or maybe I don't. You're nearly...you're...you're almost completely invisible, yet there's a silvery glow that exist around you.*

*So you can hear me, too?*

Their brief conversation was telepathic.

She looked upon him and was pleased. "You're further than I thought." Yvonne used the spoken language.

"And now you," William retorted. "Please forgive me. I'm at a loss for words."

"So am I."

"Are you here to pack your bags?" He knew better.

"You already know the answer to that."

"So, where do we go from here, Eve?"

"We don't have many choices. Time grows short, but this you know already, don't you?" She felt a shift in his metabolic chemistry.

"No. I have too many questions, and a love for flesh," he said angrily.

"William…"

He turned his back to her. "My whole life I lived in darkness. Plagued by things and feelings my soul could barely withstand.

I lived two life times and now that I'm getting a grip on this riddle, I'm beginning to put the pieces together. You come into your own, and come back here to tell me about the endgame... I don't think so."

"I'm sorry, but you know we have no control, no choice, and we must..." Yvonne tried to explain.

"Bullshit. I signed no one's contract."

"Why are you so defiant?"

"Yvonne, I feel I'm owed something here. My childhood and teenage years weren't the greatest. I could have helped people, I could have healed people, and so many other things I could have done. But no instead, I was left with a magic cube and a riddle, then told to go play. I've stole, I've hurt people, I was a teenage drunk, a fuckin' drug dealer, a lifetime whore, and I killed!"

"You finally admit it?" She was pleased to be the one to witness his testimony.

"Can I lie to you?"

"No."

"I say humanly I may have been justified. Can't say that for everyone in the room." William drew her in, seeking confrontation.

"How do you draw that conclusion? For years, you distance yourself from this family, and from me. You put me through hell, Mr. Green. Arguing, fighting, and leaving my kids home alone. Coming home with some bitch's pussy on your lips, some bitch's lipstick on your sweater, and some bitch's panties in your pocket. Come on, if anyone had a reason to be fed up, it was me. I took care of this family every time your sorry behind was out of work. You walking around like your shit don't stink, and catch an attitude when someone tells you about your arrogance; you go talking about, 'I'm going to do things for myself, because I can't count on no one else.' The nerve of you, a jobless bastard talking shit while my daughter and I supplied you with cigarettes and coffee every day, and kept a roof over your head. You played games, William, games people shouldn't play. Coming home with short money, and other times with no money, talking about you lost it while playing cards. As if you could afford to gamble with the family's money that you were supposed to have brought home.

"I'm finding some child's birth records in your bag. Yeah, you even had me out there beating bitches down over you. And that nasty *ho* bitch with your child! Oh my." She grabbed her forehead. "So what is he now, about eight years old? All the fucking drama you put me through, telling me you're taking pictures of kids. While my ass was home pregnant, and your ass was out there with some woman taking pictures of some dark skinned thang. Oh and how about Ms. Train Station, the one you had to see every night coming in from work. Or the time you had to take your camera to work, telling me you're going to take pictures of some beautiful things, and come to find it was some yellow, skinny, anorexic bitch posing for you. That shit had me hating yellow women for decades. Hell, I'm still not too fond of them!

"Why don't we just get off your picture taking days, but oh no wait, don't let us get started on your horseback riding days, or the 'I want my pilot license days', or your beeper days, or your private phone lines, or all of your cell phone adventures. Please spare me the B.S.

"It was you who drifted further and further, where I knew I only processed half of you…" She paced the floor, gesturing with her hands.

"And do you want to know why, Yvonne?" William shouted.

Yvonne made a step toward William with her chest out, and raised her voice with a touch of bass. "Yeah, tell me something. Tell me. Let me hear your fuckin' logic. What bullshit have you got for me, now?" The room temperature rose by eight degrees.

"I distanced myself from you 'cause I always found myself making plans to kill your self-righteous ass. Most of the time I thought about tacking your ass to a wall and slice little small pieces off of your body for each time I fuckin' cried over you. For each time I gave you my all, and I found out someone else was receiving my love. Each and every single time."

"What times are you talkin' about?" she asked, knowing all too well his statements were true, but she needed him to confess everything and expel his demons.

"Come on, you're a woman, surely you can recall every fucking year, every month, every day, minute and second. You fuckin' women always crying *victim* so damn much, y'all actually believe that you are. Y'all might think with both sides of your brain, but those shits ain't collaborating with each other too fucking well. I'm talking about the time you told me you thought you were in love with Louis. Remember? That shit cut through me like some giant blade. All at once, I was in pieces. Never! Never once would I ever expect to hear you say you loved another man. Maybe give me some bullshit excuse like I was hot! I was really feeling horny! I was very depressed! I was just lusting! But not once did I ever think you would fall in *love* with someone else. Yes, that was when you lost me, because I lost myself. That shit hurt me as much as it did that day when I was going to ask you to marry me.

"Do you remember that day, Eve? I was making love to you, in my bed, and you called out, 'Tyrone.' Do you remember that shit? I had nothing but love for you, Yvonne. Didn't you know that?

Only months before that, you fucked your bitch ex-boyfriend that I'd replaced, ummm," he paused, in thought. "Mark. You fucked him on the staircase while I waited outside your door for you to return. Yeah, you two motherfuckers laughed at me. Y'all thought I was stupid, and weak. And God knows how long I lived with you thinking you married the wrong man, and how you dreamed for years what your life would have been like if you would have married him instead of me. Yeah, I was able to read your thoughts back then, too.

"Or what about the time you did your other ex, Anthony, because I was spending my pay nights and my weekly wages gambling after work on the job? Hell, I just wasn't losing my check; I was also losing my girl. You really have proven to me that a man really needs to be home to watch over his shit.

"Wait a minute, no. A woman should be on her job, too. Like Ashley, that sick motherfucker you nearly killed with that asthma. From there you went back to thinking about Mark, kept in close contact with him, and planned secret rendezvous. And it was funny how you always managed to whine and tell the kids about my infidelities, but never about yours, humph?

"And I told you once before, whenever you are ready to sit down and have a discussion about my alleged son, I wanna discuss that abortion you had fifteen years ago, because I would love to sit and have a discussion on the list of possible fathers. You know that little skeleton in your closet you've failed to mention during our arguments. That was about the time you were fucking Glen and David, and me, and only God knows about anyone I don't know about. And now you got this bitch asshole, Robert, who thinks he pumps fear in my heart. The both of you, thinking I was weak. Our whole marriage I lived with you thinking I was some kind of pencil pushing nerd who was unable to defend himself, his wife, or his family, and the worse of it, you should have known better than anyone about my rage. That fucking Robert is nothing but a silly rabbit who has no clue of the pain I can afflict upon him.

"Yes, Yvonne, I do play games. I played your game, by your rules; you called all the shots. So why is it you call foul when you gotta play mine?

"And all those times…every fuckin' time I reached out to you, I was longing for you, needing you, calling out to you, wanting to love you, what would you say to me? 'Aw shit, yeah, yeah I'll give you some tonight.'

*"Give me some…* Did I look like a fucking squirrel, begging for a nut? I didn't need you to *give me some*. Why do you women think your pussies solve all of our problems and all of our issues? That shit only takes care of our constant itch to fuck.

"Yeah Yvonne, I distanced myself, because I would have done more harm if I didn't. But I never lied to you when you accused me of fucking around. You were months late, or a few months early, but never on time, and never the right woman. Even so, every time I did do something, it was always after a blow you delivered. I played your game. You never once sat down and judged your doings." He lit a cigarette.

She looked down into her empty hands, and played with her fingernails. "I'm sorry. If I had some clue…I could have…I would—"

"Save it. What is, is. What happened happened, and everything will stand as is. Those times speak for itself, whether it was right or wrong, whether it was done out of stupidity, ignorance, or lust, we will answer to someone much higher than ourselves. Like I said, I'm sorry. I have too many questions. And I've done too much shit to just comply with anything, or anyone. Besides,

I'm just getting you back, and I need to have my time to love you with what time I have left."

"That's the first time you said 'I love you,' without me asking if you do, in years," she stated.

"What good is saying it, when you're being neglected and betrayed?"

"Will, you're not an easy man to love. No, that's not true. You are a very easy man to love. You make people depend on you, you make it easy for them to feed off you, and helplessly we come to depend on you for your love, strength, security, and in a blink of an eye you change up or you just vanish, leaving a person in a very unstable frame of mind. It was easy to learn how to love you, but I never learned how to keep up with you, or when to step off, or when to give you room…"

"I know I'm complex. I don't understand myself most of the time. I just try to stay true to my heart and follow the greatest wind, which moves me. We have been together for more than half our lives, and I don't blame you for the things that happen between us. Actually, I carry that weight on my own shoulders.

"Hey, I was shady and you got shaky. That's understandable. But all my explanations were all true, well about ninety-six percent anyway. If it means anything, I'm sorry. I'm sorry for all the times I made you cry. I'm sorry for all the times I made you suspicious. I'm sorry for the times I made you feel you were alone, for the times I've caused you to distrust me, for the times you felt I needed to be replaced, for the times I manhandled you, or threw something at you. Please forgive me. I don't regret much in my life, and you know that, but these things I do."

She said nothing. A slight smile sat upon her face.

William wiped away a budding tear.

Yvonne took several steps closer and said, "Look, why don't you call the Le Centre and we'll spend next week together."

"The Sheraton, in Montreal?"

"Yes. I still have a lot of vacation time I can use. I'll put in for another week."

"I don't know. You just had a week with someone I care not to follow behind." He turned his back to her and focused his attention back to repairing the tracks.

She placed her hands on her hips. "What? You act like you never batted clean up before?" She was insulted.

"Umpped, with your track record, all too often." William huffed.

"That's because you know the best is always saved for last, zero-zero-zero." She placed a wicket smile upon her face. Triple zero was once his call numbers to his CB handle, Postman back in the days. "How about ya, Postman, you checkin' my mail? You got a grip on Lady Eve, makin' a shout for my Samurai, breaker?" She cocked her hand on her hip.

William could not resist. "That's a Roger. Roger–four to that Lady Eve, breaker. Postman got a ten–twenty on Samurai, walk it back, break, break."

"Will, that's a Roger, that's a Roger. Can you postmark my mail? I say can you postmark my mail for me, Mr. Postman? Tell him I need a slayer who can slice and dice tonight. Roger?"

"I peeped that I did. I got it postmark, I do, I said I do. That's a Roger. What you say there, breaker, break?"

Bending over, she whispered in his ear. "And you're invited, too, Mr. Postman. I'm going to need you to lick it and stick it before he arrives, 'cause Samurai ain't leaving any ends." She turned and headed for the door.

"I copied that, I did. One other thing, Mrs. Green." Their game was over, his tone turned serious.

"Yes, Mr. Green."

"What about my son?"

"What about our son?"

"I told you ten years ago about my dream of his death. If I live to be who it is I'm supposed to be, what about my son?"

"Our son is here with us today. I have no answers about any of our tomorrows."

"Where do we go from here? I'm tired of the game. Time to do you right, with whatever time I have left. Do you have the answers I seek? Do you know who I am, and why I'm here?"

She never turned around. She dared to think, knowing he was tuned into her. She continued her feminine stroll toward the door. She was pleased and felt at ease, knowing this night within itself was a triumph because she didn't have to tangle with him, or fight a battle of the impossible to destroy him, and as she stepped through the doorway, she stopped to speak.

"Yes I have the answers you seek, Dark One. All you need to do is shut up, and do as I say, when I say it. I will reveal what I can when we arrive at the hotel. Besides I just wanna do you right too, boo. Don't be long, I'm beginning to flow." She exited.

William remained silent in his prayer of thankfulness. He was filled with indescribable emotions racing through his entire being. He spent his entire life seeking the reasons for his existence, and for the last twenty-five years, he knew this woman he called wife had those answers. Finally, she'd waken from her sleep, and he must submit himself to her will totally. The troubling with that thought was each time he had in the past, she destroyed his faith and the trust he had for her. Her insecurities, inner conflicts and recklessness caused him to enter long periods of self-destructive behavior. He knew she'd changed; he physically and spiritually saw it, but could he trust her? Could he trust the one person he knew could destroy him? He had begged the Heavens for an answer to know the truth, and now it had been delivered to him as a two-edge sword.

# The Weaving

**10:42 p.m.**

The seductive voice of Kiss FM's Lenny Green filled the room as he introduced Lauren Hill's, "Cry For Me." He felt he was betrayed. Loving Yvonne has been like a tug of war, a battle, a similarity in unison with the lyricist. She left him with no options other than the one he placed in motion a couple of days ago. How dare she? Whom did she think she was? Whom did she think he was? Her, husband! If so, she must have lost her damn mind. He was no one's chump, and he certainly was not a pussy like her bitch ass husband, William. She played him once before on that night when he vowed to take care of her. She gave him a weak smile of approval, and then she was nearly killed by a bat-wheeling punk and friendly fire from a fellow officer. He'd always been there for her, to protect her. She needed his protection from the animals out there in those streets, and from the pain William inflected upon her. But no more, as he had seen it thousands of times when abused women refused to leave their abusers. Stupid bitches and now Yvonne was among their ranks. *What a waste,* he thought, as he turned the pages of his journal. *And just think. I love the hell out of her. I was going to give her the world, but now, her shit is dead and stinkin'."*

*Dear Journal:*

*It's going into day four since Yvonne and I returned from our vacation. She still hasn't told me what happened to her that night she spent out. I mean, did she talk all night on the phone with this pussy? Or did one of her girlfriends or family members convince her to go back to his punk ass? This shit ain't right. It's not fear. I spent all my time and money trying to show her she can have a life without her husband. I told her I would gladly accept her children. We'd be the little family she deserves to have. Why can't she see that I'm a much better man for her than that bitch ass William?*

*Fuck that, we ain't gotta play any more games. She should know I'm not the type to let someone fuck me over and get away with it. She should have known I was going to get her fat ass back. Silly rabbit, tricks are for kids. I'm a grown ass man, and I'm going to teach this bitch a fucking lesson, because no woman is ever going to play me and live pain-free. Hell, no. You cause me pain, I'll give you pain. An eye for an eye, motherfuckers.*

*Made me spend all my fuckin' money, got me borrowing money from my pension plan to pay my debts. And to pay this bastard to handle what I need handled. Yeah, baby, Big Daddy gets to have the last laugh. And oh boy, oh boy how I will have the last laugh 'cause her precious William is now a walkin' corpse. I'm just gonna sit back and count the days motherfucker, 'cause you're going down, down, down, down, down, bitch!*

*And it's your fault, Yvonne. You drove me crazy, over the edge. How can you fuck a man the way you did and not love him? How can you let me believe for the last two years that it would be you and I in the end? Guess you were no different from the others, just another fuckin' ho. The four-day drought from your love has caused me to take measures into my own hands. Time for me to finish what I couldn't before. Damn, the phone is ringin'. I'll be right back, Mr. Journal.*

"Hello?" Robert answered.

"Yo, it's me. Are we still on or what?" said a male's voice.

"Yeah. I'll have that package for you tomorrow. Twenty-five hundred, some photos, and some addresses. You'll get the other twenty-five after it's all said and done."

"Yeah, alright. Where's the hook up?"

"Meet me near the brown newspaper booth on Pitkin Avenue and Thomas Boyland Street, across the street from the eye glass store."

"Cool. What time?"

"Just after sundown, make it about nine."

"I got it. One."

He pressed the button on his Bluetooth headset, placed the cell phone on the desk and stared at the entry in his journal. The discussion with himself agitated him into an angry outburst. "Bitch! You'll pay for dancing on my heart. I'm not a puppet on a string, but you will respect me. I will not be humiliated in my house!" He grabbed his cell phone and started to press the numbered cubes.

The cell phone rang once, twice, three times. "Hello?"

"Hey, you're still up I see. I've been thinkin'…" the man said.

"Jake, when do you stop thinking? Go to bed. Have sex with your wife or do something constructive, just get off my phone," William begged.

"Yo, Will… I'm sorry man."

"What are you talking about, Jake?"

"Man, forgive me for thinkin' ill of you."

"Jake, you're saying sorry, you're scaring me. I'm going to have nightmares, stop it," William demanded of his fourteen-year buddy.

"Shut up before I forget why I called. Look, I've read an entry where you said…where you said that if you was to ever have an older brother, you wished I was that brother. And—"

"And so what? Man, take your sentimental ass to bed. Jake, get the fuck out the journal, turn the computer off, and get some rest. Are you home or on the road?"

"I'm in Cincinnati. I'm on the tri-run."

"Damn, next Saint Louie, then Alabama."

"Yeah, with layover's, but yo, man, thanks. Thank you for all the shit you've done for me, man. And I'm sorry for all the trouble I've caused you in the past. I've read over those early days, and I never really stop to say sorry about all the conflicts I put you through, with yo family and shit, by savin' my job and all. Thanks, man…"

"Yo, what's up? Don't you ever sleep?" William became more irritated with Jake's sentiments. He wanted to get upstairs to his wife, and forget about the world outside his doors.

"Hey, William, man, I…Something else…. rather, you lied, man. I can see a lot of shit here, and you told me you killed seven people, or people and some animals. But I count about ten bodies, man. You're a fuckin' murderer. William, why did you give me this shit, man? Why did you place this burden of knowledge upon me, man? Do you want me to go to the cops with this shit? Why don't you let your wife lock you up? You should have just kept your secrets, a secret," Jake whined.

"Jake, it's late, man, and I really don't feel like going into all of this. The *why* you will find out as you continue to read. But I suggest you stop skimming through it and start at the very beginning. Like I told you, someone needs to know the story, someone needs to know the truth, and I choose you. Good night, Jake."

"Where do I start from?"

"From the beginning—Yvonne's 'Discreet Misconceptions,' followed by Joann's 'Jo-Jo,' and then Dana's CD, which is titled *Shadows and Thorns*. Those three should give you almost all the background to near date—"

"And the last disc?" Jake asked, but William said nothing. "Hello?" Still silent. "Yo, Will, answer me. What about the last disc, Will?" Jake became a little annoyed. "I know *you* hear me."

"Yeah, Jake, I hear you, man. The last one is called *Petals in the Sand* because this tells where it started and where it will end. It's the story of Andrea. The disc says *Xzavier*. Look, everything you need to know and everything I wanted you to know is in those discs. Now go to bed, Jake, or go give your wife a call for some phone sex, you scary bastard."

"Fuck you, Will, because this is bullshit—"

"Jake." William interrupted.

"Yeah?"

"Get the fuck off my phone; you're dipping into my pussy time."

"Another prostitute?"

"No. My wife. Now, bye." William closed the lid to his cell phone, put out his cigarette, and began to put away his tools, and then the house phone rang.

♦ ♦ ♦

"How is my baby doing?" she asked.

"I'm okay. Are you coming over tonight?" He needed to know. The separation was beginning to take a toll on him. He needed encouragement, something hopeful, and something that was positive to make his deserving heart feel good.

She felt the weight of a tear hang heavy on the edge of its duct. She was missing him, too. She had been telling herself this was the way things had to be, but did it have to hurt? "No, baby, Mommy is not coming over tonight. Tomorrow night, okay? I promise. Mommy will come and get you in the afternoon, after camp, okay? We can stay together for a little while. Mommy came into some money, so we're set for a little while..."

"I hope you're not up to any illegal stuff, Ma?"

"No I'm not up to anything illegal, mister. Look, if you wanna come home, I strongly suggest you appreciate the gesture," Joann snapped.

"I'm sorry. I just don't wanna see you get into any trouble. I heard the stories about your old days. You told me lots of them and you were bad."

"Look, you're barely eight, watch your tongue. You're just too grown. Hey, kid, guess who I've seen last night?" she teased.

"Who?"

"Jonathan, guess."

"Was it—"

"It was your father." She couldn't hold it in. "And boy, let me tell ya, he was looking good, too..."

"I don't have a father, Ma. My father left us and went to take care of his real family..."

"Stop it! I don't wanna hear this out of you. Besides, he wants to see you. All he did was ask me questions about you. He still knows your age, your birthday, everything. Yo, kid, we had a long talk about you. So if he reaches out to you, you should be enough of a son and accept his hand..."

His tone changed. "He really asked about me?"

"Yes. I tell you what, I'm going to give you his cell number and you call him tomorrow and ask if he would take you to Great Adventure or something, okay? This way you guys can catch up on old times, okay? You gotta pen?"

"Wait...got one."

"Alright, here it is, but don't call him tonight, it's too late, alright?"

"Yeah, okay, Ma..."

◆  ◆  ◆

William shut off the lights and headed for the exit door into the rear of the house when his cell phone rang. He felt edgy after the very first ring. He left the unit from its pouch on his waistband, glanced into the I.D window, but didn't recognize the number it displayed.

"Hello?" he answered.

"Hi, Will, did I catch you at a bad time?" said the quite, soft almost whispering voice of a woman.

"Jo-Jo? What's up?" He had a bad feeling about this call. He could sense she was up to something. "That bastard not fucking with you again?"

"No, babe. I just wanted to thank you for the change you left for me in the medicine cabinet this morning. Oh you don't know how surprise I was and it was right on time, too."

"Where are you now?"

"I'm staying with my moms for a couple of days..."

"Good..."

"Baby, I wanna say sorry again about this morning in the shower. I feel so bad about not respecting you, and for taking advantage of you the way I did—"

"Look, it's all cool. Nothing happened, so no harm done, no foul."

"Thank you, baby, 'cause I'm sorry, even though it felt so good. You know big dicks can only get but so hard, but damn I thought my shit was wrapped around Gary Bond's bat. You felt so—"

"Jo-Jo. I said it was cool. It's a little after eleven and I'm about to lay my head, so I'll get at you later, alright?"

"Okay, baby. Oh one more thing. I was speaking with our son tonight and I mentioned how you spent the night and all. You know that kid bugged the hell out of me until I gave him your cell phone number. He's a good boy, Will, and he wants to speak to you so badly. He misses you. He's going to call you tomorrow. Please speak to him. He won't ask you for nothing…"

William was leaning against the wall, holding his head, rubbing his temples. He felt a headache coming on. "Okay. It's okay. He can call. We'll talk. No problem. Look, I'm out. I'll get at you later. One."

"Okay, love. Good night." She closed her phone, and her mother stepped out from the bodega. She stopped to pick up a few items that she didn't have in the house along with some sweets for her early morning craves.

"Who was you on the phone with?" Mrs. Garcia asked.

"My son, Ma. Why you ask? Who do you think I was on the phone with one of my tricks?"

"Why you talkin' to me like that? I'm still your mother; don't talk like that to me. Anyway, I thought they were called johns."

"Ah, Ma!" Joann was disgusted.

"What? Okay, okay, I was only playing, be easy. I joke wit' you." She smiled broadly, but Joann didn't see the joke. She wondered why she even bothered. It seemed clear this woman had no respect for her whatsoever. She didn't like when her mother started with her hooker jokes, because each and every time it would lead to them fighting. "*Mi pequeno puta hija*," said Mrs. Garcia.

The burning sensation started in Joann's heart then quickly surged through her soul. The pain felt like a hot knife slicing through her flush, dicing her into small little cubes. The knife hurt so bad, all Joann could think of was returning the pain with as much malice and contempt for her mother as she had for her, but Mrs. Garcia wasn't finished

"And which son? The little one you can't take care of or the one locked up on Riker's?"

"Ma!" Joann shouted.

"Jo-Jo? Oh, my God. Oh, girl, where you been. Damn it's been ages," said a rather tall dark-skinned woman, with breast large enough to feed a nation, and hips that molded the curves for the Indy 500. She strolled from out the shadows wearing a lilac Prada dress and shoes, a fifteen-inch string of culture peals centered with one large black peal, and a matching bracelet on her left wrist. Her approach seemed to take forever, as her White Diamond fragrance scented her path, and her shoulder length mane softly bounced in the eighty-six-degree thick, humid, moonlit night air. . "Oh, my sister friend." She extended her arms.

Joann and this woman embraced, jumped and screamed with excitement like old college sorority sisters. They carried on for what seemed like eternity. The darkness began to brighten.

"Oh wow! Damn, Keisha, girl, you look good." Joann stepped back to view the five-eleven lost girlfriend and was amazed.

"Damn, it look like you ain't aged none, child. What you been doin' with yourself? You look good. What's your secret?"

"For real? You think so? Shit, I ain't been doin nothin'. You know how I do. I still get down as often as I can, but you know I've always kept up the appearance. A sister got to be on her game. How 'bout you? What you been up to?" Keisha asked, surveying Joann with disapproving eyes.

"A little busted, girlfriend." Joann looked herself over with disappointment.

"You wanna get into something over at my place tonight? I got my superman stopping by, it's his birthday, help me give him a bangin' time—"

"I'm a mom now, Keisha." Joann wasn't sure how she should feel about Keisha's advance, but she did know it stung.

"I see that...Mommy dearest. Oh my lawd, just look at you..."

"My doors are locked in five minutes. I no open no more tonight. You stay with you people." Mrs. Garcia spoke from a distance. The girls just watched her march on.

"I see some people just don't change," Keisha said.

"Can't or won't," Joann mumbled.

"Well, anyways, how you been? You know you should stop by my apartment so we can catch up on lost time. If you like, you can come by tonight. My man and I can use the company, you know?"

"Keisha, you know I don't run like that anymore."

"Hey, Ms. Vanilla Chocolate, my domicile has become Boresville, okay? We need some excitement. Hell, I need some excitement. I'll make it worth your wild," she pressed.

"Keisha, girl, I'm not excitable anymore, child. My grove became some deep valleys. Tell your man to spice it up. Make

him get dressed into somethin', or beat him with a frying pan..."
Joann politely tried to turn her down, but Keisha wasn't giving
up.

"Damn, you're driving a hard bargain, baby. You know I want
a piece of you, too. So what you say to two bills?"

"Wh...What, two hundred? For how long?"

"Whatever you like. An hour, or two, it's up to you."

Joann considered the offer, and realized she had nearly
seven hundred dollars, the hundred and seventy left over from
William's offering, and five hundred of the seven hundred she
won, which was minus two hundred she gave to her mother.
"Noah, Kee, I'm straight girl, but thanks. Don't give up on me,
a girl never knows, you know what I'm sayin'?"

"I'll go high as *three*. Please?" Keisha begged.

"Oh, baby, not tonight. Let me think on it, but now I got to
catch up to my moms, 'cause she will lock my behind out, you
know?"

"Alright, boo. I know you don't need the drama, you get
home safe, you hear? And the offer stands anytime you wanna
do something, alright?"

"Alright, girlfriend." They leaned into one another to
exchange kisses upon the other's cheek. "I'll see ya, girl."

"Not if I see you first."

They laughed and parted.

# Rather Be With You

***11:36 p.m.***

*I*t's almost eleven-forty and the man on the phone just refused to accept the fact that the woman chose to end their little thing they had, but she didn't expect her decision to be so hard on him than it was. He was worse than a thirteen-year-old schoolboy who found out his beautiful teacher has another love, crushed. He became one serious bugaboo. She had been telling him over, and over, and over, and over she was going to keep her husband and her marriage. But *no*, he felt as if she was bullshitting him; she played him. She was just about to hang up on him when William walked into the room. From the look in William's eyes and the expression on her face read: CAUGHT. Back in the day, she could have played it off as if she was talking to one of his girlfriends, but playtime was over. She looked up at her tall, chocolate warrior and felt all warm and fleshy. He could still melt her heart, and weaken her knees.

Her mother and grandmother told her to marry him, but William wasn't the man she really wanted to marry. He was a cutie, but she was still young in the head. William and she were the same age, but he was very mature for his age. Most guys didn't know what they wanted or how to get it at the age of seventeen, which was the first time they started dating. He was singing in a group and working part-time after school. Their first boyfriend-girlfriend relationship didn't last long, a couple of weeks or less. He got caught with his hands in the cookie jar of a too damn grown lookin', hoity-toity, eleven-year-old. It was four-thirty in the afternoon when Yvonne was coming home from hanging out on Pine Street after she'd been home from school, and saw a crowd gathering in front of her building, then her man being escorted by two big large D.T.'s, with him in handcuffs. All kind of things went through her head. What did he do to get arrested? She ran up to the building, but she didn't get too far before miss Ugga-mug, Valerie Simmons, cut off her path. She had to be the one to be the bearer of bad news. "It looks like your boyfriend just got arrested."

"And why? What for?" then she felt stupid for asking this one for anything.

"He got caught fucking Regina by her mother. It's said that she's only ten years old. Damn, girl, I guess you ain't *all that* after all. Damn, you couldn't even keep your man off the babies..." Yvonne decked her in her right eye. Bringing bad news was one thing, but she had to gloat, too. Yvonne beat the half-pale yellow Valerie Simmons through the park and into her own building. She had to learn that Yvonne wasn't the one. Besides, Yvonne always wanted to bust her behind from the time she used to call her blacky, as if she was some kind of dog, back in the third and fourth grades. Yvonne should have known Valerie was jealous and wanted William, because six months later, it was told how she was all over William's jock, but as it was also told, William barely paid her any mind. She tried to upstage him one hot summer day while William was on his way to the handball courts. Miss Thang yelled at William, "Excuse me? It's me you're trying to get with, so I think it's me you want to be talking with instead of playing ball with your little gay friend there."

William stood there for a second. "Well right now I'm going to play a few games of handball, and I'll talk with you when I get back."

"No you won't." She put her hands on her boney waist, because she had no hips.

"Then I guess I won't." William turned and walked off.

"You're still a little boy. You don't know what you gave up…" She raved on, and on, talking loud, trying to disrespect William at any cost, but she was the trick because Yvonne witnessed everything and knew it was her time to get her dibs in.

Yvonne walked by the awkwardly thin looking teenager and said, "It looks like a handball and gay guy is able to beat out your time, with your tired ass self." Yvonne finally got it off her chest, but Valerie, being Valerie, turned around and called Yvonne a *black monkey bitch*. Yvonne chased her down after she made a feeble attempt to outrun Yvonne, and Yvonne spanked that ass again.

William walked up to the bed, and reached for the phone. She didn't hastate in handing it over, because Robert was getting on her nerves. Besides, if her man wanted to handle it, she was more than happy to reside in a woman's place, and she felt her place wasn't between two Mack trucks loaded with dynamite. These two men didn't like one another, not one iota, and she was not going to be arguing with William all night over a simple matter like not handing him the phone. Besides, she was moist and ready for her man, her husband, William as for whom she was craving. Even more so especially after he laid it on Robert. It was this fire that caused her to remember the things she had always loved about him, and the thought of how she never planned to marry Mr. Green. She thought she had an all-expense paid summer of free movies, parties, and hopefully some clothes out of the fling. Other than for those reasons, one would seriously have to wonder why she would go back out with a guy who cheated on her two years earlier with a ten-year-old girl. Actually, many times she had thought she was stupid for such a scandalous decision, but now she knew better. But back then, she was a young teen-aged girl who faced a long, hot summer all alone because her then boyfriend, Mark, and she broke up because he had decided to enlist in the Army. William proved to be a logical choice. He wasn't bad looking, and he had a good paying job for a young teen, which made him look even better.

Let the truth be told, there was still some love there. A love she had always tried to deny. She would tell herself, *He's one of my little brother's friends*, or *he's a player*, because she always got his local news until he started dating outside of the neighborhood, which showed he wasn't like the other bean-head guys living in the projects. William and she used to talk for hours about everything from their parents to their lovers. She would try to convince herself that they had this brother-sister type of relationship, but he broke her down. He put in the overtime and swept her off her feet for the second time, which took a whole twenty minutes. Talking about a blur. He didn't use his charm to sway her, or run the "Baby, baby, I'll treat you right, and give you everything you ask for" crap. The performance he gave was award winning. He just wasn't taking "No," as an option, and God knows how many times she said it to him. But every excuse she threw at him, he disregarded, or he had an answer for it, then lastly: "Look, Eve, no one knows you better than I do. I know what you thinking, I know when you're thinking it. I know what you're feeling, and I know why you're feeling it. Like *now* you're wondering why don't I just leave you alone, and if I'm going to hurt you again. Well, let me answer you. No, I'm not going to leave you alone, and I don't know if I will ever hurt you again. I'll say this to you; don't ever believe the B.S. that I won't, because the odds are I will over a period of time. Just don't you ever let your guard down. But if for some reason I bump my head and get stupid, it's not your fault, or something you did, because my actions will always be my own. So the truth of the matter is never trust me." She looked at him as if he was an alien with a foot dangling from the center of his forehead. This wasn't how you win a girl's heart, but he continued, "And besides you need me to take care of you. You don't cook, but I do. You can't sew, but I can. You don't handle scissors too good or iron clothes all that well. I guess that comes from being left-handed, but I know all these things and I'm more than willing to do them all for you, and for the rest of my life." He looked her in those brown, China doll eyes.

"I don't think so, besides I might be carrying Mark's baby. My period is late. We did it when he came home last month. And…and I don't know if he's ready, or even if he wants a child. I know I'm not ready, and I don't want a child right now. So I've been thinking about getting an abortion if I am…" Yvonne finally exhaled her fear she'd been carrying for a number weeks.

"Yeah, I've seen you with kids. You're not too hot in that department either." William said.

"That's not true." She had to stick up for herself.

"Oh, yes it is. You refer to them all as *little bastards*."

"That's because they are little bastards."

"Look, if it's a question of raising the child, I'm willing to marry you and give him or her my name, and I will never think twice about it down the road."

That was it. This nineteen-year-old kid was offering her his life. So she gave in, and decided to give him another chance and they started dating once again. They have been together for twenty-five years, but legally married for only fifteen of them. It wasn't because he didn't want to; it was because she didn't want to. He was right in their discussion in the garage. She was too busy wondering if Mark was going to ride in on his white horse and carry her off into a golden sunset. It wasn't as if William wasn't good to her. It was not as if he was ugly, abusive, or anything like that. William was a fine, sexy looking brother, with his dark brown tone, chocolate bedroom eyes, long eyelashes, straight nose, and almost thin pussy lips. The desire to fuck him wasn't the issue, she just didn't see him as a husband, she'd always thought of him as the godfather of her children when she decided to have some. But when you have two kids by this man, it's time to wake up and look ahead. One problem she had with William was she never felt she was in William's league. He was too much for one woman, and certainly not enough for two. He was just a handful, and that fear of him cheating on her kept her away from marriage. As long as she had a way out, a way to escape him by way of another man, she thought she would be in the best position if he ever decided to leave her, this way she would be one up on him.

That was it in a nutshell, she was afraid. Too afraid to commit to him, too afraid to open up to him, too afraid of the world, yet he knew who she was all along. For twenty-five years, her destiny was in their union, and she rejected his truth, she rejected the spirit that was within her. Always seeing, feeling, and knowing there was something great inside, yet she exchanged truth for fear, because fear kept her safe. A complete contrast from him, he faced all the same fears and dealt with them. He allowed nothing and no one to limit him, not even the one he gave his life to.

She handed her husband the phone. "Mister fuckin' Lt. Robert Wells…" William began.

"So she put the chump on…" Robert sneered.

"Look, she's home. You had your rein and now you should just move on." William was clam.

"Fuck you, punk. You bitch niggers like to fuck around, but I ain't no toy—"

"That's all you've ever been, you dumb ass. Now bend the fuck over and listen to this: If you call *my* house again I will bring you up on charges." William was getting serious. He was sticking his chest out.

*Now, that's my man*, Yvonne thought.

"Are you threatening me, you fucking wuss?"

"Shut up and spread your cheeks, bitch. If you continue to harass my wife, we will bring you up on charges."

"What?" Robert wasn't used to William talking back, but once William got tired of the B.S., all that was left was for hell to break loose.

"I told you to shut up and stay in a child's place. This conversation is being recorded. And if you continue to behave in an unprofessional manner, I will seek your job, and after I fucked over you enough, I'm gonna bust your fuckin' ass. Now you're dismissed. Good night, son."

*My hubby is such a bastard.*

William hung up the phone and stared at Yvonne. His phone demeanor got her stuff warmed up. She stared back at him. There was a time when she thought he was afraid of Robert, but she should have known better. William R. Green was afraid of no one. She looked up at him and wanted to say, "Now that's how you do it. That's what a girl wanna see. Now come here and let me break your back and make your scream my name," but instead, she slowly batted her eyes, widened them, tilted her head back and slightly parted her pouty lips. William exhaled long, swallowed hard, and released whatever tension there was.

"Why don't you take a shower, so I can funk you up again, and help you ease your troubles?" she said seductively.

"Yeah." He gave in. "I think I will." He removed his shirt; his nipples were hard and protruding, causing hers to mimic the gesture. Then he turned his back to her. Yvonne doesn't know what frightened her more, the tattoo on his back or the two exit wounds from the time someone shot him and left him for dead on New Lots Avenue outside of Brookdale Hospital where she was recovering from a hole in her head and slight concussion.

*I remember that day as if it happened yesterday. I called my daughter early that morning, and she was telling me something about all of my children were having bad dreams, and that my two baby girls were sick. I asked where William was. When she told me he hadn't come home that night, I was through. I just knew he left my children home alone, again, and spent the night out with that Joann bitch, whose ass I'd kicked in the parking lot and then arrested her for pissing me off, but this is what happened when someone tried to kill my baby:*

*I'd called home that morning. Jasmine told me William never came home. She was upset, disturb about something. I thought she was upset because she was left with the task of baby-sitting.*

*"I'm so sick of this shit!" I shouted.*

*"Mommy—"*

*"Bullshit! He couldn't wait to be with that bitch he's fucking—"*

*"No, Mommy. Something's happen—"*

*"Ain't nothing happening."*

*"Yes, Mommy, something did happen. It was about four in the morning. We all woke up at the same time, all of us." Jasmine*

was trying her best to save her father's ass, but I wasn't hearing it.

"What the hell are you talking about?" I snapped at her.

"Mommy, I felt a pain in my chest and Daddy came into my head."

"You had a bad dream. That's all." She's so dramatic.

"And what, Jayson and Jernece, too? We all had the same dream? Having the same feeling? And at the same time, Mommy? No, Ma, something happened."

"All my babies felt it?"

"Jernece and the baby got up crying. And Jayson walked into my room and said 'Someone shot my father.' Now you know that boy is strange, he's just like Daddy." She had a point.

"Yeah, he is strange. Did he go to school?"

"He left this morning saying he's going to find his father. I told him to go to school, but I don't know if he did."

"How are the little ones?"

"They're sick."

"Both of them?" I grew concerned.

"Yeah. We all are running slight fevers."

"I'm coming home." My mind was made up.

"No, Mommy. What did the doctor say?"

"Fuck the doctor. I'll be there in a little while." Those were my children. I had to do all I could possibly do to get home to them.

"How are you getting home?"

"Don't worry. Hang up now, Mommy's coming home." The pain hit me like that bat did the night before in that supermarket, which was the reason for me being there. I thought of my two baby girls, Jernece and Jerliner, with Jerliner being seven months old. I walked to the closet, looked inside and saw only my uniform.

*The nurse walked in and found me in the closet. "And where are you going, miss?"*

*"Home. I got to go..."*

*"Look at you all bent over, you can't go anywhere."*

*"I'm going."*

*"You're not going anywhere." That voice came from behind the nurse and belonged to Sergeant Duffy.*

*"I have to. My babies are home alone."*

*"You heard the boss," Robert said, as he followed the sergeant into the room.*

*They grabbed me by the arms and led me back to the bed. My fight was weak and useless.*

*"The Great William up to his old tricks?" Robert said.*

*"Something's wrong. He didn't come home."*

*"You have a big girl at home. She should be able to handle things 'til he gets back," Sergeant Duffy said.*

*They were right. I wasn't going anywhere. My head was bad. The sergeant and Robert convinced me to relax for an hour and someone would drive me home later that morning. I woke up at two in the afternoon. I called home again. The girls were feeling a little better and William still was a no show, he didn't call, and he wasn't at work. Anger filled my painful head. Then I wondered where my ride was. Why someone hadn't awakened me? I knew I couldn't trust those fools. I called the precinct and yelled at Duffy. Moments after resting my head back on the pillow, a voice said, "Someone tried to kill my father."*

*I turned and looked toward the door. It was my ten year old, Jayson, standing there, with tears in his eyes.*

*"Jayson. How did you get here? How did you get—"*

*"I said someone tried to kill my father."*

*"No, your father didn't come home because—"*

"My father is down stairs in I.C.U with two bullet holes in him."

I wasn't sure if I heard him correctly. I laid there in silence and stared at my son, and then I remembered I was capable of speaking. "Where is he?"

"Downstairs'." He turned and walked away.

I jumped for the bed, looked around for Jayson, but there was no sign of him. So I waddled my bare behind to the elevators. I tried to jet past the nurse's station, with my hospital gown flapping open in the back. The pursuit was on. A nurse chased me to the elevators.

"Where are you going, young lady... Miss?"

"My husband is in I.C.U."

"You can't go like that."

"The hell I can't." It's a hospital, who hasn't seen ass?

She looked at me and knew she was not going to deter me. She pulled off her smock and offered it to me, so I snatched the smock from her as I entered the elevator and said nothing, just gave her this nasty look when the doors closed. I get off the elevator and approached the nurse's station on the third floor, and saw a guard manhandling my son.

"Get off me!" shouted Jayson.

"Get off my son!" I shouted at this... I'm gonna be nice. So I pushed the guard from behind, and all hell broke loose. Uniforms of all kind were all over the place, including suits from the Justice Department. Don't ask me what was going on, 'cause I had no clue. Not until months later when it seemed as if all they wanted to do were to lock our asses up on murder and drug charges. But that's another story.

That was a scary time in my life. So much was going on, but as quickly as it started, it all turned around. William invented a *filter thingy and we were in the money just like that. He thought he did well when he brought this house, and it is a lovely home, but at the time I thought he was moving me all the way out here in the middle of twenty acres of trees just to get me away from my family, where no one could clock his moves. I wasn't stupid, so I thought. I only let him think I was naïve. He didn't think I knew about those he'd chosen to immortalize in the form of a tattoo on his back. He thought I was weak, but my senses were just as operational as his, maybe not as strong, but functional. I chose to shy from my abilities, and it's a good thing I did, because my looks could kill.*

*For months before this past Sunday, I stared at that tattoo, at his life. The image of four women he made love to, he had them immortalized on his back and they were in my bed, lying with us, with me, in our bed, in my bed. And he had no clue of me having knowledge of them, but it was cool. Yeah it was cool. It was all right, because I was getting mine and he wasn't getting any. He could go get whatever he was getting before from those on his back, Robert was doing all right. I mean, he wasn't as skillful as William was, but I was able to get my groove on, and at that time that was something I thought I needed, revenge.*

*Life is funny, and the curves that are the funniest of them all. Just a week ago I was happy for all the times I betrayed the man I honestly love, and this week I have the task of getting a renegade angel to repent or kill him. Now the only problem with that is this angel is one of the hardest to kill. This angel was designed to overcome everything, and I honestly still love him.*

*He sat the phone back into its cradle, and stared at me. That look, that's the look that puzzled me, because I didn't know if I should slowly back away and get into my defense mode, or relax and breathe. Truth, he only had one expression for every* situation. Detecting those subtle differences weren't always easy. He exhaled, he was about to speak, his expression didn't change, it's like the same expression he had that night I betrayed him.

# *Betrayed*

He stood outside the doorway, hawking them. The Great William was stoking her, his wife. He knew something was wrong, he must have known she was up to no good, that demon of infidelity was calling out to him from her soul.

He watched them for God knows how long before he witnessed Robert placing a kiss upon his index finger, and placing that finger between her lips where she gently suckled for a second or two. It must have seemed like a full-length movie for the hawker. The moment was long enough for him to place a value on their actions, long enough to see the expressions upon their faces, smiles of sly seduction, flirtatious sparkling of the eyes.

William calmly walked in. The music was blaring, conversations created a buzz through the air, while the waitresses were carrying trays filled with entrees, boos, and beers to their awaiting destinations. Many of the patrons took notice of William. Yvonne took note to that feeling of another, and then she felt the signature of that other. She turned her head in the direction of him. Her heart stopped, her mind raced, a lump formed in her throat, she felt heat, she thought, *What the fuck is he doing here? Oh no! This man is following me? I'll be damned.*

Her nervousness and fear turned into anger, she was pissed that he had the nerve to stalk her. Who the fuck was he to treat her in such a manner? He was the one to be watched, he was the dog. He and those bitches he ran with, then she wondered who was home with the children.

Responding to Yvonne's reaction, Robert turned to see what snatched her attention from him. *William! What the fuck is this bastard doing up in here? How did he know about this place? I hope he gets stupid so I can knock him on his ass. I've been waiting a long time to get a piece of the Great William.*

William walked up to the couple's table. His blood was boiling, but he remained cool. He wanted to turn the table over, drive his hand into Robert's chest, yank out his heart along with some other organs, but he knew this wasn't the time, or the place. William knew if he allowed himself to get caught up in the heat of the moment, he would never be able to rebound from it in his future.

"Hey, William. What's up?" Robert greeted him.

William cut his eyes and stared into Robert's eyes.

Robert felt something, but he didn't know what, but it made his insides stir.

Yvonne knew what was about to happen, and she wasn't having it. She wasn't going to permit her partner to have a sudden coronary death, or *freak* accident. "Honey, why are you here?" Yvonne said to redirect William's attention.

Successfully, William refocused his attention back to Yvonne, and reclaimed control over his emotions and anger, but still he wasn't up for the game, or the acting. "I need you to come home."

Yvonne felt his anger and she wasn't about to go home for a long, dragged out argument where everyone with ears would here William raving like a madman. That was her reason for stopping for drinks in the first place. She didn't want to go home and hear him rant on about his Filtrex project, or how it was going to make them all rich someday, or argue about his sneaky ways, and not to mention about him finding a much-needed job. Just because he was under house arrest, didn't mean he couldn't work. No, she wanted to relax, have fun, and clear her mind from all the bullshit she'd been going through. Although she couldn't understand, for the life of her, why she was comingling and receiving Robert's advances.

"Are the children okay?" Yvonne asked.

"Yeah, they're fine."

"Okay then, if everything is alright, then I'll be home in a little bit. Alright?"

"Why can't you come home now?"

"'Cause I don't want to. Go home and I'll see you when I get in."

William tried not to blow up. The nerve of her dismissing him. "Eve—"

"Yo, Will, she's not ready to go home right now. Why don't you have a drink with us?" Robert said.

"Why don't you step the fuck off." William replied.

"Hey, look, no reason to get nasty 'cause your woman has a mind of her own…"

William received a flashback of Robert placing his finger in Yvonne's mouth. "Robert, butt the fuck out!"

"Or what?" Robert stood up. William walked right into his lair. "Or what, William?" Robert stepped in to the slightly taller William's personal space.

"Robert, you don't want to fuck with me. I'm truly not the one." William's blood pressure rose.

"Fuck you, William. I ain't never like your punk ass anyhow. You talk big shit to your wife, but deal with me. Man to man. No department, no guns, just you and I, in the back, all alone. Let's go, bitch, 'cause you don't scare me." Robert began to place his shield, gun, and cuffs on the table. He was grandstanding. The mini drama quickly took center stage.

"Well what fun would it be beating a scared motherfucker's ass, Robert? It's the confidence ones, like you, I receive pleasure from, but you will never measure up to me, *son.* So step down, and step off, 'cause you can't drink from my cup."

"Fuck you. Let's go for it, if you all that…"

"Don't piss me off 'cause the fuckin' ground I walk on will void you." William stared him down from head to toe, and turned his head toward Yvonne, dismissing him.

"All I hear is talk. Let's do the walk. Be a man for once in your life, you spineless coward." Robert shoved William from behind.

William stumbled into some seated officers, who pushed him into another table, who pushed him back toward Robert.

William felt the stares, and the tension. He looked back, deep behind Robert's eyes, and whatever he saw alerted him that this moment wasn't the time, or the place. He knew only one would be left that room standing. Being on probation didn't help his fury, or his pride. He felt like shit, he was dismissed by his wife, who was just sitting there taking it all in; he was being chomped by a chump. Yeah that night he had bitch written all over his face, and Robert was the author who engraved it there.

He stepped from the bathroom smelling delicious like Bath & Bodies, Country Apple. He stood in the doorway of the bathroom for a second to what she believed, was to adore her. She lay on the bed with her short, silk komodo robe opened, exposing her dark nakedness. All except her diamond. She used her thigh that was facing him to keep her hidden from him. He turned off the lights in the bathroom, then those in the bedroom. His smoothness made her hotter. He was precise, and confident, he knew exactly what he was going to do to her. He threw his towel across the room onto the sofa. He lifted a leg and kneeled onto the king size bed, extended his long arm, took her left foot, and pulled her to him. She was frightened for a hot New York minute, 'cause she knew just what he really was going to do her.

He raised her foot higher and higher until her big toe met his lips. He kissed it. This big man who kneeled before her was so gentle, yet he held her foot firmly. She felt the heat from his breath as his head changed directions, then she felt the hot, long, wet tip of his tongue at her heal, trailed by the fatness of his tongue upward

"Oh my…mmmmmm…yes, between the toes just like that… oh yeah, baby. Shit."

As he dined on that foot, she massaged his manhood with the other, but it wasn't there long before he repeated the treatment on her.

He was driving her  crazy, and she loved every bit of it. He placed her feet on his chest so he could run his hand along the contour of her legs, and further over her knees, and around, and down her thighs, not missing one of her zones. He leaned in, pushing her leg back, widening her center, and slightly opening her, exposing her warm juices to the cool air, while his hands circled around, messaging her buttocks, to the center of her crack.

"Oooh," she moaned, as his tongue traced around her rear door. "Umm, yes, keep it moving, baby," she said, loving the feeling he was giving her. Up, up, gently combing over the tip of the hairs on her outer lips, up and over her clit. She had to bite the bottom of her lip. As his hand glided so softly up along the inner part of her thighs, her knees, her calves, the back of the legs, her ankles, the top of her feet, her toes, she knew then the Postman was in her bed with a strong grip on her.

He placed her legs tightly together, raised them with her toes pointed to the ceiling, stood, then he licked down the center of her feet, and it felt as if they both were one foot. His tongue slid from side to side, foot to foot. He forced her toes to dance in his mouth, on his tongue as if it was a carpet laid out for her.

"Woo, sweetness, what are you doing to me? Are you trying to make me cum?"

And then when he drove his tongue deep inside her, she fell over the edge from the pleasure. She screamed softly, pushing his head away, turning sideways to push him off her so she could close her legs and shut the door to her swollen clit.

But he wasn't finished with her. As she rocked from side to side, he stroked that monster of his. The look in his eyes told her she was in trouble. He parted her legs and she knew it was over for her. It was doom.

His thick head parted her lips and slid inside slowly. The pain she felt as he stretched her was pleasurable as hell. Her Postman. Her lover, her man, the master of lick 'em and stick 'em; she surrendered.

"Do as you will with me; just stay deep down within me, baby. Stay connected to me for all times and I will cream on you forever, and ever, and ever. My Postman, my lover, my husband. Ahwwwww."

# *Jake's Obsession*

**11:43 p.m.**

*J*ake didn't take William's advice. He continued poring over William's memoirs until he became frustrated with clicking, and clinking, and clicking through the maze of sentences and paragraphs. He located and placed the disc titled *Yvonne's– Discreet Misconceptions*, in the disc drive of his laptop. He skipped through this one a few times before it was where he found out about Grace Blackwell. William's young, teen-aged lover who committed suicide after William confessed his marriage to a pregnant Yvonne. William thought it would be a summer fling and would be over before the fall settled in good, but that wasn't the case. Her death held onto William for twenty-two years, just as Yvonne's summer fling evolved into a twenty-five-year union. What was it about the hard lessons one needed to learn about flings? William and Yvonne learned the hard way that people don't always exit your life and the longer they're allowed to remain attached the consequences were more substantial.

Jake knew that William and Yvonne had known each other for more than twenty-seven years, but it surprised him to learn of Andréa's presence so early at the forefront of all of this, and again, *William did say disc four, started and ended with Andréa, right? He said something in that effect. So what roll does she play in all of this? And more so, why haven't I heard of her in our many conversations 'bout him and Yvonne?*

*Wait, what did he tell me last Friday? He said these discs and that damn tattoo on his back all told the story about his life.*

Jake sat back in his seat, and looked at the contents within the dinner. He finished his steak and potatoes a long time ago. Now what sat off on the side of his laptop computer was one-third of a slice of an apple pie, and an empty coffee cup. He motioned and gestured to his waitress to refill the cup. "Oh, and another slice of pie, please."

Jake thought back to the conversation about the tattoo...

*"These eight discs are about a portion of my life, the life you don't know about, as well as about the meaning of the things on my back. Now, Jake, what I'm going to tell you is some off-the-wall shit."*

*"What are you talking' about?" Jake said, while he stared down at the discs, each one labeled The Unicorns followed by a subtitle.*

*"Just listen, will ya? Now you think you know all there is to know about me. We've been friends for what...about fourteen years or so? But you don't know everything, like who I am, what I am, or all I've done in my life. So get two fresh bottles of spirits, your juice, and me a soda and the bucket of chicken from the microwave. 'Cause I'm going to tell you something that will blow your mind, and I really want you to listen. Someone should know about this, and I love you, man. So you're elected."*

*Jake stood up. "Shit. I got to hear this."*

*William turned his back toward Jake. There were no words for a moment. Jake just stared at a mural that stared back at him. "Look closely," said William.*

*"I'm looking."*

*After a moment, William faced Jake, took a seat, and mixed a fresh glass of his tonic. "Those CDs, along with my tattoo, tell my life."*

*Jake, who was speechless, tried to make sense of what he'd just seen. "Yeah, yeah, you told me that. Man, there's a lot of shit on your back."*

*"There's a lot of shit on those discs. They tell the events of what took place in my life. There was so much happening to me, I could no longer keep the pieces together. What you see on my back shows my babies, Yvonne, my lovers, and the lives I've taken."*

*Jake stared at William, dazed, as a chill froze him in place. "Wait, wait. I don't know if I should hear this. It's, I mean . . ." Jake shook his head, and placed the discs onto the coffee table.*

*"Jake, stop bitching and listen." William turned around, exposing his back once again. "The large unicorn with its head superimposed within the moon is me. The ones on the clouds beneath me are my family—Yvonne, Jasmine, Jayson, Jernece, and Jerliner. On the cloud underneath them, off to the right side, the four smaller unicorns are four women whom I shared past lives with and have loved. These four women still exist in my life today. Now the seven angels that's spaced out beneath them, from one side to the other, are the seven times I neared death and will come near death..."*

*Jake plopped down and leaned back. "What's this shit? Who are the women? Do I know them?"*

*"I never spoke of them to you. They were in my past life. No, that's not correct. They are a part of my original existence. I also know them by their true names—Love, Sunshine, Xzavia, and the fourth one I'm still not sure of."*

Jake recalled William not knowing, or not being sure who the fourth Unicorn was. The revelation hit Jake like a ton of bricks. The fourth unicorn was Grace Blackwell. The young woman who died for him twenty-two years ago. Jake stared at her name and thought, *This tender, naïve, young girl fell victim to this monster, which means she had a role in his life. What was it?"* Will the disc reveal more about her? There was so little said about the child who gave up so much for this man called William R. Green.

Once again, Jake felt a twinge of hatred for his longtime friend, his so-called brother who turned out to be a complete stranger in so many ways between the pages of his memoir. *But what the fuck is a unicorn?* Jake questioned himself. *Are they not bullocks of some kind, cattail, yes, sure a one-horned cattail. Oh what the fuck am I doin'? Everyone knows unicorns really don't exist. William is off his damn rocker. But something is going on here, and more so why was it so important for me to know the truth about him?*

Jake opened his web browser and typed in the word 'unicorns.' He was surprised to see there were over two-hundred thousand hits on a single word. He found so much information, and most of it proved nothing. Then he remembered William said everything was spiritual. He closed the web browser, opened his electronic Bible to the King James Version and did a search on the same word. He was surprised, once again, to learn that the search revealed nine results, as where he was expecting nothing. His certainties became doubtful thoughts as he wondered the connection between William, unicorns, and the Holy Bible.

# The Same Old Me

**11:49 p.m.**

She didn't understand why her mother wouldn't open the door. She was no more than a minute or two behind her, and that was because she closed the elevator door on her when she came into the building, instead of holding it for her. Joann didn't understand her mother at times and this was one of them. It was as if she did stuff out of sheer hatred and resentment for her daughter, Joann. Well it was never a secret that Mary was her favorite daughter. But it just wasn't normal for a mother to go all out and disowned her first born. Joann's hand started to hurt from all the knocking on the door, so she stopped, leaned her head against the door out of defeat and contemplated.

*Can you believe it? She locked me out. I... I don't believe my mama sometimes. I was about two minutes behind her. I don't understand why it seems as if she has it out for me. It's a shame when you feelin' like you can't trust your own mama. I gave this woman over three hundred dollars tonight, and here she locks me out, because I said hello to an old friend? She cuts me down every time I reach out to her. Not sometimes, but each and every time. Lord, this ain't right. It just ain't right. She treats me like shit. What the fuck am I gonna do now? I can't go back home, not with that sick ass Jay Dee on the loose.*

*Damn these last two days have been so weird. I mean, crazy like, you know. Well I first get a visit from an old flame. It had been four years since I've last seen him. Now this man I would have given my right arm for, and after four years, he finally gave me enough consideration to stop by to fix my computer. How fuckin' noble of him. But I can't talk, 'cause I should have been woman enough to beat his ass, but I did smack the shit out of him for leaving his son, just as soon as he walked through my door. But instead, cursing at him, throwing kicks, and punches, what did I do? I acted like a little schoolgirl, smiled, and pretended nothing ever happened. Shit, I was even ready to fuck him, but I knew I didn't have enough time.*

*He walked back into my life and stirred up all these feelings I'd suppressed, hidden, and locked away so I could carry on. But truth be told, my entire world came crashing in on me. A few months after William dropped out of my life, my little, pimpin' ass, drug-dealing family went to war over a score William and I fucked up weeks earlier. But it really wasn't a score. It was more like self-defense. Those motherfuckers was gonna waste us, pocket the loot and keep the two keys for themselves. Thank God, William did come along for the ride, because they would have wasted me if I was by myself. Yeah so, it went the other way, instead of them knocking us off, William and I knocked them the fuck off. We offered Turtle-dove the money we'd owed him and explained how his boys was trying to pull a fast one, but he ain't wanna hear shit. And he took our people out in a whisper. Only a few of us got away, and that was because everyone thought it was my brother's operation. Damn, so many kids died, for no reason, for some shit that went down, which they had no knowledge of.*

She sighed deeply from a joyful thought that turned into self-pity, which churned into anger.

*And then this man, who has done so much for me in the past, walked back into my life yesterday. For the few moments he was there, this fuckin' man brought hope and sunshine back into my life, and then... Then he stood there. He just fuckin' stood there and crushed all the gifts he brought. He had the nerve to stand over me and announce my wickedness, my shortcomings, and my dark secrets. But if that wasn't enough for him, he had the nerve to go as far as to say I only have three weeks, or three months, three years to live if I continue on this path of self-destruction. Who the hell did he think he was? He seemed to know everything about my childhood, my father, my stepfather, and the rapes and about the abuse in detail. But who the hell is he that I should stop living? Besides, I don't work the streets, or take appointments anymore. That was how I ended up with that sorrowful bastard, Jay Dee. I thought if I play the mommy role, God would bless me and give me a man who would step up, but Jay Dee was far from a man. I learned this after time, or was it just that I didn't want to accept the fact that he was a piece of shit, and the only one sniffing up my butt crack at the time.*

*Fuck all that shit now. My man is back in my life, I got money back into my pockets, and Jay Dee wants war. Done deal, I'll just pay him a little visit at his place Friday, offer him some ass and slice his throat before we get busy. Don't wanna leave any DNA behind. Okay, with that thought I better not suck his little pee-pee either. Speaking of, it's not Friday, and I have no bed to sleep in.*

*Oh, damn, Ma, why you do this to me all the time? Damn. All I wanted to do was lay low and get some sleep. Fuck. Keisha? No, I don't feel like fuckin no one tonight. Damn, she did offer three bills and a pillow. Shit if I play my cards right, I may even get an orgasm out of this. It's a little before twelve, hell I could be finished by two, three the latest. A hundred and fifty dollars an hour or better, cool. William warned me against this same shit.*

*Oh, man. But it's three big ones, and if her man is a little dick motherfucker, it's no work at all. Just this once, God, please. Shit, I'll have a grand and it's been a long time since I had a grand in my hands that was mine. I promise I'll visit your house. Yeah, yeah I know it's been a while. Yeah, yeah and it's always for a funeral, but I'll keep this one, that's my word. A girl gotta do what a girl gotta do.*

She left her mother's building angry, but more so frightened. It was dark out. She feared the dark, because the shadows would come alive, and loved to play tricks with her mind.

Cautiously, she exited the building. Looking about, looking into the dark shadows, she had no choice but to make it to Keisha's apartment to seek refuge from the night. Her spirit felt stronger, but not enough to tickle the things she feared most—loneliness and darkness.

The tree limbs danced in the soft breeze. A strange odor swirled about and Joann knew she was not alone.

"Oh God, please get me to this girl's apartment. I promise I'll be good. I promise…"

"You shouldn't bargain with the Father," a man said.

Whoever he was, wherever he was, he startled Joann. She jumped; her heart skipped a beat or two while she looked to her left in the direction where she thought she heard him. She whipped around instinctively to look behind her. To her right, back to her left, no one there and she spun in a complete circle and again no one.

"It is said in Numbers, Chapter 30, second verse…"

"Yo, stop playin." Before her was a dark figure sitting on a bench. "Yo, who's that?"

"When a man makes a vow to the Lord or takes an oath to obligate himself by a pledge, he must not break his word, but must do everything he said."

"But I am no man." Joann engaged him.

There was momentary silence. "When a young woman, still living in her father's house, makes a vow to the Lord or obligates herself by a pledge and her father hears about her vow or pledge, but says nothing to her, then all her vows and every pledge by which she obligated herself will stand. But if her father forbids her when he hears about it, none of her vows or the pledges by which she obligated herself will stand. The Lord will release her because her father has forbidden her."

"I have no father."

"It is written: If she marries after she makes a vow or after her lips utter a rash promise by which she obligates herself and her husband hears about it, but says nothing to her, then her vows or the pledges by which she obligated herself will stand. But if her husband forbids her when he hears about it, he nullifies the vow that obligates her or the rash promise by which she obligates herself, and the Lord will release her."

"I have no husband. What the fuck is all this? Stop playin, and tell me who's this?" Joann became impatience and slowly began walking toward the man. "Sup, who's this?"

"Just a friend, Jo-Jo, who's trying to keep you out of trouble, because you know you ain't about to be good, when you're asking him to grant you something to go do bad…"

"And what you know about it? Yo, who's that? Is that, Kwan?" Joann leaned forward for a better look. The wind below louder, twirling before her, as she leaned in closer.

The black darkness of his eyes slowly became visible, then his hairline, his nose.

The hairs on the nape of her neck rose. "Yo, son, why you out here playin like that? I should hit you in your head." He ticked her off, but she extended her arms for a hug. He stood and reached for her. Their embrace was warm and friendly. She released him. "Man, why you tryin' to scare the shit out of me like that? You had me going, boy. How you been?" She looked the young man over quickly, and admired him.

Little Kwan Bartend was ten years her junior, and he always had a tremendous crush on Joann. It had been just about ten years when she saw him last. She was coming out of her mother's building when Kwan and his little friends were playing. When Joann walked by them, he stepped to her, and professed his undying love to Joann. Everyone standing around, including Joann, thought it was the most adorable sight to see.

♦ ♦ ♦

"Look Jo-Jo, I know I'm still young, but you should give a guy like me a chance. I will make you happy and protect you always…"

Joann giggled. "Oh, and you will protect me, too?"

"Yeah, baby. I will do all that for you. You're one of the hot girls around…"

"Oh well thank you, Kwan, but you do know I'm a little too old for you right?"

"No you're not; you just what, twenty-three, twenty-four?"

"No, baby, I'm almost thirty and you're not even twenty years old yourself…"

"Come on, Jo-Jo. Age is just a number. I'll get a good job, and buy you whatever you want. I'm willing to do it all for you.…"

Joann could not help but to laugh. The look on his face showed that he was serious. "Baby, that's so sweet. The women are just going to eat you up. Tell you what, let's see if you still feel this way ten and twenty years from now, after all these women get a taste of you…"

◆　◆　◆

"I've been alright, Jo–Jo. Still waiting for you to give me that chance, you know?"

"Man, you still on that? I just knew you was gonna grow out of that one, fo' sho…" Joann stated.

"Naw, you kidding. You good peoples. You always been good to me, and I ain't never forgot what you said. It gave me hope that one day we hook up and do something, you know?"

She looked at the fine specimen of a man. His anatomy was built to a woman's specifications for lust. His skin was silky brown, creamy milk chocolate. His body was hard, shoulders broad with giant caramel apples on each end, which enticed one to take a bite. She felt the warmth between her thighs, with a wicket thought, *Shit, he's old enough now, and ready like a bitch!*

"Kwan, man let me tell you. An old girl like me—"

"It's cool, Jo-Jo. I understand, and I have kinda moved on…" She felt as if she was hit in the face with an egg. "But I still hold you dear in my heart. So I just want you to think about hanging out tonight."

"Oh, I'm not hanging out anywhere. I'm going to spend the night with a girlfriend of mine and get my sleep on; you know what I'm sayin'? Why don't you walk over to her building, just over there?" She pointed to the building, just in front of them.

"You need to catch a cab and go home. You should not stay around here any longer than necessary."

"Why? What's all that about?" The hairs on Joann's neck rose again.

"I'm just sayin', that's all. I promised to protect you, to watch out for you, and I'm sayin, ain't nothing good going to come out of you hanging with your friends tonight."

Jo-Jo senses began to heighten, and her skin began to crawl. She knew something wasn't right, but she could not tell if it was his warning, or him. She quickly decided it was him. She looked about her surroundings for the best exits, if needed, while he continued to persuade her.

"Look Jo-Jo, you don't need to fear me. You should fear yourself."

"Myself?"

"Yeah. Just look at ya. It has only been a few hours since your spirit been touched and here you are back up to your old tricks."

"You need to step off." Joann tried to walk ahead of him.

"You need to give your soul a chance to mend."

Joann stopped in her tracks, turned to face him with an expression that could kill. "I am, who I am, and I'll be no other."

He stood still and watched her walk away. She was only a couple hundred yards from the building of her destination.

"Yes, yes you are hell on feet," he said under his breath, as he watched her feminine walk, sway into the building out from his site.

# You Witch

*C*urled up in the corner on the sofa, which faced the television, Dana clutched a pillow. Her eyes were bloodshot. She was still shaken from this night's events, which left her with an unnoticeable tremors deep within. She spent a lot of money on her hair earlier that afternoon, and it didn't show. Her body still ached even after the hot bath. How she managed the drive back to Kevin's apartment left one to wonder because she had no energy. There was nothing left inside of her; the only thing operating at capacity was her curiosity. She was trying to piece together the events of the day and if the visions she had seen in her mind were real, or illusions brought on by her rage she had for the open display of contempt someone had for her. The exhaustion came from her trying to convince an insecure man that her love for him was real and unthreatened.

But as she sat in the dark living room contemplating, the totality of the last few weeks was taking its toll on her. Losing tens of thousands of dollars, nearly a fourth of her trucking fleet, and customers not only had her sliding into the red, but also seeing red. Was she trying to find someone to blame for the recent events, instead of herself for poor forecasting? She knew there were increases in production, and that she had taken on a number of new clients. Should she not have had her primary mixing equipment inspected earlier? And she knew making deliveries to those new clients definitely put a heavier strain on her trucking fleet, which meant preventive maintenance should have been scheduled earlier, and the real witch was her?

Fuck no. She damn well wasn't the one tacking dead animals to her door. And she wasn't the one drawing markings in blood on her doormat, or leaving severed chicken feet under her windshield wipers. Nope, this had to be the work of someone who had no love for her, and the acts were of someone who wished to destroy her. For the last three weeks or so, every few days welcomed a new adventure. If it weren't something breaking down, customers calling and complaining, it was something tacked to her door.

The invasion on her home really had her spooked. She once considered installing surveillance cameras throughout the building. It behooved her on how this person or people were gaining entrance into the building. Settled, she decided it was time to install the surveillance cameras, as well as an intercom and keyless door system. Besides, the added security would increase the property value on the building, which she purchased two years ago from her former landlord. The upkeep of the building was okay, but there was so much that could be done with the place. And she did. She added carpeting throughout the hall and stairs. She replanted and added linen wallpaper, also in the hall, as well as changed the doorframes and doors.

The building started out with six apartments when she purchased it, but now there were only five because she combined the second and third together to create her a very large suite. The entire third floor which she occupied, were her three bed rooms, two and a half baths, entertainment room, living room. On the second floor was her den, her office, one very large garment-style kitchen, a full bath and living room. The building was an old brownstone, with twelve-foot ceilings, which helped with styling the entertainment room when she added two steps to give it that step-up feeling, giving the room a grander look. The balconies added to the second and third floors in the back of the house that overlooked the high fenced, manicured garden really gave the building one elegant effect. But the best part about this whole deal and transformation was it cost her tenants not one thin dime extra in rent.

She was also very generous to her church, partly to show her gratitude for having enough faith in her to loan her some of the money she used to get started. For the tribute of faith she repaid the loan, gave the church an outer facelift, added an upper balcony, carpeting, sound system, two television cameras, new and better seating, and a reconstructed stage. But her biggest contribution was when she set up a scholarship program. She escrowed five-hundred thousand dollars to pay the tuitions of ten teenagers who chose to attend any local city college or university. The Lord had been good to her, so she returned what she felt was due, and in compliance with God's will, while still giving her weekly ten percent.

She was considered for a deaconess position a couple of times, but unknowing to her, she was never chosen due to her loose lifestyle with her male friends, such as Clayton, William, and Kevin. The Deacon Board just didn't think it was proper for one of their elite sisters to carry on the way she did—chasing behind men, making a fool of herself, especially with William. For Heaven's sake, he was a married man! Did she not have respect for what God had joined in holy matrimony? What image was she depicting for the other young women in the church? She was manager of Customer Services Ministry, which was in charge of all the ushers, and security. How could one, who held a high position in the church and carry on in such a manner, yet no one ever came forth to challenge her behavior. There was no First Lady of *Christ Jesus Eastern Field Holy Church*. The thirty-something pastor wasn't married, and a few of the deacons were divorced and doing their thang on the down low, who was there in authority to coach her on ethics, and morals?

She was just like any other woman, searching for love, but after this evening, she felt there was no love in this relationship, just confusion. And he had the nerve to give her an ultimatum, to choose between William or himself. But what the fuck was going on here? So why was she in his apartment babysitting his two daughters who slept in his bed, while his ass was at the hospital with his ex?

*Maybe he was the only one she could call. Or maybe his daughters who called him first, they could have been frightened and didn't know what else to do. I'm sure whatever the circumstances were, his presence was needed. So were mine. I was the first he called to watch his babies. He never, ever attempted to leave his daughters and me in the same room for more than two minutes. Wow, I'm honored. Maybe he does trust me, and I have been tripping all evening. He might be right about William. Do I still have feelings for him? Am I refusing to let William go because I still want to have my cake and eat it, too. Maybe it is time for me to let William go. I don't know. This isn't something I can make a decision about when I'm not in my right mind.*

*But what about that bitch, was what I saw real? Was she putting them damn roots on me? More so, did I cause her injuries? When I smashed my fist through that bird's chest, was I crashing upon hers? Now this is some strange shit, and I can't fathom the ladder. It's too unreal, too supernatural. Yeah, yeah maybe I am caught up into William and his nonsense.*

*Oh Lord, help me! I can't think straight. I don't know what to do, because someone was tacking dead animals on my door, and that bitch came to mind. Come on, girl, the writing is on the wall. That ugly heifer is behind this somehow. There could be no other explanations, she's the culprit and I'm willing to bet on it. Or am I? William said I was going to find out the reason why I damn near chopped off my hand. But what does William know? He had my head swimming around in circles before. He did me worse than Clayton did; at least Clayton fessed up to his dirt. He took me through many changes, and had me jumping through hoops, but William made me something I never wanted to be. The other woman. And for that one fact, I hated him. I never wanted to ever be called, or have the title of being such, but that was exactly what he made me. Second to his wife, a tart to family and friends, and a home wrecker to other wives if he'd left the home he was supposed to be committed to.*

*Men; they're such assholes, and my sisters warned me. They told me repeatedly that he was married and had no intensions of leaving his wife and kids. I guess I can only blame him but so much. He never sold me my dreams. I manifested those all on my own. He never said he was going to leave his wife. He never took off his wedding band. He never tried to move in with me. How I wished he would have, oh how I wished he would have. Yeah, Kevin, you're right! I do still love William...*

# Welcome Home

**1:56 a.m.**

*A*ndréa and her mother walked into the parking lot, carrying luggage. Andréa's flight landed thirty minutes ago. Since the demise of the Trade Towers, airport security has improved much since they realized the dogs were the best idea yet. Passengers used to wait as long as two hours before boarding their flights, but since then the average security clearance time was forty minutes tops. Although lately a lot of nutcases had surfaced, trying to board domestic flights, but this nor the War of the World in the Middle East stopped those who needed to travel.

Andréa was the chief finical advisor of the southern district for Merrill Lynch. She accepted her gifts and used them to the best of her ability for prosperity. Being in the right places at the right time was never by accident, nor was coming to New York at this time. She was making a power move for the top advisory position in the firm. This was going to be the week she would become priceless. In fact, she had set up a few meetings to look over a few homes before next week's meeting.

The mother and daughter caught up on family gossip as they made their way out of John F. Kennedy Airport, and onto the West bound Belt Parkway. Andréa hadn't visited her mother's home in four years, although she had visited the city sixteen times during those years. She flew in for her meetings and flew out before evening. Her last true visit home to see family and friends was back in 2009 for Thanksgiving.

Mom was speaking, but her voice was fading away as Andréa entered into a trance, and the scene before her transformed to a place in time that was yet to pass as they turned off the Belt Parkway and onto North Conduit Boulevard. She glanced down Linden Boulevard and caught a glimpse of the short, eight-story project buildings of Louis H. Pink Houses, which were dwarfed by the five buildings of Linden Plaza Houses. The image of a 9-millimeter Gluck flashed before her. Her head jerked back deep into the headrest as emotions flooded her chest and her breathing quickened.

"Andréa!" her frightened mother screamed.

A flash exploded from the barrel of the gun.

Andréa raised her arms to void the projectile from finding its target, and in her haste, she smacked her mother in the side of the face, which caused her to lose control of the vehicle.

The car swerved. Other vehicles screamed and echoed like launched missiles over one's head, as drivers slammed on brakes.

Mrs. Hartford grabbed the steering wheel for control.

"William, run! Duck out the way!" Andréa yelled at the unsuspecting William until it was too late.

The bullet entered William's flesh and knocked him to the ground. People scrambled for cover and refuge from the crazed gunmen, who fired a second shot, which also found its way into William's flesh.

"*Noooo!*" William said after the third round found more flesh. His eyes bulged, his heart stopped, and his body began to spasm. The blood splattered on his face and shortness of breath caused him to drop his weapon as he roused onto his knees. "Oh, God," were his last words.

"Andréa! What's wrong? Andréa?" Her mother shouted while she maneuvered the car to the right side of the roadway.

Andréa's pulse was racing, her palms were wet, and heat was over taking her, as beads of perspiration formed around her lips. She lunged forward and rotated the air vent to blow the cold air directly into her face. She inhaled the cool air deeply; it wasn't enough, she needed to slow her breathing. Her fingers danced on the dashboard, finding the dial to turn the air condition to its maximum position.

Her mother had seen this reaction several times before. Andréa would have these attacks when she received the validation to a horrible dream. Mrs. Hartford was a nervous wreck, her head was pounding, and her hands were trembling, because she knew this meant death. Someone close to her was about to die. She wondered what this was all about, why had she called William's name because it was she who was murdered by the rapist in Andréa's dream.

"Andréa are you okay? Talk to me..."

"Okay, Ma! Okay! I'm alright."

"What just happened, who did you see die? Was it me, Andréa? Did he succeed in killing me? Andréa…"

"Ma, I prefer not to talk about it now. Please, I need some water. My insides are burning."

"There's a Mobile gas station down the block on Conduit and Crescent."

"That will be fine, Ma. Please hurry, please."

When the traffic light turned yellow, Mrs. Hartford yanked the shifter into drive, and blew her horn as she approached the intersection. At the red light, she floored the gas pedal, and the engine of the 2013 Mercedes Benz roared, as she blasted into the intersection of Sutter Avenue against the red light. She forced the horn-blowing, white Pathfinder entering the intersection to veer to its right, and turn onto North Conduit, as she darted left, passed it, and into the middle lane. The next two lights before her broke green and she blew through them doing sixty-five.

Mom exhaled, and slowed the Mercedes to a legal limit, as they approached a Mobile gas station on the corner of Liberty Avenue and North Conduit.

Mrs. Hartford stopped the Mercedes a little beyond the doors of the convenient store. Andréa reached for the door handle.

"Andréa, what happen? What did you see? What did you dream?"

"Not now, Ma. Not now, not ever."

Andréa stepped out of the car, and ran her fingers through her hair to tame her appearance, and it helped. Her mother stepped out to join her, but before she could make it around to the back of the vehicle, Andréa faced her.

"Give me the keys, Ma."

"What...What?," she stuttered. "Why don't we just get home and talk about this? It's not safe for you to be alone right now, Andréa."

"Ma, leave me the keys, please. I'll be home shortly. Trust me."

Mrs. Hartford just looked upon her daughter, questioning herself. She knew if she didn't hand over the keys, Andréa would not get back into the car. However, she was concerned, because she knew this revelation was bad. The last time Andréa had an attack as bad as this one was after receiving a validating sign that confirmed the dreams of her father's death. Mrs. Hartford was scared, she was trying hard not to become frantic, she knew she needed to obey her daughter's wishes. Besides, Andréa said she would be home shortly.

"Let me call a cab."

"I'm going inside for some water; leave the keys on the seat." Andréa turned and walked through the door.

While Mrs. Hartford called for a cab, Andréa walked toward the rear of the store. She opened the glass door of the refrigerated water beverage section. A light-skinned man in his early thirties was scoping Andréa hard as he reached for a two-liter Sprite soda three doors down.

"Damn, baby, you look good," the man said.

"Thanks," Andréa replied without looking in his direction.

He was insulted by her lack of attention. "Oh it's like that? What you think you're better than me? I can get a look from better lookin' bitches than you."

The remark stopped Andréa in her tracks as she was making her way for the register. She scanned the man from head to toe, and looked him in the face. "No, I don't think I'm better than you, but I don't think a real woman would give you the time of day either, least talking about showing you a little teeth, unless she's one of those desperate thangs you call *bitches*." She rolled her eyes and continued toward the counter.

The man opened his mouth to rebuttal, but he had no voice. He grabbed his throat and strained for a sound of any kind to push past his lips. Nothing.

Andréa left the convenient store with a wide grin on her face, and walked over to her mother, who handed Andréa the keys.

"Are you going to be alright, Andréa?"

"Yes, Mother, I'll be just fine. Where's your cab?"

"It should be here in another minute or two."

"Don't worry, Ma. I'll be fine. I just need to clear my head, that's all. Lately things have been flooding into my head, and I'm not able to absorb all of it fast enough. I'm okay. We'll talk in the morning." Andréa closed the door, started the Mercedes and pulled away.

Her mother watched her make a left onto Liberty Avenue, and head westbound. She witnessed what took place in the store, and she saw what Andréa had done to that man. She knew there was nothing she could have said or done to persuade Andréa to come home with her. Losing your voice was one thing, but the possibility of losing your life was another. She was afraid of her daughter's powers and never tried to challenge her, except when it came to William.

Mrs. Hartford once loved William. She prayed to the Heavens to make him the one who would marry her daughter and put her troubled spirit to rest, but instead he complicated things, and caused Andréa to go through some very bad spells. He would walk in and out of her life at will, and every time he left, her daughter became self-destructive. The day she pledged to serve in the armed forces, Mrs. Hartford felt the Heaven smiled upon her and finally answered her prayers for her daughter. She was rid of William, and she received a bonus blessing when her daughter found herself a husband of her own. But what was this? Why did she call this man's name? *I curse the day of his birth. For years, I've prayed he'd die a horrible death. He's no more than the devil's spawn from some evil dog. The son of a jackal, how dare he come back into my baby's life? Not this time. Oh hell no, not this time; over my dead body first, before I see this happen. He will not walk back into my daughter's life and destroy all she has accomplished.*

"He escaped me before. I don't know how he survived, or how he managed to escape death, but not this time, if he tries to reenter my daughter's life. Not this time, William, I will cut you so short, you will wish you never existed."

# A New Day

The alarm sounded from his cell phone. William placed his feet on the floor and made four, wide steps over to his armoire to stop the cell phone from ringing. It was seven o'clock.

Yvonne turned over onto her back. "Oh I can't say I missed that," she said, referring to the alarm on his cell phone.

William headed for the bathroom. "How did you sleep?" he asked her.

"Heavenly. And you?"

"I don't know. I felt your energy penetrate into me. It made me feel nice and warm. And I had some strange dreams."

"What kind of dreams?"

"I don't remember them now. One, I was walking in a dense forest, and the other one I was standing on Broadway, in the city, a block or two from the Twin Towers Memorial Park."

"What happen?"

"Nothing, I don't think. I don't remember. I think I was just waiting, and looking into the sky. I was all alone. No sound, no movement of any kind, nothing, just a dead, eerie silence."

William stepped into the bathroom, avoiding the mirror, as he had for over two weeks now. He no longer appreciated the reflection, which mimicked him since his image begun to turn gray, fading just as all those he had seen marked before him. He knew it would be soon, somewhere, somehow, on any given day, at any moment he was going to die. So he avoided the mirror—he avoided that chilling reminder—and stepped into the shower area to set the water flow and temperature, then returned to his side of the bathroom, looked into a drawer, and withdrew his electric shaver. With all the regret he felt, he had to face his enemy—the mirror—and groom himself.

William was still unsettled. He felt odd; the mural on his back tingled, the tattoo had changed, or something. His insides felt strange, but his thoughts pressed no further.

Yvonne scooted underneath the sheet. She didn't have to get up and she wasn't about to do so, not even to go to the bathroom. "Oh, I'll be getting up and heading into the city later on. I'm going to stop by the bank, and then go pick up my paystubs. If there is anything you need for me to pick up, just let me know before I leave," she shouted from underneath the covers.

"No. I'm good. I've have a lot of work to do today, as well. I'll be busy all day, but you can come down when you get back. Oh by the way, let me tell you who you missed last week."

"Who?"

"Mary J."

"No! For real? How she look?"

"She looks like a woman. What do you mean 'how she look?' Besides being a shorty, she looked like herself…"

"Forget it, I'll ask Jenny. She'll know what I'm talking about."

"She took some pictures with the kids and us. We had a good time. In fact, we had such a good time she might make this one of her official recording locations."

"Oh yeah?"

"Yeah. So you know what?"

"What?"

"With that, if other artists begin to flock here, I'm going ahead with my dream for this place."

"Oh, honey, that would be so nice. Now let me get some sleep, and I'll talk to you later. Okay, dear? I see you're a little chatter box this morning, but I need me some more sleep." She turned over onto William's side of the bed.

As William finished his shave, he stared at his reflection. Pity had paid him a visit. He felt pain, and hurt, and sorrow, and guilt, and ashamed, and so many emotions at once, they forced him to speak back to the image in the mirror. "Why? Why now?" However, the dark brown eyes of the image just stared back at him with no reply. He closed the bathroom door, and walked toward the glass cage where the running water in the shower awaited him.

She whispered softly to herself, as she closed her eyes. "Dream, my love. Always a dreamer."

The door opened and in came running were their two baby girls, leaping onto the bed. Yvonne's eyes popped open; it seemed she would have to find time to nap later.

"Mommy, Mommy can we come, please?" Jernece asked.

"Go where? I haven't mentioned I was going anywhere to you young ladies."

"You know you don't have to use your lips anymore, Mommy," Jernece replied.

"Oh yeah, I forgot. Well, let's just keep that a secret. Okay? We wouldn't want people getting the wrong idea about us."

"We know, Mommy," Jerliner replied.

"And how could I forget. It was you two who orchestrated that mutiny with having me exiled from my home, wasn't it?"

"It was a path you needed to take so you will fulfill your job," Jernece replied.

"Yes it was necessary. Thank you both."

"All praises goes to the Most High, for thy will, will be done on Earth because we are bind to Him as He is bind to all things," Jernece concluded.

The girls managed to worm an invitation to tag along with Yvonne to pick up her check. After which she planned to take them shopping on Jamaica Avenue, Queen's downtown shopping center.

William stepped into the shower and released a horrible scream a man could sound. The pain he felt came in the form of burning heat. While his heart raced uncontrollably, fear took a seat in the pit of his stomach, as he watched blood stream down his legs, spill off his feet, and onto the shower floor. He thought this was it. His end had finally met up with him, and he was going to die naked in his shower. How fucked up was that?

Yvonne heard her husband's whale, sucked in air, held her breath, and wondered if death came for him. Has she failed? Was she supposed to have disposed of him last night? Did she miss the sign? Or should she have known better? William was hardheaded, and always required proof. Oh, how little faith William held in anything or anyone besides himself. He trusted no man, no woman, or his God, and this she knew. But if she had distorted William last night, how would this make her task any easier, knowing that the next was equal to William. It didn't make sense, and it was her call. If death had come to take what's hers, then death would have to contend with her and battle for the short life of a man she now held much faith in to do what was right for the sake of the Heavens.

She sprung from the bed, and followed behind the girls into the bathroom. She was horrified, while the girls showed no emotions whatsoever. William was turning in circles trying to find the location of the blood, but his family was able to see clearly from where the blood flowed. It was clear this was a sign from Heaven, but it's meaning wasn't so clear other than time for all parties was getting short, death was coming. William collapsed against the wall underneath the running shower, and there it was, visible on his back, the orange and red flame was glowing bright like hot burning embers, while blood spilled from the eyes of the skeletons that laid upon the shore of his tattoo.

"Girls, go to your room. Let me talk with Daddy."

The young ladies complied.

Little Jerliner begun to shed tears. "I don't want my daddy to die," she revealed.

"It will be okay. You know we can never die, and besides, Daddy got a lot of work to do if he acts right," Jernece explained.

"I know, but I still don't want him to go," she sniffled and rubbed her right eye all the way back to their bedroom.

# Good Morning Jo-Jo

**7:34 a.m.**

Her eyes opened slowly. Her head felt as if a freight train ran through it. When she tried to move, the pain reminded her of the ass whipping Jay Dee put on her the other night. She shook her head and remembered herself, praying she would survive the experience she went through with Keisha and her man last night. Her insides felt raw, as if her organs were all out of place. She was sore from her insides, outward. Everything hurt. She motioned to move to the edge of the mattress, and her pussy screamed at her, *"You bitch!"*

"Oh, fuck. What did they do to me?" she blurted out, as she'd curled into a fetal position, holding her stomach.

She then noticed she was in the bedroom alone. The sun was shining bright through the sheer white curtains. The bedroom was small, almost too small for all the fucking that took place last night. It contained no other furniture, no dresser, no night tables, no lamps, no nothing just the mattress that lay on the floor. Her eyes filled with tears from the pain. She gasped for air, swallowed hard, and closed her eyes, as events of last night played out before her.

Keisha's man, Teddy, had his face buried deep between Joann's thighs, as she suckled Keisha's nipples.

"Oh yeah, Jo-Jo, you still got it, girl. Hmm, yes. Now show my Teddy's dick some love while we tongue everything you got down here, girlfriend."

Joann and Teddy changed positions. Teddy lay on his back while Joann positioned herself for the 69, spreading her outer lips so Teddy could get back to his business, and then bent over, spreading her left butt cheek for Keisha, who did not disappoint her with her unbelievably long tongue. They licked and suckled themselves into a hot, sizzling frenzy.

The room was filled with smoke from the lighting of blunt after blunt, which was laced with blotter. Joann didn't smoke, nor did she drink, but she got a good buzz from inhaling the pollutants of narcotics in her atmosphere. She became dizzy, her world had no anchor, and then the texture of their voices became ominous. Then that dreaded moment came, the one that Joann was trying to avoid the entire night...fucking Keisha. Joann feared Keisha, and with good reasons. Keisha really wasn't all the woman the world would believe. Keisha was packing a piece of equipment most men would be envious to have. This transvestite cock was so large; one could place a crown upon Keisha's head and present her—*him*—with his own cock for a scepter. She was massive, but worse, she was reckless when she used it.

Joann screamed and screamed. She gasped for air while Keisha drilled for gold. Pushing her monster into places no man was meant to go. Through Joann's tears, she thought she'd seen the figure of dragons or gargoyles or something she would classify as demonic, and they were laughing louder and louder with every thrust they rammed into her. The site was so horrifying she closed her eyes to wish it away, and when she opened them, it—the beast—spoke to her. She tried to move, she wanted to get up and run, but the snake that slithered around her breast had her pinned down, with its fangs lodged into her right nipple. She screamed and screamed louder as the snake continued to swallow the breast. When she looked again, only half the breast remained.

"How was your little conversation with little Kwan Bartend? You know, he's still madly in love with you, and I hope you know he's also dead. Yeah, he's just a little, spoiled, dead kid, who refuses to leave this place for the sake of saving his one true love, and that would be you. How fucking sickening," the beast said.

Joann looked upon the beast. It had Keisha's breast, her shoulders, her arms, even her hands, but not her face, and when it bent down to speak to her, Joann could smell the rot of dead flesh upon its breath.

"After all these years of being dead," he continued, "he still loves you, doesn't he? What a shame he can't save you from your fate, you little misunderstood tramp! William can't save you; he can't save himself, the pathetic fool. Come with me now; let go of this pitiful life you have. You know you don't wanna be here. Come with me now and let me fuck you in your ass, in the midst of the golden embers straight from the flames of *hell* forever. Would you like that? Would you like to ride my giant, fucking cock forever and ever, and ever, and ever, and ever? Say yes, you little dumb bitch?"

"No. I will never!"

"Come on, bitch, look at what I'm offering you. A fat cock up your ass 'til hell freezes over. What? You want me to offer you some dollars to go with that, you're such a little fuckin mutt whore. Always got your mind on the dollars."

"Never! Get off me! Y'all get off me."

"Come on, this offer won't stand all night. When daylight comes your three weeks starts ticking. You're such a dumb cunt, any which way you look at it, you're fucked! If you stay with William, you'll lose all you cherish."

"You're just a bad dream, now go away!"

"You're such a dumb, bitch, you know that? I'm not your bad dream, I'm your fuckin' worst nightmare ever since I fucked you in the girls' bathroom back in public school, and I've been fucking you in your ass ever since. Why do you think you've never been able to hold on to a man? You should have known you were cursed when every man who offered you a ring died."

"I don't believe you. Not William. I love him with all my heart, and he loves me, and he didn't die like the others."

"William, William, William. Yeah right. He never offered you a ring. Oh sure, you two talked about life as a married couple, but he was never going to pop that question to the likings of you. I guess it's true to what they say: always a wifey, but never a wife. Well he got his coming. His own doings is about to catch up with him. He will destroy everything connected to him. Right now, he's our best ally. Hell may never welcome him in, but nor will Heaven. He'll be an outcast, no place to call his own. Forever bound from world to world because of his independence. Much like your mother, Lilith."

"My name is Joann! Now get off me! I said get off me!"

"Oh shut up, you stupid whore, and fuck me, bitch. Fuck me, fuck me, fuck me, fuck me, fuck me…"

Joann reawakened with a weak scream, more of a weak cry. She swarmed and kicked wildly, as she emerged from her nightmare. She grabbed hold of her forehead, which felt as if it was a giant vibrating bell.

*Oh my God, I will never hang around motherfuckers who smoke that shit again. My fuckin' head is killing me. Shit, so is my whole damn body. I will never do this shit again. My hooking days are over; I can't do this shit no more. Messing with these big dick mothers who don't know how to use them, they don't do nothing for you but bring you pain, by ripping a sister's inside apart. I will never understand why God gives these useless and confusing motherfuckers such big dicks and give the real men little tiny wieners. I can only guess it's for us stupid bitches to understand what love is all about, because you really would have to love a little dick motherfucker to marry him and then stay with him after he cheats!*

She opened her eyes to the bright sunlight flooding through the now, bear windows, nearly filling most of the room. She tried to focus on the walls. Slowly all came into view. She gasped in shock and disbelief. Last night the room had furniture, and the mattress was on a frame. She stared at dried blood, which trailed a path from the bathroom to the mattress, which is where she lay, wrapped in a sheet. She removed the sheet with no hesitation, and screamed at the sight of her bloodstained legs, thighs, and entire midsection.

*What the fuck did they do to me? Where the hell am I? There was furniture in this room. We listened to music from the CD player that sat over...* She looked in the direction of an empty corner. *Damn, I know I'm not going crazy. Those motherfuckers drank, smoked, and acted as if we were having a party up in here. Oh, God help me.* She grabbed her head in an attempt to make some sense of it all, and then her eyes traveled downward, snapping her back into the moment. *Blood! Why the fuck is there blood all over these sheets? All over me? What went on in here last night?*

She sprang from the mattress. Her body slammed against a bear wall. Her heavy breathing was loud, but not as loud as the whaling of angels crying for mercy, the screams of agony and pain, and Keisha's voice screaming in her ears. She grabbed her head in an attempt to block out the sound.

"There's no help of you, Jo-Jo. Accept my offer or face your doom with the others. 666 will never be fulfilled. You and William will not fulfill your destiny. William will fail you and the rest of them. You will never come within your own again. Come with me now, and let me save your sexy ass."

"Oh God, please…"

"God doesn't hear you anymore, you dumb bitch. You're a fucking home wrecking, whore. You lay in too many married beds and separated too many couples he joined together. You sold drugs to weak-minded individuals who sought happiness in a fucking weed and powder. You murdered that poor defenseless boy. It was his first time out, and you shot him in cold blood. You could have let him go, but you just had to be a cold-hearted bitch. Actually, I admired you greatly for that shit. You're good at killing the young and innocent. And on that note, let us not forget how you stink as a mom. Motherhood was never in your blood, but you're such an *artist* at bending dicks. Come join us in Hell!"

"I will never…"

All went silent.

She looked about the room. She smelled a foul odor, and the air was stale. Her left leg was shaking uncontrollably until she placed her hand upon it. She did not want to believe what she just experienced had actually happen. She was never demonically attacked in the light of day. The event puzzled her, yet it left her more frightened than anything else.

*God talk to me, please. Tell me what's going on here. Tell me what to do. I can't take this craziness. All of this can't be real. How does that bitch know about William? How does she know about the three weeks? William said I had three years. No, he said he seen the number 3, and if I repent I might have more time. William called me Sunshine, this bitch called me Lilith's, daughter. God, I need to know what to do. Do I follow William, do I keep trying to win his ass back, or should I just leave him alone and move on with my crazy, messed up life that you've given me? It seems so much like I'm on a path to nowhere.*

She wrapped herself in the sheet and headed in the direction of the bathroom where once inside she started the water to the shower. After adjusting the temperature she stepped up to the medicine cabinet, opened the door in hopes of finding something for her splitting headache; nothing. She closed the door and peeked in the mirror to see what she might look like. Surprisingly, she looked better than she had the day before, in spite of the pain she felt from her broken insides. Her skin looked healthier with a much brighter glow. She pulled back her hair, to look at herself in the mirror for another moment, and felt a cozy warm feeling return from the image, and then she turned toward the shower and stepped in.

The water was warm and soothing. She closed her eyes to let the water wash away the visible signs of a night gone badly. She could not help but wonder about the statements Keisha made as she tried to convert her. She knew something was wrong, she had a feeling she was cursed by someone, or something. She knew those evil forces was after her, and that was why she was unable to sleep during the hours of darkness. She knew the shadows was after her, she knew those who was within the shadows were up to no good, but what was worst is that she always had the feeling those shadows was killing off her husband's to be. Each time her hand was asked for in marriage, and she was given a ring, they would somehow end up dead, rather murdered to be more precise. Suddenly she jerked, and then crouched into a ball. She lost her footing and slid backward in the tub. "Frrth, ssshitt!"

The painful cramp caused her to grit her teeth and fight for air. "Oh God, help me…"

The cramps knocked up in several areas of her abdomen and became visible, as they traveled downward. She screamed, and began to breathe with short rapid breaths.

"Oh, God."

She slid along the bottom of the tub to the rear where she fought with the water, the blood, and the slippery surface to get to her feet. She screamed, as she tried to find something solid to grip. She inhaled deeply, grabbed her stomach, and pushed down hard upon the traveling, the crawling object. She screamed, and screamed, but continued to push downward upon her belly, forcing the mass into her carnal, and with one deep breath, she held upon it, spread her legs, and pushed.

She strained and screamed, "Jesus," as the massive blood clot emerged from her and plopped down into the tub. The shower rained on the clot, causing it to move slowly toward the drain. Joann, with her back against the wall, just watched as the blood dissolved and flowed down the drain. As the last clump of the foreign mass slid down into the drain, for that brief moment, Joann would swear she saw a tiny hand and fingers balled into a fist, and placed its middle finger up. Joann inhaled, her eyes widened, and she collapsed to the bottom of the tub, where all went black.

# Twelve Down and One To Go

The brown delivery truck pulled up in front of the two-family detached, brick home. It was a little early for deliveries, but this was an above average working class, upper middle class, section of Queens where concessions and certain allowances were made to appease the small mass of residents living on Ditmars Boulevard in the East Elmhurst section of Queens, New York.

The lawns were neat, clean, cut, leveled and green, which said a lot for the record-breaking heat wave suffered by most of the country. In fact, the climate around the world had become very sporadic, somewhat unpredictable and uncertain despite the advances made in meteorology.

The six-foot-three, dark-skinned deliveryman rang the doorbell. The thirty-three-year-old woman dropped her hairbrush into the basin. Her senses kicked into red alert, her skin began to crawl while the hairs on the nape of her neck rose. She didn't know what to do, answer the door or call someone for help.

The five-foot-seven, chocolate brown-skinned woman stared at herself in the mirror, frozen in place until the door rung again, forcing her to make a decision. However, she wasn't sure if it was an enemy at the door. She had been spooked for the last two weeks with false results. She had never been wrong compared to the countless times she had been recently. Her dreams had become nightmares. She knew they were just visions, but she never received such horrible images of such death and mutilation of men and beast alike.

Last night she dreamed she saw herself kneeling before God herself. She was beautiful and magnificent in all of her glory, for what was revealed of the Holy one. The woman was not surprised to see that God was feminine. God spoke to her, and told the woman to go to Cookies in Queens Village on Jamaica Avenue and at the register will be a woman dressed in all pink and blue jeans. God said for her to tell the woman, "The flames has regenerated, and taken to flight. The prophecy of 666 needs to begin, the Lamb awaits you."

She had no idea who this woman was or why she should go to this store to meet with this her other than to deliver the message.

The doorbell rang once again. She exited the bathroom, crossed the hall into her bedroom, opened the door to her closet, reached far back in the corner of on the shelf, and withdrew a metal box. She placed the dark green box on her bed. She sled the dials up and down until she lined up the correct combination of numbers. Once the lid ajar, she opened the box and quickly grabbed the .380 semi-automatic and a clip. She popped the clip into place, loaded a round, then tucked the weapon behind the waistband of her pants behind her back, and made her way to the front door.

When she opened the door, the man in the brown uniform was walking down the pathway toward his truck.

"Excuse me, but may I help you?" she said beginning to feel at ease once she noticed it was a delivery. She had been expecting a Cherry Wood, China cabinet she purchased from Lowes online catalog over the weekend.

"Yes I have a delivery for this address, for a Mrs. Saunders."

"Yes, that's me. I'm sorry it took me so long to answer the door. I was preparing myself for work."

"It's okay, ma'am. Are there any men in the house that would be able to assist me with the hand truck? The box is very heavy.

"No, my husband and son left for work already, I'm sorry."

"It's okay I'll make due. I'll be right back."

The driver continued his walk toward the back of the truck. He stepped inside the vehicle, being careful not to step in the puddle of blood, which gathered there from the bound, semi-nude man who lay among some fallen packages, bleeding from his skull. It was clear the man was dead. The imposter placed the hand truck on the ground, slid a large carton to the edge of the tailgate, jumped off the truck and proceeded to bring the large box off the truck carefully and slowly.

She watched him struggle with the large carton and thought he was right in asking for help. She knew she was not about to give a hand with that package, and then she prayed it was not a sidewalk delivery. All seemed normal, but she still wasn't able to shake that feeling of alertness. Her senses had been on high alert for a couple of weeks now, and her dreams were making no sense to her at all. Her psychic abilities were malfunctioning, giving her false signals, which almost led to her stabbing her husband when he silently came up behind her while she was cutting up potatoes for her beef stew.

After the driver had the carton balanced on the hand truck, he wiped his forehead with his right forearm, and proceeded to wheel the hand truck up the path to the front door, which sat behind three steps he would somehow have to get the package up, before he could enter the house. She pulled the door open wide when he reached the bottom of the steps.

He angled the box where all he needed to do was tip the top over, sitting the package on its side on the top landing, where he then pulled it through the entrance. She wasn't too happy with the way he dragged the box over her wood floors. She looked hard for evidence of scratches from his negligence, but she found none, and came up with an idea.

"Can you carry it into the dining room just ahead of you, please? Thank you."

He looked before him, and then looked at her; he wasn't too pleased. "Yeah, sure."

He dragged the box into the dining area and leaned it against the wall, withdrew an electronic key pad from his back pocket, the wand from his shirt pocket, and handed both items to her.

She placed her signature in the box provided, looked up at him and noticed the beads of sweat running down his face. "Can I offer you some water, or orange juice, something?"

"Oh yes, if it wouldn't be too much trouble?"

"No. No trouble at all." She walked into the kitchen. "That box was heavy and I really appreciate you bring it into the dining room for me."

As she opened the refrigerator door and leaned in to grab a medium bottle of Deer Park water, she felt the sense of urgency, and then an angel yelled to her, "Behind you!"

She stopped breathing, turned around, her eyes widen in disbelieve and terror to find the man who now appeared to be larger than she'd first realized, swinging a very large dagger at her.

She ducked and moved away from him as fast as she possibly could, but her attempt wasn't good enough. He caught her by the left shoulder. She screamed, as the blade sliced through her flesh.

Like a mad man, he raised the knife and continued his pursuit of her. She threw the bottle of water at him, as she ran around to the other side of the center island. "Come here, bitch," he barked at her.

"I got your bitch right here," she yelled, reaching behind her back and pulling out her .380. She tilted the piece to release the safety button. She raised the gun, placed her finger on the trigger, and tried to take aim, but her eyes widened as she saw the dragger release from his hand and sail through the air, across the twelve-foot island.

The dagger hit her in the center of her chest; she fired a shot but missed her target due to her shaky hand. She looked down at the object sticking out of her chest, dropped her gun and placed both hands on the island for support. Her shortness of breath brought tears to her eyes, but she tried to keep her eyes focused upon him, as he walked toward her, slowly unzipping his pants.

Once upon her, he turned her around to face him. "Did you really think you were going to warn that Eve bitch? My master is stronger than your weak God. You will never succeed. These monkeys will never obtain Heaven's wealth. Your kind should have joined us, but no instead you choose to serve a Master who would put the lowest before you."

"They are not the lowest, but the last of her great creation, which your master and the others refuse to accept."

"Accept them as great! Never! Accept them as our leaders and representation of our kind? You must have lost much of your identity during your journey here."

"Even if so, I am still of the pure, I am magnificent, I am loyal, and even more so I am *good*… What do you say, demon?"

"Bitch, I say… *Ahhhh!*"

With both hands, she clawed at his face. Her final attempt to make sure he would remember her each time he looked into a mirror.

He punched her in the face, grabbed her and threw her across the room, while holding on and ripping her pants right off her. She slammed into a utility cabinet and slid along its door to the floor.

"I usually like my prey a little cold, a little stiff, but I want you warm and full of what little life you have, so I can fuck it out of you."

She tried, in an uneventful attempt to get to her feet. Once he was upon her, he lifted his right 14-sized boot, and swiftly kicked her head against the cabinet, and then again. Then he watched the blood trickle from her left eye, as she fought to breathe.

He bent over, grabbed her left arm, and with the incredible strength he possessed, he flung her into the air and slammed her body, face up, onto the center island. Looked about the counter area, then back at her, where she laid trying to cling what little life she had in her, and ripped her panties off her. She offered no resistance.

He reached behind him, grabbed the bottle of extra virgin Olive oil off the counter, reached into his pants to pull out his erect penis, and poured the oil upon it.

After he lubricated his member, he placed the bottle of Olive oil back onto the counter behind him, climbed on top of the counter, got on his knees, grabbed her legs and pushed them back to give him full access to her rectum.

Once inside her, he placed her legs over his shoulders, and continued his assault upon her. With every stroke, she grew weaker and weaker, and he watched her. He stroked his manhood deep inside her, and watch her facial expressions.

His torment went on for another thirteen minutes until the moment he was waiting to come, and when the moment arrived, he leaned forward, looked into her eyes, pushed his member deeper and deeper until she exhaled her last breath, and he sucked it into his nostrils, capturing her last essence of life. It was not until then did he ejaculate inside one of his victims for the first time.

He withdrew his knife from her chest. Grinned at the corpse, and backed off the center island, feeling completely blitzed in fulfillment. He grabbed the bottle of Olive oil, and slid a piece of paper between her butt checks. She received the grade of *E*.

# Don't Mess With The Wife

*W*illiam placed the bloody towel onto the counter. He stared into all the mirrors, viewed all the angles, all the various images of himself from those angles only to see there were no answers, no conclusion, or insight to his demise. Deeper wonderment only left him with a single question: *Was it all a dream?* Hell, he knew better. It was real. His wife and daughters witnessed his sight. They saw tears of blood flow from the eyes of all the unicorns, blood that streamed from the eye sockets of the skeletons, the waterfall that spilled various winged creatures into an ocean of blood. They witnessed the hand of God spell out a message before them. They knew the message spoke of pain. They knew this man they called father, husband was coming into his own and they knew they weren't ready to receive him, so they consoled him, but the reflections within the mirrors said nothing happen. He didn't understand the event. Was it the work of Satan, or of Elohim? He received no revelation, or signs whatsoever. He knew he was going to die. He knew death was closer to him than he liked, but he also felt the Heavens was fucking with him, which he believed was more likely than the possibility of Heaven actually trying to tell him something.

He sighed, grabbed his leather toiletry bag, reached inside and withdrew a number of items, such as his shaving razor, shaving gel, a jar of petroleum jelly mixed with cocoa butter, three bottles of Giorgio Armani colognes and after-shave lotion.

He picked up the can of Aveeno shaving gel, sprayed a small amount of the gel into the palm of his left hand, and applied the gel to his face. He worked it into a thick lather, as he wondered what if it wasn't the Heavens messing with him, but something he suffered from one of those he was connected to. He closed his eyes in a daze. He stumbled backwards a step or two, opening his eyes to a blurred room filled with a blinding, bright light and a deep ere voice. "Go onward from the Host, Dark One, or suffer alone in the destruction of the gifted one and their monkeys."

William grabbed his head, rubbed his eyes, and stumbled back to the counter in darkness.

She shook her head once again to clear the dizziness, the blurriness, and sting of the bright sunshine, which shone in through the uncovered windows. She didn't understand any of the events that took place last night, nor the ones that took place earlier this morning like the voice of a demon in her head, or the miscarriage she experienced of what looked like a partially formed fetus. She didn't understand any of it. What did her girlfriend, Keisha, know about William? How did she know so much about her when it had been so many years between them?

Joann searched her cell phone's address book for William's number. She needed answers. She needed to know if he had something to do with what transpired hours ago with Keisha, and that shit she told her about her having only three months to live. She needed to know if this was his fucked up idea to get her into church, or to torment her. Tears slowly flowed from her bloodshot eyes, while her hands shook uncontrollably, unable to scroll through the name list. Then she remembered she had him on speed dial. She held down the number 8 button, placed the phone to her ear and listened to the ringing tone.

♦  ♦  ♦

The ringtone from the movie classic, *The Good, The Bad, and The Ugly* sounded, and she stared at the BlackBerry. She knew the signature of the caller. She debated with the temptation whether should she answer it, or let the opportunity pass so there could be a brief moment of peace between them. She resisted the itch of answering, but the echoing of the tone beckoned intensely. She waited to see if William would rush from the bathroom, but after so many rings, she gave into her urge. She looked at the bathroom door one last time before rushing to the phone. Then she answered, "Good morning, Joann."

Joann was floored. With everything that had happened to her, now this *bitch*... Her mind raced, everything within her told her to end the call.

"Don't hang up, I can help you..."

"How you gonna help me? What you got to do with me? Where's William? Where is my baby's deadbeat daddy?"

"Look, Joann, we need to talk..."

"I don't wanna talk to you. We ain't gotta relate ever, just share the man..."

"Why do you have to always act like an ignorant bitch?"

"Who the fuck you callin' an ignorant bitch? William didn't think so while I was all up on him the other night—"

"You're lying..."

"Am I? You had to taste my cum when you sucked that dick, because I came as hard as a bitch straight out of lockup, and I enjoyed every fucking inch of him."

Yvonne closed her eyes to yield to a quick silent prayer, and then sighed in submission. "Joann, I'm sorry if I came out my face on you like that. We have to put aside all the years of fighting and getting grimy with each other. We need to build a better understanding and relationship between the two of us."

"There ain't shit I need to build with you. You fuckin' trifling bitch, you had me jailed, and I'm never gonna forget that shit. And I know in my heart of hearts you had a hand in having my son denied a relationship with his father. So where the fuck in *hell* do you get the notion I would ever want to relate to you?"

"Because…you and I no longer have a choice. Either we work out our differences, or the both of us will lose everything we ever love…"

"I ain't losing shit else, bitch, because I ain't dealing with your tired, rundown ass. Now put my baby's daddy on the phone, bitch!"

"I'm sorry, but try him later."

Yvonne disconnected the call, and placed the phone back where she retrieved it. She forced back the tears, which tried to swell up in the ducks of her eyes. She stepped out onto the balcony, looked up into the clear, light-blue sky, inhaled deeply and fought back the tears once again, but with every second she managed to do so, increased the pain within her chest.

*Father*, she started to pray, *I will need Your great strength to curve this child's bitterness. We have been at odds for eight years with a child and my man between us. The first time we met, this chick actually tried to run me over. But I am far from fault. Our troubles do extend from my evil hatred I had toward her. I beat that woman's ass that day in the parking lot, and then locked her up for a weekend. I was angry, I was pissed, you damn right I was bitter and I found pleasure fucking up my husband's mistress, and I enjoyed every bit of doing so. I was being a pure bitch when I locked her ass up. I did that shit to her because she claimed her pregnancy was William's. She told me she was going to keep the bastard child to fuck me for the rest of my life, so I just had to show her the power I could wheel by keeping her away from my man, even if it was for three days. But that was only the beginning of my obsession to destroy everything about her. Each night while she was in lock-up, with the help of some of my Correction friends, I arranged nightly visits for her the whole time she was locked up. The idea was to beat her into a miscarriage, but the dumb bitch wasn't pregnant.*

*I knew William was taking care of that woman's child because his money didn't add up. Lots of unaccounted hours he said he spent doing overtime, but the hours didn't match the paystub, and somehow the bonuses were always getting shorter, and shorter. The thought of him making love to that bitch ate at me day in and day out. Then she called one day out of the blue to rudely announce my worst fear that she mothered my husband's child, and was carrying another one of my husband's seed. When we fought, I tried so hard to kill any possibilities of life ever having a chance to grow inside her. I kicked and stomped that chick as hard as I could, but she was like New York City's homegrown cockroaches and rats, resilient. I dropkicked the chick and she bounced back on the offense.*

*I found out the chick was messing with me. The first kid I checked up on was too old to be William's. I was also able to get a copy of the child's birth certificate, showing the name of the accused father. I said accused because this chick was into lies.*

*Her name wasn't Holly and the bun in the oven was a lie, too. She had already given birth five months earlier to a handsome baby boy, which meant there was a very good chance the child could belong to William. That shit hurt. I always feared and never wanted to see that day come, which I placed at the top of my list of "The Ultimate Betrayals."*

*I tried hard to make her life a living hell. How I seen it was, she was the other woman taking away my peace and happiness. A home-wrecking bitch that sucked the life out of a family's happiness, well-being, and future. So I decided to score one for all the wives who was losing sleep over those bed-bug bitches like this one. Get one in for the wives who was getting their faces punched in, for the wives who couldn't get their ends to meet, for the wives who lived and loved invisible husbands because the number two chick had her man's nose wide open. I thought it was time for the wife to stand up and pay back these backstabbing bitches with some sleepless nights. I felt it was time for a wife to return a home wreaker some heartache and pain. It was time for a wife, no, time for me to take away all those around her that she loved.*

*It was easy, child's play really, because she was so ghetto. The chick never lived an honest day in her entire life, so everything about her, her family, and her friends was nothing but a bunch of lowlife critters. She and her peoples were into everything from selling crack cocaine to prostitution, from grand thief auto, robberies, to loan sharking.*

*My girls and I staked out all of their locations. We logged their movements, took pictures of all the comings and goings of her pimp-daddy, Sunny, and his two sons whom ran the organization. It wasn't a large-scale operation, but a small enterprise, which was bringing in about thirty thousand a week.*

*My plan of attack started with some community service and those horrible looking prostitutes. I actually believed I saved some unsuspecting woman from AIDS, or some other STD. I had those bitches corralled and off the streets so many times, it allowed them the chance they needed to concentrate on themselves, to think better of themselves. Well they had no choice. I had those nasty, stinky hos locked up so many times they almost were assigned permanent beds. Then I moved to their little two-bid bookie, which was no problem at all. I had him out of business after three busts.*

*My real challenge came when I went after the ones on the top. It was nice shaking that tree, but I wasn't satisfied with nice. I wanted to see that bitch cut down, so I went after her roots. I was so hell-bent on destroying her I didn't care if my husband got caught up in it or not. He had no business messing with the bitch; he needed to be taught a lesson or two about loyalty. But like with every evil act, the seeds you spawn will become your monster.*

*The oldest brother, Jamar, was making a Jersey run for their dope. He ran into a little trouble when he tried to cross back into NYC. New Jersey's State Troopers busted him at the tollbooth leading to the Holland Tunnel. This was where the stupid bastard tried to make a run for it. Needless to say, they shot him. He damn near lost his life. He survived his wounds and was given a year to heal. Why a year? Because the bastard wasn't carrying any dope! It turned out he never connected with his source, and was returning back home dry. The year was charged to him for trying to run and evade State Troopers.*

*My crew and I figured baby brother would try to pick up big brother's duties, but that wasn't the case, so we focused our energy on their lieutenants. Yet days turned into weeks, and weeks* into months. Someone was bringing in drugs. I was no closer to uncovering their new pipeline then I was to knowing my man was knee high in the mix of it all. So I had three male friends lean on Sunny. They kidnapped the man for three days. They tried to beat it out of him, tortured him with water, electricity, fire and a hammer. They went a bit too far and put this piece of shit, motherfucker in the hospital with no information on his operation whatsoever. Our operation fell apart after that; Sunny and his crew got into some kind of drug war, then my world came crashing in when I found out William was leaving my children home alone while he ran the streets to be with this bitch, no doubt. A few weeks after learning of William's night-flights, we had a blowout. William and I got into a real bad argument, which was at the center of us both nearly losing our lives. I came close to being a victim of friendly fire, and William was shot after visiting me in the hospital.

As if that wasn't enough to contend with, the Feds stepped into our world and really turned my family lives upside down. They accused William and me of being high-level drug dealers running Brooklyn's eastside, and several jails on Rikers Island. Apparently, my investigation was being investigated, as they were investigating Sunny, Joann, and William. They accused us of killing three rival drug dealers up in the Bronx. It took two years for William and I to be exonerate of all charges. The incidents forced William and I to repair our marriage, once again, as we had a few times in the past to stand together, to stand strong against impossible odds, to stand as victors as we had so many times in the long history we shared together.

## *I Can't Believe
the Bitch*

**8:30 a.m.**

Joann shivered outwardly, yet her heart was toasted inwardly. She couldn't believe the conversation, which had just taken place. Her emotions were divided from the very beginning, she knew better than to call a married man cell phone before nine in the morning. She knew the game, shit she help put it together. Back in her days, she played the game, hell she was the Game, Ms. Diggity, no doubt.

One night, many years ago when she was seventeen years old, she was working the Caribbean Bar in the Downtown Brooklyn's, Fort Green area when a belligerent drunk disrespected her by calling her a, *ho*.

🌢 🌢 🌢

Joann was shouting the joint for potential dates. She was really feeling herself this particular evening. The place was packed. The men were thick, wall-to-wall. The dancers were hungry and being fed well, so they were putting out their best stuff. The atmosphere was electrified. The DJ had the place rocking hard, the floor bounced, the walls thumbed, the stripers had the men shouting, peeling off fives, tens at their feet, as the ballers stuffed their ass cracks and G-strings with fifties and hundred dollar bills, and Joann was in the zone.

The men and women was hot in their asses and seeking relief, one particular man stood out because he was loudest talking buster who was saying nothing. Joann strolled by his table and friends, "Damn this ho is fine." He said loud enough to piss Joann off. She didn't like that *ho* word. She was a businesswoman. She seen a Ho, as a stupid bitch who fucked out of stupidity, as where she fucked because it was services being rendered, unless she was on a mission of destruction.

"Yo, bitch what would it cost me to get a piece of you?"

Joann stopped in front of him, "You mean a piece of me?"

"Ain't no one else I'm talkin' to, bitch, what's your price?"

"You ain't no cop, are you?"

"My dick too big to be po-po…"

"Sure you can handle me?"

"Hell yeah. You ain't sayin' nothing…"

"A piece of me will cost you a bill, can you handle that?

"You ain't said nothing but a number…"

"Put your money between your lips and pull out your Johnson."

"What right here?"

"If you ain't got the balls…" she looked at his friends around the table.

He friends egged him on, but he was hesitance until Joann lifted her mini-skirt, showing she wasn't wearing any panties. He eyed her beaver, and nearly broke his fingers reaching into his pocket. He counted off fives and twenties, placed them between his lips, and then wrestled with his zipper. Joann bend over to assist him with his struggle, once she unzipped his pants, she reached into his crouch to expose his manhood. She stood upright, looked him in the eyes and licked her lips; he winked back. She lifted her skirt, saddled him, and then held back his arms as he tried to hug her.

"No touching! That cost more. Now, where is that hundred for a piece?"

He used his eyes to point toward his mouth; he couldn't wait to get this show on the road. The warmth from her diamond caused his manhood to harden rapidly.

"Ahhh, my pussy feels good, don't it?"

"Damn good, baby, now let's do this..."

She withdrew the bills from his lips. "Keep your hands behind your back. No touching." Joann lifted her blouse to expose her bare double D's. She took her left breast and placed its nipple upon his lips, as she spied two bouncers heading in her direction. No sooner as the man started to suckle upon her breast, Joann stood up. "You got your piece. If you want some pussy it's gonna cost you two hundred..."

The man stood up. "Bitch!"

"Let's go Jo-Jo, you know that shit is not allowed here," said one of the bouncers, as he grabbed hold of her left arm.

"Hey, that bitch just took my money..."

"No I didn't, he agreed to pay for a piece, and he got a lick."

"Sir, put your johnson back in your pants, and sit down or leave with her."

The man bitched, but sat back down in his seat, listening to the laughter of his friends and strangers alike.

♦ ♦ ♦

Hell yeah she knew better than to call this man when there was a possibility the wife could be around, but shit, he was her man, too, far as she was concerned, and it was high time for all the bullshit to come to a head.

She dropped the cell phone, wrapped her arms around herself to fight off the shivers. Suddenly a light went on inside her; she knew this feeling—shivering, hunger, confusion. She was suffering from hypoglycemia. She looked around the room for her purse; it was nowhere to be seen. In a single bound, she leaped for the bedroom door from her crouching position.

She stumbled into the hall, her body banged against the wall, she cried out with a weak, "Ouch."

With both hands, she used the wall to hold herself up, as she made her way through the living room. She looked about the bare room. She turned and headed for the kitchen. It was there she spotted her purse sitting on the counter near the sink.

On wobbly legs, like a drunken sailor, she staggered toward her purse. Her eyes began to play tricks on her, as the kitchen disappeared, so it seemed. She tried to refocus, shook her head, looked about once more, and the room began to stretch before her. She reached out, attempting to grab on to her purse, but she stumbled over her own foot and fell.

*Oh, God, why is you fucking with me? I am so tired of these games. First, this bitch calls me back and wants a fuckin' truce. I can't believe this bitch! Why should I ever think about coming to an agreement with her trifling ass? All I got for her is snake eyes, and a hard way to go.*

"Die bitch, die!" she said aloud, as she crawled across the floor.

She labored for breath, hammers pounded her skull, and the dizziness caused her eyes to roll and swim backward in their sockets. Her head hit against the cabinet door, she smiled with the feeling of hope. Her limbs shivered wildly, as she climbed her way up toward the counter top. She tried hard to place her feet firmly under her. She was rapidly losing her motor skills. She knew this feeling; she was losing consciousness. The last time she experienced these systems she found herself laying in a hospital bed.

Like a blind woman, she felt her way about the counter in search of her purse. Once she laid hands upon it, she clutched it with both hands, and snatched it to her bosom. After falling to the floor, she pulled back the flap, and rumbled through its contents. Like a fiend, she brought forth a Baby Ruth candy bar, fought with its wrapper for entry, and concord the feat to be rewarded with its sweetness of chocolate, caramel, and nuts.

It took no more but a minute and a half to finish off the candy bar before she was back to rumbling around in her purse. This time she withdrew a black pouch. She unzipped the pouch, and it spread open like a book. Although she was momentary blind, she instinctively reached for a small red box that read: Lilly Glucagon Emergency Kit for low blood sugar. She withdrew its contents, and immediately began the preparations needed for an injection.

She popped the seal off the vial of glucagon, removed the protective cap from the syringe, which wasn't too difficult of a task as when it came to her trying to insert the needle into the bottle of glucagon. She knew she didn't have much time before she would lose consciousness, yet the weakness in her arms and the trembling of her hands made it nearly impossible.

"You can do it, Mommy. You can do it if you try hard enough..."

"Jonathan... Is that you? I love you..."

"Try again, keep trying. Don't leave me like Daddy did..."

"Mommy's trying, baby. Mommy won't leave her baby."

With her hands lying in her lap, placed her left thumb and index finger together above the cab of the glucagon. Then she placed the needle between the thumb and index finger of her right hand. "Mommy's tryin," she said while slowly bringing her hands together, allowing the finger tips that were holding the objects to kiss so she could slowly glide the syringe needle into the vial.

Once the needle was fully inserted, she pressed the plunger to insert the contents within the needle into the vial. She held the two objects together between three fingers and gently shook the vial to mix its contents. After a minute she stopped, prayed the contents within the vial was clear, and withdrew it all back into the syringe, and gave herself an injection in her right thigh.

She sat on the floor of an empty apartment all alone; leaning against a kitchen cabinet, covered in sweat, with a syringe lodged in her thigh, fighting to stay awake. Her body was on the verge of shutting down until she felt a wave of tingles surge throughout her. Her lips curled up to form a weak smile. "I'll be okay, baby. Mommy is still with you. I'm getting sleepy. Don't forget to call your father…"

*Oh, Father, why was I stricken with such a dreaded disease? Say what? What did you say? 'I thank you often for not letting me catch AIDs, so why do I now question you about having Diabetes?' Well shit, I heard that, I did. I got my nerve. I thank you for living, yet I wanna bitch about how I'm living. Just the way ungrateful motherfuckers roll. And I'm no different, just another grimy bitch, too. Hmph, I tried to get William's sympathy by telling him about my eyes. It probably would have worked if I had told him the truth about me being a diabetic. Instead, I tell him some shit that I'm bleeding from the back of my eye and the doctors don't know why. Shit, they know perfectly well the reason for my partial blindness, a byproduct from my pet disease, diabetic retinopathy, Proliferative retinopathy to be more precise. My condition is so severe I have retinal detachment in both eyes.*

*I'm a Type II diabetic who failed to manage my condition for so many years. I was like so many other first-time diagnosed diabetics. I refused to believe it was true, and all I needed to do was cut back on the sweets. What a rude awakening it took for me to accept the fact I had this disease. I was hyperglycemic with a blood sugar over 800, which launched me into a diabetic coma and a two-week stay in the hospital, learning I had high blood pressure, kidney scaring, neuropathy, and retinopathy, but not even that made me take care of myself. I saw how my self-adopted father, Sunny, was living with his diabetes, and that was as if he didn't have the disease. I didn't become serious about my diabetes until I seen what happened to my adopted dad.*

*Sunny went missing for about a week. No one knew where the man was until after I got a call from him, telling me to come pick him up from Kings County Hospital. When I asked him what happened, he told me he was kidnapped by three guys posing as drug dealers, but he said he could smell cop all over them. He said they tortured him for days about his operation, who, where and how he was getting his dope. Sunny was old school, and didn't give them nothin', but they messed him up bad. They fractured several bones in his body.*

*The doctors told him the healing of his body was going to take some time due to the severe condition of his diabetes, and it was then when I found out how horrible and unforgiving diabetes can be. I literally seen it in action when Sunny came home in a wheelchair with two broken ribs, four broken fingers, and a broken left foot.*

*Well, six weeks after coming home, he went to get the cast removed, and it was there diabetes showed its ugliness. Sunny would use the tip of a hanger to starch his itch within the cast, and it was then I saw and smelled the effect of diabetes in the form of gangrene. My stepdad suffered every living day of his life after the discovery.*

*First went the foot, followed by the leg up to the knee. Then the same happened to the other leg. He got tired of the cutting, all the hospitals, and all the doctors so much, he decided to stop all the treatments and let the diabetes run its course with no further interference. He gave up and the diabetes claimed him painfully. I didn't want to die like that, so I decided to get my shit on track, but it looked like I started a little too late, also. I can't believe that bitch wanna be my friend. Hmph, after all the shit she put me through. I don't know how, but I'm gonna pay that bitch back for living on the same planet as me, and take back what's mine.*

*You hear that, Keisha! I choose, William. You fuckin' man-bitch! William is the only one who ever made me feel like a person, like a woman without sin. He never called me a bitch, never called me a ho. He never called me out my name, not even when we argued, or disagreed. He was always good to me. He saved my life a few times, not just up in the Bronx, but he saved my life the very first time we met.*

*I had just got kicked out of the Caribbean Bar for geeing some idiot out of a bill. He said he would pay a hundred dollars for a piece of me, so I told him to suck a titty for that yard. Well, technically, he never said which piece he wanted. So I got kicked out the joint, and decided to scout out the Baby Grand further down Fulton Street and Nostrand, sometime referred to as Babies Grand because it was frequented by a large number of teenage prostitutes.*

*I hopped the A train headed to Bed-Sty. I let a few of my sisters know where I be, because that was how we rolled. We always watched each other's back, dropped the 411 so we all know what was what.*

*When I reached the front doors of the Grand, I felt him. His presence hit me like a ton of bricks. His signal was strong, the strongest I had ever felt. When I walked through the door, my world shifted into slow motion. My breath became heavier with each step that got closer to him. The place was packed, but he pulled me toward him. I was frightened, my heart was pounding the shit out of my chest, I wanted to turn and run back through the door, but I wasn't in control. He was. Don't ask me why I believed that, but I felt as if I was bonded to him, I was a part of him, I knew of him, but even more bizarre, I felt as if I belonged to him. Then suddenly there he was, staring at me.*

*I did my bounce, took long slow strides to give the cheeks of my ass time to catch up to my hips. When I walked by him, I tucked my hair behind my ear and licked my lips, and damn did I get his attention. The tension between us was so electrifying. Damn I swear I seen lightening within inches of each other.*

*The tall, dark stranger had a sex appeal like no other man I have ever encountered, and Roberta Flack and Donny Hathaway singing, "Back Together Again," sent my head into a spin. I knew this man. I knew him intimately. I knew we weren't strangers, yet I held my head up, kept my eyes straight, and passed him by, along with all the, "yo, baby," "hey, sexy," shouts from the drooling dogs and vacated the joint. Before I could reach Nostrand Avenue, he was behind me, trying to get my attention.*

*"Excuse me, love, can I buy a minute of your time?"*

*"Buy what? Do I look like—"*

*"Look," he interrupted, "let's not play games. I don't mean to offend you, nor am I trying to waste your time. I'm just looking to spend whatever time I can with you."*

*"How do I know you're not a cop?"*

*"A fucking cop would put away his badge for a moment with you, so what's the difference? Name your services."*

*"What you looking for? Half n' half, straight?"*

*"That's the best you got to offer?"*

*I giggled. "What you looking to do? I'm not into all that freaky shit, unless you want me to spank you. Now I can beat up on that ass all night if you got the change."*

*Now he laughed. "Woo, back up now. I'm not into pain. I'm just asking if you—"*

*"What? If I take it up the ass?" His eyes popped. "Sure. You can fuck me in my ass, and I'll let you have it at half price if you let me strap up and fuck you in your ass."*

*"We don't need to go that far; I'm just trying to get inside you. I want to know you."*

*"To know me will cost you thirty bucks, plus the room and tip. Can you handle that?"*

*He agreed to all my terms, then I took him around the corner to a spot on Hagerman Avenue, where the price was cheap, but the place was kept clean.*

*After all the money exchanging was completed, we went to a bedroom in the back of the apartment and got undressed. My stomach was all up in knots. This man intrigued me, even though there was a respectable level of fear within me. I wanted him inside me so bad; I was willing to pay him if I'd failed to hook 'em.*

*We stood facing each other nakedly, awkwardly, impatiently, each waiting for the other to make a move, flash a sign, something that said, "Come, and get at me."*

*He moved in closer. I didn't know what to expect. He leaned down; his move didn't startle me because men always tried to lock lips. What was surprising was I didn't resist. He grabbed hold of me, wrapped his arms around me, and something came over me. It felt as if I've been there before, within those arms. I felt his warmth. I felt his heartbeat, and when he kissed me, I felt...I felt loved.*

*We lay on the bed; I kissed his nipples, while he ran a hand through my hair. I love it when a man plays in my hair while I'm sucking on him. We kissed some more, then he entered me. I moaned, gasped, and nearly spouted a tear. Oh my God, I had never climaxed on entry from any man my whole life. That was the greatest feeling I ever experienced, but bliss was short lived once I started receiving unbelievable images from him. I knew they were from him, as I looked up into his eyes. I mean real deep, far, far back, I was able to see the blue flame ablaze. I saw what appeared to be angels. I'm not sure what he saw, because from the look he gave me, he saw something within me, and withdrew himself from me.*

*I thought maybe he had cum like I did, but that wasn't the expression on his face. He looked at me as if he did something wrong. He even apologized. I didn't know what that was all about, but he hopped off me in a snap, then handed me another hundred if I would go home, and stay off the street that night. I agreed, but that was my plan, too, after our little get together. I violated two of the rules: never, ever get personal and never, ever cum.*

*I did as he asked; it was not until the following day that I learned the stranger saved my life, when I heard Jeannie was murdered by her john. It turned out that john was the asshole I played at the Caribbean. He stabbed up little Jeannie because she looked a lot like me, and her outfit almost looked the same as mine. That bastard came looking for me. He was going to kill me. To this day, I wonder what William saw to frighten him, and to pay me a hundred dollars to take my ass home. I can't believe that bitch wanna be my friend.*

*Oh, Lord, no! I can feel...No!*

Joann's body began to tremble. Her eyes rolled back into her head, as her head banged against the cabinet. Seconds passed before her limp body slid to the floor. The seizure was mild; she would lay on her side, naked on the kitchen floor unconscious.

# Husband, Lover, Daddy

*W*illiam's nerves had finally settled down from his early morning drama, which frightened the living daylights out of him. He was so sure that was the moment he was going to die, and what a way it would have been for an exhibitionists to leave this world, lying naked in a running shower. Well, he figured dying in a shower was better than dying while sitting on the toilet, taking a dump.

While William struggled with his nerves, Yvonne also struggled with understanding the message behind Williams' early morning event. For her, she knew it to be a sign of danger, but danger was no different from every other moment in the day. She was convinced the symbolic message meant their lives were not just in immediate danger, but worse. She believed it meant every individual on William's back was in danger, but her error would to believe it was just her family and those four women he portrayed on his back. She should have known immediately it would also involve his friends, his business contacts, his guardians, the three hundred nine rocks tattooed on his back, and countless angels on, below, and above Earth.

William had managed to come in contact and touch the lives of so many guides and guardians from the time of his birth. From his doctors, his nurses, his caretakers, the teachers, the drug dealers, the hookers, his wife, even his children had been placed in his life for every decision he ever made, and none of them was the wiser. So much for freewill. William knew better than to believe in *free will*. How naive was mankind to think they could do, say, go, and behave as they wished, with little or no thought for their God who already made preparations for their decision, whether it be favorable toward him, or not.

Yvonne sat on the sofa in her bedroom, teary eyed. She could still feel the pain in her chest from the rapist's blade, but it was not the pain in her chest, which ailed her. It was just that this woman, as well as the other eleven messengers, whom she desperately needed, had departed the earthly realm. All killed by a knife-wheeling lunatic who was working closely with the Fallen-One. Her two baby girls entered the room in an attempt to comfort her.

"Mommy, will she be okay?" said her youngest, Jerliner.

Yvonne dried the last of her tears before facing her daughters. "Yes, baby, she will be okay." She sniffed and cleared her throat.

"But she wasn't always a pleasant person, or did she visit the house of the Lord much?" injected her middle daughter, Jernice.

"You two should know better by now. She was a spirit and not of man. Her spirit was in communication with the Holy Father, whether she was conscious of it or not. And you should know by now that we are not judged the same as man, but judged as spirits. Our failures are our markers for judgment. Man was given a written guide on how to awaken their life force, but that is not our concern. We are here for one reason and one reason only. Now you two go get washed, we need to get outta here, if we want to have time to do some shopping."

The two little ladies looked into each other's eyes, and screamed in unison "Shopping!" and ran off toward their bedroom.

Yvonne watched her two daughters bolt from her room and smiled to herself for a brief moment for being blessed to have such beautiful children, inwardly and especially outwardly. She was once very shallow; a dark-skinned woman who believed she could only marry a light brown or high yellow-skinned man whom she felt would produce beautiful children. William was dark chocolate, almost as black as she was, and she shivered at the thought of bearing his children. The reason for her feeling this way stemmed from a traumatic experience at the hands of her very wicket ex-boyfriend, Michael.

She dated Michael in her late teens, and he put her through hell. If the distrust in her life had a root, he was the spike that anchored the entire structure. Not only did he forge the foundation for distrust when he dated two sisters while dating her, he also broke the inner core of her self-esteem when he verbally attacked the darkness of her skin for being the reason why he cheated.

"But what have I done wrong? I give you sex every time you asked me." Yvonne spoke through the tears and congestion in her chest. "I have never denied you anything. I give you my money. I bought you a leather coat. I don't even own a leather coat. I do your homework for you. I let you be with your friends. I never ask you for much of anything!"

"So you bought me gifts. Roxanne makes me feel like a man!"

"And I don't make you feel like a man?"

"Hell, no. You don't cook for me. You don't listen to me when I tell you what to wear, and you don't—"

"I'm only seventeen! I have five siblings, I can't replace my clothes. You never want to come to my home. You never let me come into your kitchen to cook for you. You just bring me down here to this basement, into this room to fuck me!"

"Look, I said what I had to say. If you still want to be my girl, it's up to you. As a Muslim, I can have up to seven wives, and you can be my third wife."

"But I was your woman first!"

"Yes, but Sharon is having my baby, and Roxanne is lighter and much prettier."

She was crushed. "Sharon is having your baby?"

"Yeah, and don't you ask for one, because I don't want no kid as black as you. You can never have beautiful children..." His voice faded into a distanced echo.

◆　◆　◆

His words became seeds of destruction and torment, which only caused her to date light-skinned men, but during her recklessness, her body rejected those eggs, which became fertile. One of the unborn belonged to Mark, and the second unborn belonged to William.

She first learned of her pregnancy from Mark just before William's reign. He asked her to be his woman, and she declined, stating that she might be with child. William offered to give the child his name if the father did not want to step up. She was flattered, but when William made the offer, she did not see William in that light. For her, she already had William picked out to play the role of godfather, or a close, family friend like Uncle William. Two weeks after William's offer, she miscarried. Although Mark was a light-skinned man, the stress of giving birth to an ugly child proved to be more than her body could handle. So her body rejected Mark's seed, as it did William's a year and a half later. However, on William's second time around, her stress of having an ugly child was replaced with the stress of William's infidelity, which left her with more anger than self-pity. It also gave her the desire to repay the bastard for all the pain he was putting her through. But if the events of the infidelity had not have taken place, Jasmine would have never been born. She knows this now, but back then, she would have never considered it even being a possibility of the truth, let alone to think that God would have a hand in it.

She found it odd that she was not able to see William's other child, his son. He said he had no outside children, but she would bet everything she owned that William had a child with another woman, and all her senses pointed to Joann. If so, that would explain why her senses would fly off the charts whenever she were in Joann's presents. She could not see into William or Joann because they were not of her kind, which would be the reason why she couldn't see their bastard child.

She stood, walked into her closet to retrieve a never worn black bra and panty set that hung on a rack with eight other colorful sets that she picked up the day before at the second lingerie store she visited.

She tossed the bra and panties on the bed, along with the outfit she'd prepared to wear: dark blue jeans, a pink belt, a striped pink and white blouse, pink Sketchers sneakers, and white Bobbie-socks that had a pink ball on the back.

The death of the warrior didn't bother her as much as the fact that once again she had been denied the message. She knew whoever this demon of death was, had to be stopped before time ran out. She walked over to the phone and dialed her husband's number.

William's cell phone rung twice before he answered. The moment he touched his phone, he knew the signature of the one on the other end. He tried hard not to respond to the beckoning ringtone, but it was as if he was on autopilot. He couldn't help himself. Before he knew it, he found himself speaking to the person on the other end.

He was caught off guard, and not prepared to respond to the person on the other end. He didn't have a plan, nor did he prepare an outline for the conversation he dreaded to have. He knew he owed this person, yet he did not have a clue on how he was going to repay that debt. Thoughts ran through his mind. Should he beg for their forgiveness, or bribe them with a lot of money to subdue the guilt that ran through his veins. Guilt, which caused his body heat to rise, which caused his throat to dry, which caused sweat to bead in the palms of his hands, while the images flooded into his mind. They were putting up wallpaper with blue skies, soft white clouds, green grass, tall trees, and a village of little Smurfs. The couple decorated the nursery in a theme, which was centered around the Smurfs, because it was Joann's favorite cartoon. After the wallpapering, William went back to finish putting together the crib he was working on just before giving Joann a much need hand with wallpapering the room. They had so much more to do before the little one arrived, which also included throwing a baby shower, which didn't sit well with William. He searched through his mind night and day for a solution so he would not have to attend the baby shower, without disappointing Joann. Her heart was set on them both wearing the same outfits, opening the baby's gift, and her showing off her man. William had always managed to keep their relationship as quiet as possible. To most of her friends, he was too good to be true, while proving to be very elusive. They wanted to know who the man was, this phantom lover whom tamed this she devil of a woman, and had her happily ready to give birth to a male child.

Yet, William mysteriously had to work that weekend of the baby shower. William always felt bad about disappointing Joann, which did not compare to the shame and disappointment he felt with himself as he pulsed to speak into phone. He didn't want to drop out of their life, but he could continue on that path with Joann. He was in too deep. He wasn't just cheating on his wife any longer. He was selling drugs, making buys, transporting and then, in the blink of an eye, it moved up to killing. With Joann he wasn't just breaking all the rules, he was breaking his rules, crossed boundaries; the ultimate lines of betrayal and when he realized how he was endangering his children, to permit their relationship to continue was beyond comprehension.

He sat back in his chair and remembered when he first held Jonathan in his arms that night at Brooklyn's Hospital on De Kalb Avenue, downtown Brooklyn.

William fed him his first bottle of Joann's breast milk. He had to exchange the nipple three times on that one tiny bottle for him before he would drink from it, and it was then William knew. He knew the child was gifted just as his mother and himself. William didn't know what role the child would play in his life, but he felt a dark, cold shiver run up his spine, which gave him a clue to his wonderment.

"Hello, Jonathan."

"Hey," the eight-year-old boy responded, who was feeling just as awkward as William.

"How have you been? It has been so long since I last saw you, what about three years now?"

"More like four."

"And like you can remember it being that long?"

"Actually, yes. I remember a lot when I was a child."

"When you were a child? Boy, you're still a child, but I know there have been a lot of things going on which forces you to mature beyond what's normal for a child your age."

"What is normal? I don't know what that is. I don't have a father, and I don't even have much of a mother—"

"Yo, stop that. Your mom loves you more than life itself. She gives you all that she has to give, and she begs for what she doesn't have. So respect her, and the things she had to do for the little she received for doing it. So how is Summer Camp?"

"It's okay, but that's not why I called."

William was taken aback by the child's tone. "Why have you called, Jonathan?"

"More than I need you, my mother needs you. If you still care for her—"

"I'm beginning not to like your tone, Jonathan. What's up with your mother?"

"She's having seizures, and about to go into a diabetic coma. She's lying naked on the floor of a..."

William's entire body became flushed with heat. "In a vacant apartment on the sixth floor, at 622 Montrose Ave. I can see her."

"I tried calling her phone, but she's not with us anymore." He began to sob. "She needs your touch. Will you help my mommy? I'll be good. I'm sorry for being mean to you. I...I—"

"Stop crying." William took a deep breath. His head thumped from the stress for knowing he was about to break all the rules, once again, and cross the lines which would surely jeopardize all the blessings he received with the return of his wife. For a brief moment he wanted to shed a tear for himself, but he couldn't reject a child's cry for help, which wasn't just any child, nor was the woman just any woman. They were a part of him, not to even mention, he owed them. "I got this. I'll get her home, and maybe this weekend you and I can spend some time together so I can catch up on what you've been doing. Go shopping and just kick a few things around. Cool?"

"That sounds great. Thanks, Dad."

"You don't have to thank me. I'll have your mother call you later tonight. Of-One."

"Of-One."

Jenney looked at him. "So I'm doing these police samples by myself?"

"Yeah. You don't mind do you?"

"William," she took a deep breath, "I'm not sure what's going on with you, but I think you need to step back and look at the shit you're getting yourself into…"

"Lady, that sounds like some good advice, but the ride had already begun, and the fucked up part about it is I'm in the damn middle of all this shit."

William stood, placed his blackberry into its case, and proceeded to the staircase leading out to the parking lot on the side of the house.

*What the fuck am I doing? Well I couldn't tell the boy no. I am responsible for all this shit that's happening around me. Damn, Venasay told me to keep my dick in my pants. Why out of the blue would Jonathan call? I know his mother put him up to it, it's in her nature. Besides how uncommon is it for Joann to be at the center of everyone's major fuck up?*

*This shit comes at the best time, just when I've finally reached the crest of my journey. Last night I was touched by an angel. I was touched by a lifelong dream. My whole life I lived for this woman to come into her own and touch me. Oh my God, she touched me! I felt all of Heaven awaken. All the angels that once cried out apart from each other in agony, came together and*

*hummed in harmony, in unison, they became Of-One. How can*
*I be in my right mind, and I'm doing some dumb shit like this?*
*God you know I'm stupid, please forgive me. I hope you know I*
*don't want to do this, but I am compelled to do what I'm about to*
*do by my nature, not by my desire. My woman holds the answers*
*I've been seeking, yet she's no longer my woman. She's not even*
*a woman. No woman possesses the ability to make me feel like*
*I did last night.*

*From the moment I entered her, I saw time stop. The voices*
*and crying of beings ceased. Eve's soul and mine twined into a*
*single consciousness, which broadness was as expansive as the*
*universe. We were filled with the lights of many worlds, yet I*
*knew we were far from the One.*

He reached his truck, dared not to turn his head, nor look in
any direction other than straight. He opened the driver's door,
climbed inside, started the engine, backed out of his parking
space, and drove forward toward the road. Yvonne watched his
every move from their bedroom's balcony.

◆　◆　◆

**9:52 a.m.**

$\mathcal{W}$illiam was over the Tri-Boro Bridge and in Brooklyn
within less than an hour time. When he reached 622 Montrose
Avenue, he looked about; he knew this housing complex and
knew Joann's mother lived just a couple buildings over. He
parked behind the building and made his way inside the secured
building by assisting a woman with her shopping cart while she

tried to control her two snow white, curly haired Bichon Frise puppies, which were more than a handful for the woman.

When he got off the elevator, he let his senses guide him in the direction of the vacant apartment, and stopped in front of 6M. He nervously took a deep breath as he turned the doorknob, but entrusted his senses to guide him. He ajar the door just enough for him to get his head into the apartment for a peek, and was quickly greeted with the unmistakable thick, foul odor associated with the presence of departed demons.

All of William's senses kicked in to action as he entered the apartment with caution. He looked up, down, sideways, back, and front as he made his way to the kitchen to find Joann lying on the floor. He quickly ran to her, bent down, placed two fingers on her neck and searched for a pulse, which he found, but it felt weak. She was cold, stiff, and lifeless with a syringe attached to her right thigh. He immediately started checking the rooms for her clothes, and for something he could wrap her in to raise her body temperature.

When he stepped into the master bedroom, he was taken aback by the gruesome sight of bloody sheets, liquor bottles, and beer cans strolled about. A chill ran up his spine, causing his entire body to shiver. The dead, musty odor filled the room as well, except it was more concentrated. He grabbed her clothing, her underwear, and a bloody sheet. Once in the kitchen, he placed her clothing on top of the counter, got down on his knees, removed the syringe from her thigh, laid the sheet over her, sat on the floor, and scooped her into his arms. Repositioning himself by turning his back around, he leaned against the cabinet, and rested her in his lap.

He stares upon her, sweeps her hair off her face, touched her neck for a pulse. "She needs your touch," he remembered

Jonathan words. He tilt her head back, looked upon her once again, and placed a kiss upon her lips, a kiss upon her cheeks, another upon her forehead, rested her head upon his chest, rocked her as if she was an infant, and hummed no particular tone, then shortly followed the words of  Steve Winwood's "Angel of Mercy."

His energy surged to her aid. He held her close while his breast was filled with song, his soul admitted to the love he had for her. As much as he tried to deny it to the world, to Yvonne, he could no longer deny it to himself. He had always loved her. They were two A's, trump only to each other. Their sex was phenomenal, their passion was unquenchable, yet their love was forbidden; it was not in God's plan. Like all thorns, their purpose was to protect the bush as a whole, the stem, and its precious petals. They were designed to bring harm, draw blood and mangle all threats.

Thirteen minutes after he finished the song, she showed signs of her return. Her breathing became stronger, followed by strong twitching of her limbs, murmurs of fright, and streams of horror.

"It's okay, it's okay," he whispered in her ear, holding her closer to him, and softly rocking her. "I'm here, baby. They won't bother you anymore. I got you…"

"Get away from me!" She flung her left arm into the air, motioning for him to stop.

"Come to me, Sunshine, come to me." Then he wondered if that was her true name, her angelic name. Then he remembered his conversation with the others; he heard her name mentioned several times before. "Sun'na, come to me, Sun'na!"

"William? William?" Joann replied.

"Come to me…"

Joann's nails of her left hand clawed into his chest, breaking skin.

William released a sound of pain. Through his grimace of puffs and grunts, he traveled through a portal that placed him within a space and time he knew nothing of, but was instantly joined with Joann.

"William!" She fell into his arms.

"Sun'na…" William looked into her frightened eyes.

"They're here; they're trying to take me away with them."

William looked up at two figures resembling giant trolls, with dragonheads, dressed in leather and fur, long tails, holding large swords in both their hands.

"Get behind me, Sun'na."

"Release her, and be gone," said the larger beast. Its voice sounded like that of Joann's friend Keisha.

"No."

"She is pursued by another who is willing to grant us many things. Stand not in our way, be gone, or be slain."

"If you want her, come get her, but be assured, not Heaven, nor Hell will stop my fury upon you."

"Who are you?"

"I am the Dark One."

The smaller demon took steps backwards. "We are not his level. We should go."

"I am not afraid," Keisha replied.

"Do battle with me and feel what all fear…death."

"He is, and he knows. Let's be gone."

Within a red flash, the demons were gone. Joann collapsed, and William turned to catch her, while at the same time back within the earthly realm he was in tears of pain, and gasping for air with short breaths. He removed Joann's grip from his chest.

"William…" She opened her eyes and looked up at him. "…I had a dream you were with me. I had a dream and you're here."

"I am here Jo-Jo. I'm here, now you rest. I need to get you home."

"No, take me to my mother's over in the next building."

"I remember where, now relax and get your strength back."

"You came for me; does this mean you still love me?"

"I have always loved you."

"Don't stop loving me, William. I know I'm not the easiest woman for you to love, or that I even deserve your love, but I swear before God, I will give you my all to stay in your heart."

"You have shadowed and lived within a chamber of my heart for a very long, long time. You have been a part of me, and I believe you will remain with me until the Heavens figure out they must do away with the both of us."

"You still say some strange shit, but I think I know what you mean, and its sounds good."

She buried her head deeper into his chest. He embraced her lovingly and securely while closing his eyes in acceptance of whatever the faith that lay before him, while at the same instance Yvonne exited the bathroom, startled by the bright flash of the Katana sword. She stopped in her tracks, with many things racing through her mind, knowing that if his sword flashed, he was about to go into battle against other spirits. Was he injured? Who did he slay? Will this affect Heaven's plans? Her job was to protect William until she could convince him to transcend back before the Father.

Yvonne knew if the sword remained in its stand, then William would still be among the living. She closed her eyes and reached out for him. When she felt him, she felt Joann's presence as well, and then oddly she felt their embrace.

**10:33 a.m.**

The two young ladies heard the jingle of keys, followed by the clicks of the tumblers as a key evaded the lock's cylinder. The occupants within the small, stuffy apartment sat in the living room, with a clear view of the door, and waited with baited breaths to see who was on the other side. There had been no phone calls, text messages, or any other type of updates of what was going on with that woman.

Dana waited with just as much anticipation as the two young ladies she'd watched during the night. It was more like they watched her. It seemed as if the two young ladies took turns sleeping and watching Dana's every move, which kept her from doing what she went there to do. These were the same two little girls she thought were so adorable, yet they seem totally different; loveable little darlings they were not, to say the least. They were rude. When Dana tried to have a conversation with them, they ignored her, stared at her as if she had two head. They whispered in each other's ear, before rotating their short naps in their mother's bedroom. Dana desperately wanted to get into that bedroom. So much so, she thought about spiking their Arizona Fruit Punch with some Nyquil to knock them out so she could get into that room, which was the only reason why she agreed to watch Kevin's two princesses.

Kevin called and asked if she could watch his two daughters while he rushed to the hospital with his ex-wife. She agreed because she thought she would have access to inspect the premises for some sort of signs that the woman was a witch. She wanted to find something to prove that she wasn't losing her mind, and then throw the shit in Kevin's face that his ex-wife was a real witch and one nasty evil bitch.

Dana did not sleep one wink, or close her eyes the entire time since she stepped into that apartment. She didn't feel comfortable. Better yet, she didn't feel safe. In her heart of hearts, she knew Kevin's former wife was a Pentium circle, chanting bitch, and she was flying her wicket broom over her business and the core of her life. She knew 'The Witch Bitch', aka ex-wife was the one causing the sudden chaos with her business, her man, and her purse.

Dana and the two young ladies heard a woman's voice say, "Okay, okay," as the door slowly opened. The girls jumped from their seat and ran toward the door. Their father stepped in, followed by their Aunt Leona and two plain-clothed detectives. The girls were totally disappointed, while Dana became more curious.

"Where's Mommy?" the oldest daughter asked.

"Your mother is still in the hospital recovering," Aunt Leona replied.

"What happen to her?" the youngest daughter asked, which was in sync with Dana's thoughts.

"Your mother won't be home for a few days." Kevin tried to make it sound as nonchalant as possible. "She got four broken ribs, and both her lungs are bruised. Are you girls sure no one was—"

"Mr. Walker, I have to ask you to reframe from questioning the girls until we have had a chance to do so ourselves," a detective stated.

"Yeah sure, but I have the right to be present during questioning."

"We'll talk about it down at the station, sir."

Kevin focused his attention back toward his daughters. "You girls go put on some shorts and sandals."

"Can we bring our PSP?" the youngest daughter asked.

"Yeah and bring your chargers, I got a feeling we going to be down there for a while. Leona this is my fiancée, Dana. Dana, my sister-n-law, Leona."

"Dana."

"Please to meet you, Ms. Leona."

"Church girl aren't you?"

"Yes, ma'am. I worship at The Holy Legion of Zion in Brooklyn."

"Oh with Reverend Jefferies, so you must be their deaconess?"

"Hmm, yes I am."

"That Reverend Jefferies is a good lookin' man. When he spoke at the Coliseum last August at the Gospel Super Fest, I could barely keep myself still in my seat." She giggled.

"Yes, he is a cutie."

"And I was so proud when I heard the news that they voted a woman to the title of Deacon. And I heard that they honored you with a plaque, a party and all that good stuff. Us sisters are movin' up in these churches, and it's about time. I'm talkin' about a new season here now, halleluiah, bless the Lord."

Dana was taken aback by the woman's knowledge about her and her church. "What church are you with?"

"First Ladies of Eden Church of Worship, over on Springfield Boulevard, in Jamaica."

"Yes, with Sister Reverend Mathews…"

"Yeah. Child let me tell you something about this woman—"

"Leona, we're ready," Kevin interrupted, as he placed his arm around Dana's shoulders. "Can you take the girls down while I thank Dana, and lock up here?"

"Sure can. Come ladies. Nice meeting you, Dana."

"Nice meeting you to, Ms. Leona."

"Daddy, you comin'?" the youngest daughter asked.

"I said I'll be right behind you, didn't I? Now go with your aunty, you hear?"

The young lady complied, but not before giving Dana an ugly look which spoke volumes on her contempt for Dana.

Once the door closed, Dana faced Kevin. "Sounds like she's in serious condition?"

"She is. She's not doing so well. The police think she was attacked. They found bruises all over her chest and back. I told them everything that I know, and how the girls called me when they found their mother lying in a pool of blood, but I don't think they believe me."

"Why wouldn't they believe you?"

"One reason is because I have cuts and bruises on my hands."

Dana looked at his hands with surprise and suspicion. She knew his hands weren't so battered when she left his apartment, as they now appeared. "Oh, my God, Kevin?"

"What? You too? I got these marks from punching at those boxes, and that machine I bought for you."

Silence parted them, and then guilt surfaced upon Dana's conscious.

"Look I gotta get down stairs before they think I'm trying to make a great escape or something."

"Kevin." Dana looked up into his eyes, and upon his face for the right words to say. She couldn't find any. "Kevin, is your wife a witch?"

"Ex-wife, ex-wife, get it right! And what kind of shit is that to ask me? Have you lost your damn mind or somethin'?"

"I...I don't know how to explain this. I...I saw her at my apartment. Not her, but a vision of her when I found a dead bird tacked to my door."

"Dana, I don't know what kind of shit you're trying to start here, but I ain't got no time for your nonsense."

"Are you seeing your wife?"

"Ex-wife, and yes I do see her. It's every other week when I come to hand her twelve hundred dollars, and to see my girls, which you insisted that I do."

"Don't get coy with me. You know what I'm saying."

"How fuckin' dare you stand here and accuse me of fucking around with my ex when it's you who can't seem to get enough of your ex."

"Bullshit. There is nothing going on between William and I."

"Bullshit is right. You ain't got that motherfucker out of your system, so who are you trying to fool here?"

"How many years have I been with you?"

"How many years have you been with him? If you ain't fuckin' him, you gotta be keeping him around for somethin'! If it ain't so then tell me why you won't replace that outdated piece of shit of a computer he gave you years ago?" He was in her face. "You make motherfuckin' millions, you can have the best of every fuckin' thang, yet you won't get rid of that old, tired, run-down fuckin' machine that's still running XP. But I know why. You keep that shit so you can get him over to your apartment when it breaks down every couple of months."

She took a step back from him. "That's not it."

"Then what is it?"

Dana didn't have an answer for him, so she questioned herself. Could Kevin be right after all?

"I…I keep it because…"

"Here let me help you out. You hold on to it for sentimental reasons, because you still wanna feel attached to him. I ain't no fool, Dana."

"But, I—"

"I done told you, either him or me. One of us got to go. I'm not living another marriage of confusion. Figure it out and get back to me. Now leave this woman's apartment, so I can lock up."

Dana looked at the anger upon his face, and uttered not a word. She quickly collected her things in silence, while fighting back tears. She was not going to let him see her cry. She held her head up, in order not to show just how confuse she really was, and then she exited the apartment without looking at him to declare her independence and self-worth.

# She's Mine, Dead Man

"Pastor, am I wrong for having these feelings?"

"Jerome you must come to grips with the understanding of your path. You have the unique opportunity to do God's work here and to destroy the beast before he comes into power."

"Pastor?"

"You have said she calls him 666, did you not?"

"Yes, I heard her refer to him as 666 and something several times while in her trans."

"You know your wife is a powerful charlatan who tries to cloak the truth from God's servants."

"But doesn't the bible speak against killing Pastor? I promised my God, Jehovah, after I left the army, I will never kill again, Pastor."

"King James, Exodus 20:13 says: 'Thou shalt not *râtsach*, or kill,' which means not to murder. You cannot bring the death of another by terms of premeditation, or to slaughter while engage in a sinful act. When God sends out his Angels for a task to destroy an evil city, or an evil host, it is not murder, but the commandment of God. You have been chosen to do the work as an Angel of God, how can you deny yourself such an opportunity to serve the Lord?"

"I'm sorry Pastor, forgive me. I will not disappoint my Lord. I will do as the Lord my God has asked of me. Grateful am I for the opportunity to fulfill his word. Pastor once I have killed the beast, what should I do about my ex-wife, Andréa?"

"Your wife, she is still your wife. What God have joined together, can no man undo…"

"But how do we know if God joined us…"

"Are you still questioning that? For Heaven's sake, I married the two of you; do I not represent the Lord?"

"Yes, Pastor. Sorry, Pastor."

"What you must do with your wife is bring her back here to me so I can perform an exorcism, which is something I should have done many years ago."

"Yes, Pastor."

"Well then. Now you must be off to handle your assignment, and trust in the Lord, my son. He will guide you and protect you from any and all harm. Now let us pray."

Jerome got down on his knees, bowed his head before his pastor, who placed his right hand upon Jerome's head, raised his left hand and recited Psalms 23:4.

♦ ♦ ♦

Jerome returned to his home still confused from the meeting between him and his pastor, but even with the dough, he concluded who would know more about this situation other than a man who walked with God. Anyone with a mind could see that there was a spiritual battle unfolding right before their eyes, with his wife being an agent for Satan on the frontline of this battle, and William being Satan himself in the living flush.

He prayed, after which he opened his bible to Revelation chapter 13 where he read of how the great dragon went to capture man. He focused his reading upon verse 7; *And it was given unto him to make war with the saints, and to overcome them: and power was given him over all kindreds, and tongues, and nations.*

He heard her say that he will go out into all the nations and conquer. He figured William will unleash his two agents to do his bidding and capture all the souls of Man, but not if he could help it.

William was going down. He will not sit upon the throne, which was meant for his Lord, Jesus, not if he could help it. He was going to kill this beast and the U.S. Army taught him well in the regards to killing his enemies.

He listened to the ringing tones in the phone's receiver until it was answered. "Good day, and thank you for calling Delta. My name is Julie, how may I assist you today?"

"Hello, Julie, I'm calling from Dallas and I need a flight out tonight for New York's JFK International. Can you help me with this?"

"Yes I can, sir, just give me a moment while I check that for you, sir." There was a slight pause. "I'm sorry, there are no flights available out of Dallas tonight, but I do see a couple of cancelations for a flight leaving tomorrow at 7:15 a.m., with one layover in Saint Louis and arriving at JFK at 1:10 p.m. Friday afternoon. Would you like for me to book that for you, sir?"

"Yes, that will be fine."

"What credit card will you be using to book this flight?"

After Jerome hung up with the airline, he quickly dialed another number. It was to a New York City area code, where the phone was answered by a gentleman with a deep voice.

"Hello?"

"Hey, Kevin, what's up man?"

"Hey, what's up, Roe? How you been? I haven't heard from you in weeks now, what's poppin'?"

"Hey, here's the deal. Andréa left me, man, and went back to her mom's to be with her ex."

"Yo, I'm sorry to hear that, man, so what you doin' about that?"

"I'll be in town on Friday, and I will need some help posing up while I'm there. I heard her ex was a real bad-ass, I just wanna bring her home."

"No problem, my brother, say no more. I know some peeps, but they're gonna put you out about 15, on a double 9."

"Whatever, I just wanna keep the game even, you know?"

"I feel ya, I feel ya. So holla at me when you get in, I need to be out, so I'm gonna get my walk on. You got a place to stay?"

"No, but I'm sure I can find a hotel, motel or something."

"Yeah, no dough, but you're welcome at my crib anytime."

"Thanks, man."

"You're my peeps, man, no problem. So text me your arrival info and I'll see you when you get in. Alright, bro?"

"Cool."

*Evil*

*N*eighbors kept a vigilant eye on the unfolding events, which interrupted television programs on eighteen major networks, tri-state, and countless news outlets nationally, but most of the neighbors pulled their blinds and locked their doors, for they were horrified. How could such events take place among their kind? This sort of stuff didn't happen in their neighborhood; a visit by a modern day Jack the Ripper who was on the loose to frighten all the residence of this great city, less the fact he was also striking fear in the hearts of women globally.

Law enforcement was at a loss. Hundreds of cops, agents and CSI technicians from around the world were working together to find the identity of a monster, to learn the whereabouts of a man who was on a mission they dared to give thoughts to. It was as if he didn't exist. He left no fingerprints, no hair samples, no fibers, no drops of blood, not even a trace of semen after he brutally sodomized his victims. This man was a true monster that had to be stopped. Law enforcement was tired of following the carnage this man left behind.

Detectives, FBI agents, and international inspectors poured over the crime scene. Hundreds of pictures were being taken along with video footage, while Detectives Wells, Long, and Tait, along with FBI Agent Williams and Bradley combed over every trace of evidence they could find with the naked eye.

The world's top profilers all agree; the victims are not random. They were selected for this person's monstrous challenge. They were selected to fight for their lives, each one rated on how well they fought for their life, and his reward for the victory was to tie them to furniture, in their own home, with articles belonging to them, so he could sodomize their lifeless corpse.

Mr. Saunders, the victim's husband, sat on NYPD's couch bus, under the cooling air-conditioner. The temperature was already at ninety-eight degrees, just four points off from the predicted one hundred two degrees high set for the day. He was not considered a suspect. The police knew this monster's method of operation. He liked to kill servicemen-technicians to gain entry to the premises of his prey.

Agent Bradley finished his call, placed his cell phone back into its pouch, and assembled the others.

"What you got?" Robert asked.

"We need to talk with the husband to complete a theory," Bradley replied.

The men walked onto the bus to conduct another interview. Agent Bradley took the lead for the questioning.

"Mr. Saunders I have to ask you a few more questions and I need you to be totally honest with me. Totally, no matter how ridiculous or embarrassing it may sound, I need you to complete this picture for us."

"I'll do the best I can, officer. I believe I have told you everything I know to help…"

"Yes, we know and we appreciate your cooperation. Sir, could it be possible your wife was a psychic?"

The other detectives shared looks, but remained silent to see where Agent Bradley was taking this line of questioning. Mr. Saunders hesitated to respond.

"Sir, Mr. Saunders I needed you to answer."

The husband turned away from them. "There might be some who would say she had the ability to see certain things."

"So you are saying she was a psychic?"

"I...I...I don't know. She was more than a psychic, as we know them to be. She was stronger, powerful, spiritual even, although she wasn't the church going kind woman. She knew and was aware of her abilities or gift."

"Powerful. How was she powerful?"

"This might sound crazy, but her visions, the places she would go into, you would think she was right there beside those she was seeing. There was one time I would swear she was in the presence of God himself."

"What do you mean?"

"I cannot explain it. You would have had to witness it for yourself, because it was the feeling you got, it was the change in the atmosphere around you, it was the fear that ran to the core of your very being."

"You said she used to receive visions. Now tell me the truth, Mr. Saunders, she saw this coming? She knew she was in danger, did she not? Tell me the truth, Mr. Saunders?"

"Yes. Yes, she knew she was in danger, but she could not see from where or from whom. Whatever dreams or visions she was getting had her spooked. She nearly stabbed me a few days ago."

"How so?"

"She was cutting some potatoes for her stew, and I walked up on her from behind. I guess she didn't hear me come into the kitchen. The look on her face when she turned around, she was so frightened."

"Did she see the killer's face?"

"No, she never said she did. All she said was, 'Evil is coming for me.' I didn't like the sound of what I heard. Her words scared me so bad; it forced me to attend church services this Sunday just passed."

"Thank you, Mr. Saunders, you've been very helpful. Excuse us, please."

The group of men departed from the grieving husband so they could speak among themselves.

"What the hell was all that crap and mumbo-jumbo about psychics and spirits?" Robert questioned agent Bradley.

"Well, collectively between the US and the other countries, they have been able to come up with a single profile for this guy. They found there is a single, common link between these women. They all were psychics, they all seemed to have a powerful ability to see the future, and they also seemed to have a unique gift. They all seemed to have the ability to communicate with God directly—"

Detective Tait interrupted. "Come on, do you really expect us to sit here and believe in this other world shit?"

"All I'm saying is a connection has been found between all the victims, and secondly it is of a spiritual nature. When you look closely at the positioning of all the victims, the killer did not pose them this way for easy access to sodomize them. Their heads, arms and legs form or symbolize a pentagram, and their heads were positioned to point toward the Middle East, Israel."

"So what are we dealing with here, gentlemen? Do we go find other psychics to pick up a lead, or a priest to read us some scriptures?" Detective Long, asked.

The men looked at each other in silence.

"I tell you what we need," Robert blurted. "We need to put away this bullshit and go catch this crazy motherfucker with some good, old fashion police work. Are all the agencies and Interpol sure they have no video footage of a similar person entering and exiting more than one airport? Are there not any passports that can be linked to all or most of the countries that fit within our timeline? Do we know when and where the actual driver made his last delivery? He whore the driver's clothes and left the truck, so did he walk away or drive? Let us scout for video cameras within a half-mile radius. This bastard might be evil, but he's not a ghost. We're missing something—"His cell phone interrupted him. He glanced at the ID screen. "Excuse me, I gotta take this."

He walked to the front of the bus and stepped out into the blistering heat. "Yeah, did you get the package I sent to you?" Robert asked the caller.

"Yeah, I did. Look like I seen this guy before."

"Don't worry about that, just get the job done. I don't want him breathing any longer than he has to."

"I'll take care of it, just have my money."

"Come pick up half tonight, and the other half when the job is done."

"Cool. Where at?"

"On the corner of Pitkins Street and Thomas Boyland Boulevard."

"Right down from the precinct."

"Yeah, about nine o'clock."

The two men hung up their phones, and Robert started to laugh. "Oh yeah. The Great William will soon be no more. Enjoy the time you got left, you oversized punk, because soon I will be rid of you, and I'll be the one there to comfort Yvonne through all her pain. Then I will show her how a real man lives. I'll give her some strong love to erase all memories of you, have your two little girls calling me Daddy, and kick those two older, good for nothing, deadbeats, out into the street, or have them arrested for breathing."

♦ ♦ ♦

*12:30 p.m.*

The room was dark. All windows were covered up. No light shone nowhere except for the single candle placed in the center of the floor before him. His eyes were centered on the flame, while his mind zoomed somewhere deep out into space, and his lips spoke words into the darkest.

"Yes, Master. Yes, oh, Great One. I will always be obedient to you, Master. I live to serve you. Thank you for choosing me as your disciple. I will not fail you. I will forever obey you, oh Great One. I will kill them all. I will leave none alive to stand in your way. Especially him, Master. Leave him to me. Let me savor his blood from the sharp edge of my blade. Sorry, Master. Sorry, Master. As you say, Master. I will leave him alone, as you say, Master. I will continue to eliminate those who carry the message. Yes, I will remove those who pose a threat to your cause, Master."

He looked at the dagger  between him and the candle. In an instance, he took it up in his right hand, and slowly sliced into the flesh of his chest. The blade slid from the top of his left chest, down and across his heart over to the right side of his belly.

"My Master has awarded me with great treasures, and pleasure beyond my imagination. I have drunk the blood of my Master's enemy, and desecrated their empty shells, which brought joy to my loins. I love my job, Master! Thank you."

◆ ◆ ◆

**1:12 p.m.**

*M*rs. Walker watched the nurse change the near empty bags that were attached to the intravenous tubes, leading into her right forearm and hand. She wasn't feeling much pain, just some discomfort. The codeine kicked in about fifteen minutes ago, and was doing its job. She has been thinking the entire day how she ended up in that bed. What happened? What went wrong?

*She put me here, the little fucking slut! She's getting stronger. I have to finish her before she gets too strong and I'm left powerless against her. I have to keep her mind, body and spirit occupied while making her ineffective against my Master.*

*She got my man, so I'm entitled to a percentage of everything she owns, and she owns millions. Shit, the cost for dick is high these days. She should have listened a little more to her pastor and followed her precious Lord a little closer. She should have learned when she was dealing with that William, messing with married men could be detrimental to your spirit. It leaves you open to all kind of things, and when I'm finished with her, she will wish she were never born. I will cut her off from the flowing waters, and destroy that light which shines in her. I will engulf her with darkness and rip her fucking heart out! The bitch will never know what hit her. She fucked with my man, and now I'm going to fuck her inside and out. And I got just the item I need to do her right.*

# Let The Games Begin

*Y*vonne and the girls reached the station house just as the afternoon shift had started their tour. She was handed her check by Sergeant Duffy, while the girls captured a few officers' attention, telling them all about their shooting experience; how well they could handle a gun when they go with their parents to the shooting range in Pennsylvania. This was during Family Weekend that came around every three months in the Poconos where they spent time together horseback riding, bowling, playing videos games at the video arcade, and target practice at the shooting range.

"Hey, can I speak with you for a minute?" Sergeant Duffy asked Yvonne. She turned around to see where her girls were. He took her by the arm. "They'll be okay, come with me."

They walked around a corner, down a hall, and into an interrogation room. He closed the door behind them, and turned to her. "Look, I know it's none of my business—"

"Sarge—"

"Let me speak. Now, you know how crazy rumors and things get out around here. Just what in the hell do you think you're doing?"

Yvonne stepped away from him and propped her behind on the edge of the table. She's dressed in blue jeans and a knitted pink, lightweight V-neck pullover that teased the cleavage of her double D's.

"How can you be so disrespectful to this department and to your marriage, and run to the islands with that fool of a man, and then have the balls to bring your daughters under the same roof where you practice your deceit?"

Yvonne lowered her head in shame, took a hard swallow while she gave thought to the embarrassment she'd brought upon her family, her job, and herself. "Steve, you're right. I'm sorry. I made a mistake—"

"Yeah you did; a real stupid one."

"Yes, it was a stupid thing for me to do, but I broke things off with him when we returned a few days ago."

"You know half the department still thinks you and your husband are some kind of drug lords."

"I don't see why, all of those charges were dropped. We were convicted wrongfully on those charges; besides, they found the real perpetrators of those heinous crimes. It was a simple case of misinformation. They had the wrong people."

"Well, you driving that damn car and your husband paying all the expenses on our parties ever since, might cause a few of them to think otherwise."

"Look, it's just a car. My husband owns a business, a record company or something. Hell, he even works with law enforcement and helps solve cases and find lost children, for Heaven's sake. He created an invention that put his face on talk shows and magazine covers, so how can they still think such things? It should have all gone away by now."

"Yeah, well, it should have, but still you guys got money to burn, and being Black with that kind of money don't help."

"Don't tell me you white folks still think us niggers are po'?"

"Don't get smart, and besides, what the hell could William have done that was so bad for you to do this to him?"

"Actually, he didn't do anything. It was just one of those things a woman goes through at one time or another. It's something a man would never understand."

A brief moment of silence, then Sergeant Duffy found it necessary to express the concern of his untold fear. "You don't know this, but years ago when you first started working here, I tried to get you...umm, transferred."

She chuckled. "Stop lying, you tried to have me fired."

"Yeah, well. Like I was saying, back then when I was trying to take your shield from you... And I...I never mentioned this to a soul, and I certainly never mentioned it to you, well no one but my wife. He...your husband...he came here to the station to have some words with me."

"Excuse me?"

"I said, we had a talk, can't you hear?"

"You two had a talk? About me? Is that why after a few months later you had a change of heart all of sudden? You two *MEN* came to an agreement?"

"A change in my life, actually."

He walked to the far end of the room to tell her about that visit that took place just after the incident of the baby being thrown from the window. Sergeant Steven Duffy was convincing the necessary people that Yvonne was emotionally unstable for her position.

◆ ◆ ◆

Sergeant Duffy and his driver had just gotten into their car, and on their way to assist the fire department in closing off the surrounding streets and redirect traffic elsewhere, when they were approached by William.

"Excuse me, Sergeant Duffy, I would like to have a word with you," William said, as he walked up to Sergeant Duffy's window.

"Who are you?"

"William Green, Yvonne's husband."

"See me when I get back. I have to be somewhere now."

"I don't have the luxury of time. We need to speak now."

Sergeant Duffy didn't blink and instructed his escort to drive on. Oddly, when the car began to roll, the engine shut off. The officer tried to restart the vehicle.

"It won't start. Our conversation is a little more important."

"I don't know who the fuck you think you're playing games with, but, nigger, let me—"

"My wife happens to love this job, and the shit you're planning to do to her will cause her pain, and that wouldn't be a good thing. You see, it hurts me when she hurts, and I don't like to hurt. I hate pain. When someone hurts, and causes her pain, it really pisses me off, and I hurt, and sometimes kill a lot of people who need not suffer my rage," he warned.

"Look, why don't you go find a good job and support your nappy-headed wife and your little monkey kids, and leave policing to the real cops. I don't need that cunt on the force, taking up valuable positions that a good man can hold down."

"You know, you and your kind sickens me, niggers."

"So you share my pain. Now go before I get out this car and throw the cuffs on you and put you, where your nigger ass belongs."

"Where my nigger ass belongs? Where, in a cage? You're so damn ignorant you didn't even understand my statement, and to think you took a damn test for this job. Don't stir my emotions more than what they are. I might hurt you, instead of helping you."

Sergeant Duffy reached for the handle to the door, and opened it, hitting William on his knees. William reacted by slamming the door shut. The two officers attempted to exit the police cruiser, and in an instant they were paralyzed, frozen in their odd position of reaching for the door handle, yet their heads were allowed to move.

William looked into Sergeant Duffy's eyes. "I should stop your fucking heart from beating, you trifling piece of shit." William leaned into Duffy's face. "Now this is how your world is going to turn. You will recant your statements you made to certain individuals. You will not complete those forms waiting on your desk for your return. In fact, you're going to recommend an accommodation for her bravery and courage in the attempt to save that child's life. Now let us shake on it."

William extended his hand. Duffy eyes popped when he saw his right hand extend slowly out the window toward William's, by no will of his own.

"Why should I do this? Why should I not just see her gunned down in a drug bust gone wrong?"

"Because I am about to save your pitiful life, you bastard. You have cancer in your colon, and you have passed the stage for treatment and hope. So I'm going to take your hand." William took hold of Duffy's hand. "And I am going to force your cancer into remission."

Heat surged into Duffy's arm, then through his entire body. Duffy looked into the tall black man's eyes and saw an endless void of darkness, as the temperature of heat intensified.

"Sarge! Sarge! Steve!" The officer cried out to his sergeant who shook and jerked, as if he was having a seizure.

Duffy continued staring into the darkness of William's eyes, which turned into a portal for his spirit to escape.

It was there, in a dimension of nothing, which voided space, time, anything, except the voice. "By my Grace you are healed. Go and sin no more."

A black sludge dripped from Duffy's nose, while blood dripped from William's nose, then from nowhere, a spark of light separated the two men.

William stumbled backwards a few steps and grabbed hold of his hemorrhaging nose, while Duffy fell backward into his driver, holding his nose in awe over the exiting black sludge. "Get me to a hospital!"

The officer turned the key, surprisingly the car started; he slammed the lever into gear, and the pedal to the floor. As the police cruiser sped away, the lightheaded William tried to focus on their exit, but it all was a blur. "This I do for you."

🌢 🌢 🌢

"...a lot of things became clearer to me after that. I still feel that warm sensation every day of life since he touched me. The only time I don't feel it is when I'm thinking or doing something that's not quite right. So I know he's not the simple man he appears to be outwardly. And he knows he has this ability and all, so he must know about you and Robert."

"He knows, and we're working it out."

"Good, 'cause I don't ever want him in my woods again, and I don't ever want to be around him if he chooses to get upset. So as a friend I'm telling ya, get your head out of your ass. Robert is not worth the trouble you're heading for. And just so you know, I will fire your ass if you bring a scandal to this office."

"No problem, Steve. It took this trip to open my eyes to the truth. That's why I'm going to need two more weeks to straighten out my home."

"Two more! Oh no. No can do."

"I have the time."

"I don't have the coverage. No."

"I've worked the last two years straight, I need time off."

"No." He walked toward the door.

"I'll go over your head," she said to his back.

"You'll have to, I don't have the authority." He stepped out of the room without looking back.

She sat with her thoughts for a moment to formulate a story that will give the captain to have him sign off on an additional two weeks of leave. She had nothing, so she figured she'd call out sick for two weeks and suffer the consequences when she returned. She lifted herself from the table, walked toward the door, and reached for the knob just as Robert walked in.

"Need time to patch things up with hubby?"

Yvonne stopped in her tracks, and realized he must have been listening to the whole conversation from the intercom in the room on the other side of the two-way glass. Then her senses heightened. "Hey, Rob."

"Officer Duffy, where is our mommy?" asked little Jerliner.

"She's down the hall." He directed the two sisters by pointing. "Count five doors on this side of the hall, and she'll be in that room, okay?"

"Thank you," Jernece replied.

The two girls made their way down the hall. There was no need for them to count the doors, as they sensed exactly where their mother was, and with whom. When they stopped at the interrogation room, they exchanged looks, and shook their heads in agreement. Whatever it was they agreed upon, it was between them and God.

Jernece reached for the doorknob, turned and attempted to open the door. The door jarred just enough for them to see their entry was being block by Robert. Jernece looked Robert square in his eyes and frowned. Jerliner looked between Robert's legs to find their mother at the back of the room.

"Your mother will be out in a few minutes. Go back up front with the sergeant and wait for her there." Robert took a step to his left and closed the door.

"I don't like that man," Jerliner stated.

"Come on, Mommy wants us to go back and stay with Officer Duffy."

"Why? I don't want to leave her; he's going to hurt my mommy." Jerliner refused to budge.

"She'll be okay, and besides this must take place…"

"But why? This is going to make Daddy angry."

"This is how it has to be."

"But Daddy kills people when he's angry."

"Okay, let's get back to Officer Duffy, he'll help us. So come on, I'm the oldest." Jernece finalized the dispute.

Jernece turned and walked back to the front desk with Jerliner reluctantly following a couple of steps behind her.

"…the least you can be with me is honest. If you want to break this thing off, fine. But you played me; I feel so fucking stupid. You could have just let a brother know his faults. Give me a chance to improve on my shortcomings."

Yvonne was trying not to let her anger partake in this one-sided conversation, but he closed the door in her children's face. She silently prayed for Robert, and then prayed some more.

"Robert," she paused. "I don't know how to say this to you without being brash. You are not giving me the space and time I need to put my thoughts and feelings into words where we can sit down and speak about this..."

"William must be the better man. How does he put up with this bullshit you do?"

"Must you raise your voice?"

"Then speak to me, bitch. Tell me something."

The girls walked behind the front desk to confront Sergeant Duffy.

"What happened, you ladies couldn't find the room?"

"We found it, but that ugly man closed the door in our face," Jerliner replied.

Sergeant Duffy quickly realized that *man* she was referring to had to be Detective Lieutenant Wells.

Yvonne decided to step off before the meeting became confrontational. She held up her right hand in surrender, and walked toward the door.

Insulted and put off, along with feeling he was being disrespected once again, Robert grabbed Yvonne's hand with a standard tactile maneuver, bent her hand backwards and forced her arm behind her back, while twisting her wrist a little more than needed. "Don't diss me, bitch!"

"Argh! Robert you're hurting me, let go of me."

"I'm not your fucking play toy. Talk to me, Yvonne!"

Sergeant Duffy leaned over to his assisting officer, Officer Tabbit. "Johnny, take care of these young ladies, and watch the desk, I'll be back in a moment."

"Sure, Sarge."

"You little ladies stay here. I'll send Mommy out, so you guys can get on your way. Alrighty?"

"Tell her to hurry; I have to go use the bathroom," Jerliner whined.

"Here, let your big sister take you to the bathroom, it's over there." He pointed to a door at the far end of the room. "See that door?"

"Yes," Jernece replied.

"Take her there, and lock the door when you go in."

"Okay," Jernece confirmed.

Robert had Yvonne faced down on the table, still applying pressure to her wrist and arm. Yvonne strained to lift her head.

"Robert, release me, don't let your pride write a check your ass can't cash."

Robert twisted harder.

"Arghhhhhh!" Yvonne gritted her teeth.

The door burst opened. "Take your hands off my officer."

"Leave the room, sergeant, this is personal. That's an official order."

Sergeant Duffy stepped into the room and closed the door. The six-foot, forty-seven-year-old, white man stared Robert in the face. "Take your fucking hands off her, before I throw the cuffs on your black ass for assaulting my officer."

Robert released Yvonne and took two steps backwards. Yvonne fixed her clothes and shoulder length hair.

Sergeant Duffy looked at her. "Your girls are in the bathroom up front. I'll speak with the captain about your two weeks. Now go home, and let us two talk."

Yvonne opened the door and left without saying a word. She tried to collect her thoughts within the short walk to the front of the station. She was so ashamed and embarrassed for what took place, having the sergeant come to her rescue, but she knew it was for the best. If it had gone any other way, she would have hurt Robert and brought on that unnecessary attention she was trying to avoid. She retrieved her paycheck from officer Tabbit and thought shopping would make for the perfect distraction from her current events, but more so, she wondered what was to come of the evening when she returned home. She looked at her wrist and bit her bottom lip.

**3:33 p.m.**

*W*illiam wrestled with the spasm in his right wrist. He has been massaging the hand since mid-afternoon. Jenny was pissed with him because the hand was getting in his way of operating the controls. If he would had gotten out of her way, she would have finished the project twenty minutes ago.

William wondered if Joann or someone else connected to him was in trouble, but no one's face popped into his mind with the first initial burst of pain. It was less than two days ago when he last felt a burst of pain across his face. That pain belonged to Joann who was being beaten by her lover, Jay-Dee, which caused William to run off into the night to rescue her from her attacker. He was prepared to kill a man that night if it needed to go that far.

"Shit!" said William, after he over panned on the horns with too much treble near the end of the mix down. Now they had to reset and remix the entire twenty-eight tracks.

"You want me to do this?" Jenny asked hastily.

"No, no. I'm okay. We just have to do the shit all over again. You delete the file and I'll reset the tracks."

They reset everything and restarted the process of producing a master.

♦   ♦   ♦

**8:07 p.m.**

*W*illiam and Jenny finished all that they needed to do, and were heading to the kitchen for dinner. Yvonne and the girls were at the top of the stairs when William and Jenny came up from the studio.

"You guys been gone all day," William shouted up the stairs.

"Your brats are something else, let me tell ya," Yvonne declared.

"Daddy, we got new color Game Boys," Jerliner said, with a big smile.

"And we got lots of new games, too, Dad," Jernece added.

"And not *one* thank you, at all. I'm beat. I'm going to take me a shower and watch my T.V. with the door closed. Hi, Jenny. You hear me fussing up here?"

"Sup. I can't believe all that you said about those two angels. They wouldn't do that to Mommy." Jenny laughed.

"Yeah, right. Mommy is done for the rest of this evening."

"I'll be up after I eat something, babe. You want me to bring you something up?" William asked Yvonne.

"No. We had Red Lobster."

"And you ain't bring me none back? That's messed up, Eve," Jenny said, with disappointment in her voice.

"I'm sorry, girl. With all the bags and these two wanting everything, all I really wanted to do was get home. How about you and me tomorrow?"

"Bet. Your treat?"

"Hell no. I had mine. It's you who want yours, so you gotta pay for my company."

"Your company?"

"Yes, you know how us girls treasure our time."

"Alright, I got you, but you're getting a kiddy meal."

"*Shit*, you can call it what you like, but Eve is gonna be eating, licking her fingers, and rubbing her overstuffed stomach."

They all laughed. Jenny and William entered the kitchen and surveyed the pots. Maria fixed up William's favorite dish: meat loaf, mashed potatoes, corn, collard greens, brown gravy, and buttery biscuits. They grabbed their plates and dug in.

William turned to Jenny. "Hey look, I know I've been a pain in your ass this evening so let me make it up to you. Why don't you knock off early tomorrow? This way you and Yvonne can go clothes and shoes shopping."

"Oh hell yeah! Like what, you buying?"

"Yeah, it's on me."

"Hey, you can be a total dick every day as long as you pay."

"Now picture that…"

"You got Red Lobster's, too?"

"Nope, you gotta pay for your own food, so good luck with that. Oh, next week, Yvonne and I will be taking a trip up to Montreal."

"Hey that's nice. Just you and Eve?"

"Yes."

"That's nice; you two haven't been spending anytime together, alone, without the kids and the outside lovers…"

"Excuse me, miss?"

"Hey, no disrespect, but you two guys are a piece of work. That's all I'm saying. But I love y'all."

"You know, I don't have to be nice and you can pay for your own shit."

"Ha, too late. Don't be like that, and you should pay for lunch, too, you really should."

"You should stay out of my business. Go have some fun. You may find a new dick while you're out there."

"I don't need a new one. I just need the old one to stop acting like a prick."

"There is another matter we need to talk about..."

"I'm all ears."

"I want you to know that if something was to happen to me, I have provided well for you."

She dropped her fork on her plate, disgustingly. "I don't wanna hear this. Nothing is happening to you, so eat. Please, eat."

"Will you stop acting like a little cunt, and hear me out?" She picked up her folk reluctantly. "I just need for you to know these things. No one knows what might happen. I left the studio in your name. My kids don't want anything to do with the business, and we're into the money, so keep my dream alive. And lastly, I would prefer if you kept everything here, the studio, your room and parking space, but if you don't, I understand..."

"What's all this? You got cancer or some shit? Sup with all this?"

"I'm just saying if something was to happen, that's all. You're my bud, and we roll like that. Okay, so relax and eat your corn."

Jasmine walked in. "Hey, peeps."

"Hi, baby girl."

"Hello, Ms. Wall Street Executive."

"Humph, I wish. This proxy shit is getting boring," Jasmine retorted.

The three conversed over dinner for thirty minutes until they departed to their bedrooms. The baby girls were in their room with the door opened; arguing over whose game was whose. William chooses not to intervene. They'll work it out, or Jerliner will choose to come to him for an appeal.

Yvonne was enjoying her bath. William took off his shirt, turned on the television, burped a few times, and took a seat on the sofa. Minutes passed; he tried to wait for Yvonne to emerge from the bathroom, but it was as if she fell asleep or something and he needed to go really bad.

Another minute passed and he could not wait any longer, so he got up and jogged into the bathroom to break water.

"Hi, honey."

"Hello, babe. I'm sorry, but I can't hold it." He lifted the seat and began to relieve himself. "So the girls got their way with you, or was it guilt?"

"I don't know. I think it was both. I was feeling guilty, and they ran with it."

William walked over to his side of the vanity, as he turned the hot water knob to wash his hands. He looked in the mirror at Yvonne's reflection. "Yeah, that guilt thing will get you every time." He sees Yvonne's face quince as she tried to lift herself. "Hey you okay? Need some help, old woman." He walked over to the tub to assist her.

"No, no, no. Let the old lady be, she can do it on her own."

"Yeah, sure you're right."

William scooped her out of the tub. She screamed, and then laughed in excitement. He stood up straight, with her cradled in his arms. He looked at her with equal excitement that she was back where she belonged, within his arms. "Not bad for an old man, ha?"

"You still got it, baby, but you better put my heavy behind down before you break something."

William turned toward the door and felt the strain on his weak right knee. "Yeah, you might be right, it must be the excess water."

"The water? Well yeah I can go with that, because it can't be me and my slim hundred and eighty-three-pound frame."

He lowered her slowly to the floor, while she held on to him with her arms around his neck. Once her feet were firmly placed on the floor, she grasped his face and kissed his lips tenderly. "I love you, Mr. Green. Well sometimes, no most of the…naw, for the moment."

They laughed, although William took her statement seriously.

As she lowered her arms, William spotted the bruise on her right wrist. He grabbed her by that arm. "What's this?"

Yvonne was speechless. She didn't know what to say, so her mind raced for an answer, for a lie, for something, for anything other than the truth. But she didn't have to say a word; William read her mind as she visualized the event she was trying hard not to think of.

He saw Robert applying pressure to her hand and causing the slight sprain. It was clear to him now, as he remembered the burst of pain he felt when creating the master this afternoon. He saw this man willfully touching and hurting his wife with no regards to her having a husband. No respect for his own position of being the other man. He hurt his wife because he could no longer be the other man and possessing some small part of her. William watched it play in her mind and he felt the tension in the atmosphere just as it grew there in the bathroom.

William released her arm and turned for the door, with Yvonne giving chase. William reached for his shirt he'd thrown on the bed earlier.

"William, no, stop! Don't go. He's not worth it," Yvonne pleaded, but William refused to hear her. William reached into his closet and withdrew a safe box, placed it on the bed, and worked the combination while Yvonne continued her attempt to reason with him. "William, baby, sweetheart, please… Please, baby, I can handle this, you know I can. Leave it to me, don't go down there!"

The lid popped opened, he reached inside, and pulled out his .45, automatic Glock 21, a ten-round magazine, and turned toward the door. Yvonne grabbed his arm and snatched the magazine from his grip. William took hold of her, lifted the woman off her feet and threw her on the bed. She bounced once, twice, and spilled onto the floor. Her one hundred eighty-three pounds were no match for stirring raged that was building inside her husband. William reached into the gun safe, withdrew another magazine and was out the room. Yvonne jumped to her feet, spinning around in circles, looking for her robe.

William was half-way down the stairs when Yvonne burst from the bedroom, screaming his name. Jasmine and Jenny exited the kitchen, responding to the commotion.

"William! Stop! Don't go, in the name of our, Father, stop, please…"

Jasmine's eyes widened, her heart stopped, and became dizzy when she saw the gun in her father's hands. "Daddy! Mommy what's wrong with him? Daddy!"

"Yo, Will!" Jenny shouted for his attention.

William slapped in the magazine, loaded the camber, and placed the safety back on. from the top of the balcony, their two baby girls watched William head for the front door, and their mother's efforts to advert William from his certain act of suicide.

"William, those cops will kill you dead if you take that gun. Think of our babies!"

"Daddy, stop!" Shout Jasmine.

William stopped, looked around at everyone, as they stood frozen in place, He looked at his weapon, withdrew the magazine, opened his hands, and watched the gun and cartridge drop to the floor. He lifted his head and stepped over metal pile.

"Oh, my God. Stop him, Jasmine. They'll kill him…"

"Where is he going?"

"To kill Robert!"

Jasmine could feel her father's rage, and was terrified. "I'm not getting in front of him. Oh no I'm not."

"They're going to kill your father, do you hear me?"

"Only you can stop him, Ma. Damn! You know how he is. He's crazy. Why did you have to be so stupid and fuck around? Damn! Mommy, damn!"

Jasmine ran from the house and into the driveway. William jammed on his breaks to avoid hitting Jasmine, as she crossed in front of the truck's path. The truck strikes to a halt. Jasmine was missed by inches.

Shaken, yet more fearful, she slowly approached William on the driver's side of the truck. "Daddy, I'm scared and feeling sick. Please get out so we all can talk about this. Please, Daddy, please."

"Baby girl, I'm just going to bust his ass, that's all."

"No, Daddy. Those are cops. They can shoot you and say anything. No, don't do this; we need you more. They might kill you."

"So be it. Step away."

"No, Daddy."

"Jasmine, move from the truck!"

"No. I'm going to hold on." She locked her fingers together around his neck.

"Then it's on you."

William shifted the gear-stick into first, and slowly accelerated. Jasmine slowly walked alongside the vehicle, and then quickly skipped, then jogged. She wondered when he was going to stop or if he was actually going to drag her to her death. William wondered just the same, was she going to let go, or was she fool enough to sacrifice her life to stop him? He figured the only way to find out was to speed up and put her to the test. Jasmine could not believe her father had her running alongside his truck, and he showed no signs of slowing down, or stopping. When she began to stumble, she released him and fell onto the pavement. William watched her tumble, and roll across the pavement into the grass. His body tensed up, he wanted to stop and go back to see if she was okay, but he knew the guilt of putting her through the ordeal would have accomplished her goal, so he looked forward and forced the image of her fall out of his mind.

William made the right turn onto the main road, as if someone or something kicked life into slow motion. The phone was sounding like a trumpet, the two little ones was crying out from the pain that begun to raffish their bodies. A huge streak of lightening lit the cloudless sky, after which thunder roared so loudly, it shook the ground beneath it, and spoke, "Send him home to me."

Yvonne emerged from the house taking aim with William's weapon in hand. Her facial expression was cold and stern. She stared down the sights of William's .45 Automatic, and centered in on her husband's skull. William turned to look her in the eyes.

The sky roared again, "Now," it sounded. Her finger started to squeeze the trigger; she looked into William's dark brown eyes and hesitated.

Jasmine was on her feet yelling at her mother, as she ran towards her. "*No!*".

William and Yvonne's eyes were locked on each other. Yvonne knew she had to do what she was commanded to do. A thought entered her mind, the thought of William and Joann's embrace, which had taken place earlier that morning. She squeezed the trigger, releasing a kill shot at her husband of twenty-five years. The sound from the gun seemed to have resonated just as loud as the thunder. The bullet raced toward its target. Yvonne squeezed off another, and another, while William watched on and waited to be struck down.

"Mommy, *no!*" Jasmine screamed.

Jenny came bursting through the door. "Eve!"

Yvonne fired again, and again, and again and was about to empty the clip until Jenny grabbed Yvonne from behind, and Jasmine grabbed the gun.

"Mommy what's wrong with you? Have you lost your damn mind?"

Their struggle was brief; Yvonne released the gun to Jasmine's grip.

"Better me taking him, then them killing him." Yvonne pushed Jenny off her, turned around in her robe and slippers, and said to her daughter, "Jasmine, get my keys off the table and bring the car around while I go back upstairs to get dressed."

"Why, you're going after him?"

"We have to."

"We? I'm not going anywhere with a mad woman who's trying to kill my father!"

"You have to. He's not going to listen to me, and I'm going to need all the help I can get."

"He's not going to listen to you? Hell, you're trying to kill him! What's wrong with y'all, he almost ran me over and you, and you...ahh!" She buckled over in pain. "My head is killing me!"

"I know it is, baby. It's your father's rage. That's why we must stop him before he hurts, or kill all of us."

"What are you talking about, crazy lady?"

"You are so far from knowing. Your spirit is so weak, and the weaker the spirit the more his rage hurts; it might even cripple some of us."

"Mommy, I don't feel good."

"Bring my car around; I gotta stop him before he kills you."

# The Ripples

She picked up the telephone receiver. She knew who it was. "Yes," she answered. Dana was totally drained; it had been a long day. She slipped off her pumps, and rubbed her tried feet.

"I guess you knew it's me, huh?"

"Yeah. Who else would it be?" She spoke with sarcasm and bitterness. "None of my friends want to call me anymore."

"I guess I really turned into a monster, lately, huh?"

"More than."

"I don't know what's wrong. I'm not myself. I never acted this way before. I have never been so insecure, not even with my ex-wife."

"Look, we went through this earlier today. You called me six times already. You've made it perfectly clear what it is you expect from me. You left me with a decision to make, but you won't give me a moment of peace to think. Now when you feel you can trust me to make up my own mind without perversion, or persuasion, to let me deal with this "*thing,*" you just need to sit back, rest in peace, and I will call you back."

"Dana, don't hang up on me, please, baby—"

"I have a terrible headache. My inside is on fire. This really is not a good time…"

"Look I've taken the computer back. I'll get my money back. I will never try to persuade you that way again..."

"Persuade me? You threatened me. You're trying to control me. But it's not your fault. It's mine. I should have put an end to it when you first started—"

"I never tried to control you."

"Haven't you? Telling me how to dress, what to wear, scrutinizing my friends, questioning them all the time. What's with all of that?"

"I haven't told you what to wear, I only told you what I like seeing you in. The clothes I bought I thought you would look good in, and I only questioned your friends about one person, and what they think of the guy—"

"What is that telling you?"

"Look, I don't trust the guy, that's all."

"No, boo, it's not him you don't trust. You don't trust me. And look, I'm not your wife. I'm sorry, I won't go there, but there's something you need to realize, baby, and that is people are going to do what they choose to do, even your ex-wife made her own choice. You failed to trust a choice I made years ago, and I chose you."

"I understand that now..."

"No, you say that now. I've told you before, he will never get this again, he will never. Yet you think he can screw my head on and off at will. What the hell is wrong with you men? You believe women don't have minds of their own while they're away from their man. Y'all act like women aren't capable of making logical and willful decisions all on their own. Well here's a wake-up call; he can't yank my chain, and neither can you. Now, bye."

She hung up, stood and struggled to place one foot in front of the other as she made her way to her bedroom to get a change of clothing. She knew he would ring her home phone again and blow up her cell phone until he parked his car outside her building; her only choice was not to be there when he arrived. She decided she would take refuge in her mini apartment, which was attached to her office, on the sofa bed. Her headache was getting the best of her. She knew it was due to a connection to someone close, but her pain was too intense to focus on its source.

When she passed her dresser, she decided to listen to her messages awaiting her on the answering machine. She received calls from her sisters, her mother, her brothers, and Kevin had called nine times. The fourth time he called he left a message on the answering machine informing her he'd bought her a present—a brand new computer system for her home office—a message which she received too many hours too late. She stepped back into her shoes, slid her feet over to the coffee table, bent over slowly to grab her bag and keys. She dragged herself out from her apartment and into the hall. Through heavy breathing, blurred vision, and sweaty palms, she managed to lock the door then turn toward the stairs. She carefully placed one foot in front of the other, while using the wall and handrail for support. Half way down, all went black; she collapsed and tumbled down the remaining steps. Her body ended up at the bottom of the staircase, twisted and lifeless. The noise she created going down caused the occupants in a first floor apartment to investigate.

The man opened the door and found Dana lying at the base of the staircase. "Oh, my God! Dana! Dana!" He placed his ear to her chest to listen for a heartbeat. He heard none. Franticly with his right hand shaking, he placed two fingers against the arteries on the side of her neck. There was no pulse. She had no breath. He pulled her body away from the stairs and stretched her body straight, and made sure she lying flat before he started giving her chest compressions. After several minutes, he was no closer to bringing her back to this world than when he first found her lying outside his door. Then a cold, horrible chill shook his soul when he saw the blood pooling underneath her head. He rushed back into his apartment for the phone.

# A Mother's Love

Joann's vision became blurred while walking into the kitchen, where her mother was finishing the dishwashing. "Mommy, do you have any aspirins? Man, I got a mad headache."

"Yeah, go look in the medicine cabinet. There's some Advil in there you can take."

Joann turned around to walk back toward the bathroom, using the wall as a guide. Her hand searching for the medicine cabinet, she found it and opened the door, and then she quickly realized she couldn't see the labels on the bottles. At that instance, her mother came walking down the hall. The pain battered the insides of her head intensely; she couldn't help but wonder if death was trying to reclaim her once again. Would William be standing outside in the hallway ready to break down the doors to come to her aid? He was her knight in shining armor, her lover in arms, her man 'til death, never to part. Far as she was concerned, William was on loan to Yvonne, and her reign was ending. She and the bitch were going to have to settle up, and the interest was taxed.

"Mommy, help me, I can't see the labels. Please help me."

Her mother entered the bathroom. "Why are you so helpless?"

"I'm not helpless, I'm sick. I have Diabetic Retinopathy, which was caused by my diabetes. The blood vessels in my eyes are bleeding. I told you I've been legally blind for three years now, but you always seem to hear something different."

"Here, where's your hand? Give me your hand, I said." Ms. Garcia placed the small tablets of Advil into Joann's palm. "Now drink from the faucet to wash them down."

Joann sat on the toilet seat looking like a drunken sailor who was begging for some sort of relief. She found it difficult to drink from the faucet; she couldn't keep her head down long enough to sip the water because the pain would pulsate throughout her brain, and down her spine.

"By the way, I need forty dollars for bingo tonight."

"I gave you a hundred dollars last night before you so rudely locked me out the apartment. What happened to it?"

"What? You're questioning me young, lady?"

"Ma, it's not that, it's…"

In an irritated voice, Ms. Garcia snapped. "I used it. I needed to buy some things for the house. What's next? You want to know what I bought?"

"No. I just asked. I don't have any change left. I need to get some sneakers for Jonathan."

"You should buy some sneakers for your son who's in jail. I can't keep sending him things, and money, and food, every two weeks. I can't do it anymore; I told him I could only send once a month from now on. You haven't seen him, wrote him a letter, you haven't done nothing. I have to send him my little bit of money to call you, his mother."

"Mommy, don't start this. My head is killing me, my body is burning like I'm on fire, please don't do this."

"It's always about you. You have two sons, you know?"

"Fuck this. I'm not going to argue with you. You start this shit every time you don't get your way."

"When I can't get my way! What kind of life did I have? Don't you forget I raised your child, don't forget that."

"No, Mommy, you took my child. You convinced me that I couldn't raise him. And soon as the papers were signed, you kicked me out. Telling me I wasn't fit to be around him."

"I did what I had to do."

"Which was what? You told me that I was too young for a child, Mommy. You say you want it all, your babies home with you, but you lied, you just wanted my male child. I was only fifteen, Mommy, and you kicked me out. You sent me back out into the streets as if I was a stranger you turned away from the door."

"It was because you're a whore! You're a filthy, little tramp that tries to ruin my life with every little chance you get, over, and over, and over again."

"I thought so." Joann placed the tablets into her mouth, placed her lips under the faucet and turned the cold-water knob, while her mother raved on.

"You have always been nothing but trouble to me ever since you were born! You have been nothing but trouble to me. You never meant me any good. Why were you ever born to me—"

"It was the odds."

"What?"

"I don't know how I know that, but it was the odds being stacked against me."

"It's always you! You, you, you! You never thought of anyone other than yourself!"

Joann used what little strength she had to lean against the wall and slide her way to the door. "And what about my father?"

"What about your father? He died just after your sister was born—"

"No, Mommy. He left you. He left you because you're a nasty, evil, wicked woman, and because—"

"Aha!" Her mother attacked her from behind, beating her in the back of her head.

Joann tried to cover her head, but the punches became unpredictable.

"Get out! Get out of my house! Get out now!" Ms. Garcia shouted as she kicked Joann in her back.

Joann's body slammed into the wall outside of the bathroom. Ms. Garcia was in full attack mode. "Destroy." She ran and body slammed Joann up against the wall as if she was in a roller-derby rink knocking those bitches over and out the rink. Her assault continued with kicks to Joann's mid-section, followed by fury of slaps about the head. Joann tried to protect herself, but she was no match for her mother. Blood spewed from several areas of Joann's tender facial flush.

"Mommy, stop! Ma! Ma! Mommy, stop!"

"You ungrateful little bitch. I gave you birth and you gave me nothing but heartache and pain. I knew you were the Devil's spurn the very moment I conceived you. You, you, you night owl, and I want you out of my house and my life forever!" Mrs. Garcia grabbed Joann by her hair, walked her over to the front door and slammed her forehead against it several times. She reached around Joann, opened her door and threw Joann against the adjacent wall, while in native dialect yelling, "No va cada vez un pie en mi casa o matará muerto!" She tells Joann to get out and if she ever returned, she'll kill her.

Joann's blouse was ripped, her hair was a mess, and her heart had been crushed beyond repair.

Mrs. Garcia waved Joann from her sight, but Joann couldn't move away from her fast enough, as Mrs. Garcia encouraged her by connecting three kicks up Joann's ass, moving her far enough from her door, making sure she was at a distance. However, with the force of the last kick, Joann bounced off the wall and fell backwards, so she delivered several blows to Joann's head and body for her disobedience.

Finally, Mrs. Garcia returned to her apartment, slamming the door loudly to sever their maternal connection.

Joann heard the door slam, the echo vibrated through her soul while she crawled on the floor toward the elevators, with blood oozing from her busted lip and busted nose, and still she could hear her mother rave from inside the apartment. She knew she didn't have much time to move far away from the apartment, or risk getting attacked again. With one hand against the wall, she stood and limped within ten feet of the elevators.

After a brief rest, she lowered herself to the floor and crawled the remaining distance to reach the elevator door, and positioned herself under the elevator call buttons. All busted, she reached into her pocket for her cell phone. Feeling around the keypad for the right buttons, she dialed three numbers.

"This is a nine, one, one operator. Where is the emergency?" said the woman on the phone.

"Hello…"

"Where's the emergency?"

"I've just been beaten and robbed by two men, help me please. I'm a diabetic, and they beat me really bad, my insides hurt, and I'm also blind. I can't see, please send me some help…"

"What is your location, ma'am?"

The 911 operator retrieved Joann's information and location. While Joann waited for help, she reached into her back pocket to remove one hundred seventy-two dollars, and shoved it into her panties. Before she could rest her head against the wall, she heard the deadbolt locks disengage. Like a bat released from hell, her mother flew from her apartment, wearing steel-toe Timberland boots. Joann knew it was her mother. She tried to stand; she slid up the wall slowly in pain. A figure appeared before her. "Mommy…"

Joann screamed from the kick to her pelvis. She collapsed on the floor on her side only to receive multiple kicks in the midsection. Her mother said nothing, but she left no area of Joann's body unvisited. To add insult to injury, she lifted her housedress over her bare ass, lifted her leg, and blessed the unconscious Joann with a golden shower.

Hearing a group of male voices descending in the elevator, her mother dropped her housedress and quickly ran back to duck inside the apartment before being seen by the two police officers and two EMS technicians who stepped off the elevator to find a woman who was badly beaten, unconscious, and soaked in piss.

# Die, William, Die

"*A*ndrea, tell me what to do? Baby, please! Andrea, talk to me!" Mrs. Hartford cried to her daughter who was beating her fists and head against the refrigerator.

"William! William! Stop it, please. Please, stop!"

Mrs. Hartford stared at her daughter helplessly, but with much anger. *That damn William! How is it that he still manages to bring my daughter all this pain? I hate him so. I thought we were rid of him. I thought my daughter was rid of him. Andrea has only been home for a few days and already the madness has begun. I can't believe he would have such a grip on her after so long. He must be stopped; he has to be dealt with before he kills my baby.*

"Andrea, where is he? Do you want me to bring him here? What do you want to me to do? Andrea, speak to me now, baby, come on, talk to your mother."

"There's nothing you can do, Mother. We are Of One, we are of his order, we are connected to him and of his order, and we must bear his anger, his wrath. If we fail to contain his fury, then we have failed Heaven. Only *Ona* can stand against him if the Father stands behind her." Her eyes bulged as wide as they could get; she grasped for air, her entire body shook. Suddenly her body tensed and froze her in the middle of some sort of spasm.

Her tear-glazed eyes were wide and staring up into a blank ceiling, mouth open, body stiff.

"Oh, my God, *no*! Oh God, no! Not my baby. No, you wouldn't do this to me. Damn you! Not my baby! Please don't kill my baby. Please, oh God no. I'll do whatever you ask, oh Lord. Please, oh please don't let him kill my baby. William, you give her back to me! You hear me, William? I said give her back to me!" She lowered her head and cried into her daughter's chest. "Motherfucker, you give her back!" She hollered at the top of her lungs. "I'm sorry I tried to have you killed. I'm sorry. Please, Lord, forgive me. Oh, God, please forgive me. Don't let that evil motherfucker, William, take my baby for my mistakes," she cried.

*I'm a mother that would do anything for her children, even if that anything included murder. I'm not proud of what I've done, but I can't say I wouldn't do it again. I had no choice but to try and rid that evil bastard from my baby's life. He was killing her; I couldn't just standby while he was ripping her apart from the inside out.*

*It was twelve years ago when I witnessed this god-forsaken vampire sucking the life from her, literary!*

*It was on a Tuesday, late in the evening when this motherfucker stopped by out of the blue. Out of nowhere, like pigeon shit that just plopped from the sky, this slimy piece of shit landed on my couch. Andrea knew the contempt I had for this man, yet she asked me to be civil toward him. Because of my love for my daughter, I agreed to keep the peace. That snake knew I didn't like him. He could've asked her out for a cup of coffee which could be far away from my neighborhood, but we knew why he didn't. Because the motherfucker was married with a house full of kids, that's why. I am so certain that damn wedding band of his would shine brighter than the sun when it came into my presence, just to taunt me. I also knew him being there had to have a tremendous effect on my baby because she loved that bastard to death, and I damn well wasn't going to let it come to that.*

*They sat on the couch laughing about the short two years, which had passed since they last saw each other. It was obvious they must have had some phone conversations prior to him showing the fuck up. Her eyes were all dreamy. She hung on his every word, so girly… she was so happy. But I knew he was going to hurt her once again, he always did. Their relationship was an odd one, yet quite emotionally tensed. They met so many years back when they were teenagers. At first, he seemed to be good for her. She smiled more; she was even happy most of the time. Then suddenly everything changed after William broke off their relationship, and ever since then he caused my baby heartache and pain.*

*Like I said, it was twelve years ago when this bastard came-a-callin' and they sat and talked for hours like old friends trying to catch up on each other's life. When they finally got their behinds up, she walked him to the door to say their 'goodnight' and all, while I'd went down to the basement to bring up the laundry. When I came back up the stairs from the basement, I heard the sounds of heavy breathing, so I looked around, and then decided to investigate. I was not ready to absorb what I witnessed. This motherfucker had his entire head buried between my daughter's thighs. I gasped and nearly threw up. He had her legs over his shoulders and her ass lifted up in the air with her back against the wall. She was rubbing his head and pulling his hair, while he was acting as if he hadn't ate in days.*

*I wanted to bust through the door and beat this bastard in his head, but I had promised my daughter I would be on my best* behavior, and how could I justify myself for spying on her? So I quickly and quietly rushed myself to the safety of my kitchen. Fifteen minutes later, I heard Andrea running up the stairs to her room. It sounded as if she was crying, but I wasn't sure.

She had one of those nightmares again that night so I knew that bastard had hurt her, and that was the very first time I gave thought to the idea of committing first-degree murder. Luckily for me, a week later she signed herself into the United States Army. I had mixed feelings about the whole ordeal. Here it was I was losing my daughter to go fight in a war, but I was getting rid of William, which was a much pleasing thought than my daughter leaving. But even more satisfying was witnessing the pain and disappointment on his face six years ago.

This juvenile delinquent showed up at my doorstep looking for Andrea. My daughter, Andrea's younger sister, Linda was sitting on the stoop watching her daughter play in the front yard. I was a little nervous at first because she had a thing for William also, but her honesty did my bidding. I was sitting in my reading chair when a bright light flashed into my living room, distracting me. I got up, went to the window to investigate. The sun was shining brightly, so I figured it must have reflected off of someone's windshield, but when I peeped through the blinds I was hit by a burst of light that damn near blinded me, but I saw where it came from, that motherfucker wedding band. This fucker came out from his car carrying a huge bundle of long stemmed red roses. They were beautiful. Big, dark red petals, bursting with enough warmth to melt the coldest of hearts. Well, except mine and the only reason for me being the exception was because he held them.

Another flash from that damn ring, damn near blinded me again. That damn wedding ring of his was taunting me.

*There he stood, chatting and charming Linda with his small talk, and then came the crushing of the Great-One. He asked if Andrea was home. Linda gave him that dumb look followed with, "You don't know?"*

*"Know what?"*

*"William, I thought you knew Drear doesn't live here anymore."*

*"Oh? Wow, I guess it's been a minute. Where does she live these days?"*

*"William, Andrea moved out and went to serve in the Army six years ago."*

*Then I saw the shock on his face followed by the look of sudden pain. "Yes!" I jumped with joy and did a little dance.*

*"Woo. I... I... I had no idea. I didn't know. I came by a few times but your brother only told me she wasn't home. How long did you say she was gone?"*

*"She's been gone for six years now, and...um..."*

*She hesitated and I practically willed her to continue. Bring the climax to this show and bring the curtains down on William's reign over my daughter.*

*"William, she's...she's married."*

*And I saw him take what I thought would be his last breath. This motherfucker was crashed. I saw reality fade, and his whole world tumble into a sea of chaos and uncertainty. If I didn't have so much contempt for the bastard, I would have felt sorry for the motherfucker. But, instead I jumped far back from the window and did the James Brown dance while singing, "The Big Payback!"*

*Moments later after my victory dance, I went back to the window and found this bastard in his car. I watched closely to see what he was up to.*

*Three long minutes later, he emerged from the vehicle, placed a letter into an envelope, and grabbed those damn roses off the hood of his car and approached Linda. Forgetting to put on my slippers, I ran for the door.*

*I knew I scared the shit out of them because they jumped for their dear lives when I swung the door open and snatched the envelope from Linda's hand, while William was handing her those roses.*

*"Give me that, and you take those damn flowers away from here!"*

*"Mrs. Hartford, I—"*

*"You, nothing. I want you to stay away from my girls, you hear me? Leave Andrea alone. She's married and she don't need no parts of you in her life. She's happy and she's living a normal life without you. Now leave here, and don't come back!"*

*"Mrs. Hartford, I don't know what I've done to you, but I mean you no harm, or Andrea—"*

*"Shut up before I spit in your face!"*

*"Mrs. Hartford, whatever I done, I'm sorry, but what Andrea and I have will never keep us apart for too long. We are 'Of One,' and that's beyond you. Goodnight, Linda."*

*That was when I thought the unthinkable. I permitted my mind to sink into the mindless abyss of ignorance, chaos and lawlessness. It was so clear to me; I knew this man had to be stopped. I knew there would be no peace for my daughter, unless I had this man stopped.*

*I hid the letter and put together a plot to see that Mr. William Green would never re-enter Andrea's life ever again. It took me months to profile and select the prefect killer.*

*I was glued to my television, watching, awaiting to hear news of a Brooklyn man being shot and killed. That night was unusually cold, dark, ominous even, just damn eerie. Then just before the crack of day, the latest news bulletin stated a man was found shot twice in the section of Brownsville and was undergoing surgery, fighting for his life. He was listed to be in critical condition. When I called the hospital to see how critical he was, I got no straight answer. I was told the hospital was crawling with cops and federal agents. I couldn't understand how one man could cause so much commotion, but again it was William, and somehow it made sense.*

*That hit cost me five grand. You would figure two shots in the chest and the bastard would die, but no such luck. He lived and is still after my daughter.*

◆ ◆ ◆

**8:36 p.m.**

"*M*ama!"

"Call him and try to talk him down."

"I've been trying, he won't answer his phone."

"The older ones, like myself, will not survive his rage. We can hold him only for so long. He is much too strong for us. When he comes to, let him know I don't blame him. Let him know I love him always."

"I will, Mama, I will. But hold on. Try to hang in there, Mama."

"Eve will have a difficult time with him from this moment. She revealed her hand to him. He will no longer trust her and he will be guarded. Turning him toward the Father will cost us dearly, and we are already losing against the fallen ones."

"I know, Mama, I know, but if we are not able to turn him, and if Yvonne cannot achieve her objective, we will all suffer."

"Remember, my daughter, Isaiah 55:11, *'So shall my word be that goeth forth out of my mouth: it shall not return unto me void, but it shall accomplish that which I please, and it shall prosper [in the thing] whereto I sent it.'* The Father has sent out his word, and it must not return void. William will comply, or William will be destroyed," she confirmed, followed by a painful outcry

"Mama! Mama! Ma!"

Mrs. Simpson burst into tears.

# Never Touch Mine

A cell phone rung numerous times before a blonde-haired woman angrily answered. "Hello?"

"Good evening, ma'am, can I speak with Donny, please," the heavy breathing man rudely requested.

"He's in the shower. I'll have him call you back."

"I need to speak with him now. Tell him it's Agent Ramsey on the phone, and we have a situation."

"Hold on, hold on." Reluctantly she complied, but if she would have listened to that little voice, she would have disconnected the call and turned off the cell phone, but instead the woman walked upstairs with the cell phone, down a short hall and into the bathroom. "Honey, theirs a man on the phone name Agent Ramsey, who must speak with you."

A hand came out from behind the red, black, and purple shower curtain that didn't match the décor, or the yellow walls of the bathroom. The hand was gesturing for the phone, which she handed it to him, and crossed her arms over her chest and waited.

"Yeah, what?" asked Agent Donovan.

"Sir, we got trouble…"

"Speak to me, Ramsey."

"William, sir. He's going after the cop."

"He's what! What the fuck do you mean he's going after the cop! Damn it; stop him. Arrest him if you have to." Donovan quickly stepped out from his shower, knocking his wife backward and over the toilet with no concern if she might be injured. He continued his naked sprint toward his bedroom.

204 | Lord' Williams

"Sir…"

"Shit! He cannot get himself killed by those cops. Damn, I was afraid of this. I knew I should have stepped in months ago when we found out she was fucking that piece of shit lieutenant."

"But, Donovan! We lost him."

"Shit! What the fuck you mean you lost him? You find him. Find him! You find him, Richard. Get to that precinct before he does. I'll call the precinct and have two officers meet you outside the precinct. I want you to call that cop commander and place the cop in protective custody. Prevent this from happening…"

"What precinct?"

"I don't know. Are you fucking kidding me? You have his file."

"We're on the Buckner Expressway."

"The…the twenty-third, no, no the seven-three. Yeah, that's it, the Seventy-third on East New York Avenue and Thomas Boyland, in the Brooklyn's Brownsville section. Step on it, I'll meet you there."

He dropped the cell phone on the bed then rambled through the middle drawer of his armoire in search of underwear and socks.

"You're leaving?" his wife questioned.

"Yes, Maureen, I'm leaving. I can't find shit here. What, I thought you did laundry yesterday?"

"I did, I haven't had a chance to bring them up from the basement."

"Are you serious? With all these little people I feed around here, put their asses to work and make them earn the food on their plates." He stormed out the bedroom. While he was heading for the stairs, he heard the shower running, and realized he'd forgotten to turn it off when he first received the call. "Hey,

Maureen, why don't you go turn off the water in that shower, and go do something with yourself?"

"Why don't you go tell the little people to shut it off? I'm done!"

♦  ♦  ♦

Jasmine and Yvonne raced toward Brooklyn; they were about twenty minutes behind William, certainly not enough time to stop him from this suicide mission for the sake of vengeance. Yvonne tried to reach out to him, but his mind was blocked, incoherent from his rage. For years, she questioned his manhood, bringing on the notion of him actually being a punk long before Robert ever came along. For her, smart, pencil-pushing men weren't fighters. She believed he would stand up for her, but he would never fight for her honor. However, if the truth was told to her, William was on the frontline fighting for her on a daily bases in a world filled with many unseen opponents. She believed he didn't have the guts to get into a man's face or push on him if she were pushed, or manhandle a guy the way he would manhandle her. He would push on her then dare her to call one of her boyfriends, or someone to come to her rescue, but she resisted the temptations of his offers many times. Yet, in her heart she knew William had no middle ground, no shades of gray; he was either hot or cold, extremely nice, caring, understanding, or nasty, belligerent, and spiteful, '*a nasty Sagittarius bastard*', as she often quoted, referring to his reference of character.

Yvonne's Lexus Coupe was just reaching the Grand Central Parkway when William was about to exit the Jackie Robinson Expressway. If she continued doing eighty-eight miles per hour or better, she would narrow the distance between them by ten minutes.

"Mommy, my head is killing me! Stop hitting the potholes."

"I'm sorry, baby. I know it hurts. It's your father. I have to reach him and calm him down before he kills us all…"

"Excuse me! Mommy, you shot at the man. I mean, you actually shot at him. I don't think he'll be willing to speak with you without his gun! Why? Why would you shoot at him?"

"I don't know how he did it. How he managed to deflect all my shots? My aim was perfect, yet neither he, nor his vehicle was scathed."

"I don't understand you! Did you come back home to kill my father? Why, Mommy? Is it because he's going after your little side action?"

"Jasmine mind yourself."

"Mommy, you shot at him!"

"He's alright, right? So don't worry about it, okay?"

"What a dysfunctional family. The only reason why I came with you is to make sure no one shoots my father. I can't take this pain!"

"Just hold on for a few more minutes, we're almost there." She tried to comfort Jasmine.

◆ ◆ ◆

On the other side of Brooklyn, racing up on the eastbound side of Eastern Parkway, were two NSA agents. The one on the passenger side was on the phone with Sergeant Duffy, asking to be connected with Captain Bradley, or Lieutenant Wells, but neither of the two men was in the building. Robert informed Sergeant Duffy he was stepping out for lunch. He had his mind set on sinking his teeth into a turkey breast and Swiss cheese hero, topped off with shredded lettuce, sliced tomatoes, diced hot peppers, green peppers, onions, and mayonnaise. However, before he would sink his teeth into his heartburn sandwich, he had to keep his appointment with his hired hit man.

"I told you he's not here. He stepped out for lunch. What about that don't you understand?" Sergeant Duffy said.

"Look, all I'm asking for is his cell phone number."

"And who are you again?"

"NSA Agent, Faraday, New York Office, and this call is of an urgent matter!"

"Yeah, I thought I heard you say that…"

"Can I speak with the commanding officer there?"

"How many times do I have to tell you? You're speaking to him, as long as the captain and lieutenant are out of the building. Now stop wasting my time, pencil dick. Bye!" Sergeant Duffy placed the phone back its base, while shaking his head in belief.

Robert stepped up on the sidewalk on the corner of the Pitkin Avenue and Thomas Boyland Street, walked several feet in the direction of a man who was wearing a dark green T-shirt, black Rocawear jeans, black Jordan's, and a Rastafarian hat stuffed with dreads, which still managed to spill out and down his back. Robert joined him in leaning against a large gray building that used to be an East New York Savings Bank in the seventies and eighties.

"What's up?" Robert greeted the man who appeared to be in his early thirties.

"Ain't nothing. So we still good or what?"

"Yeah, we still good. Here take this." Robert handed the man a large manila envelope. "Everything you need and payment is in here. Half now the other half when it's done. You will need to stake out his home and catch him while making a run to some local spot up there where he live, is preferred, but if you have no choice, hit him when he comes back here in the city. He moves around a lot, so you'll get a lot of opportunities to take care of business. Any questions?"

"You got a time limit?"

"Nope, I just need it done. Don't contact me until then. If you get sloppy and get caught, don't contact me at all."

"Gotcha."

The two men separated with the man heading east toward Rockaway Avenue, while the lieutenant crossed over on the other side of Pitkin Avenue, heading up Thomas Boyland Street toward the precinct.

Approximately fifty feet away from the precinct front door, William came up behind Robert, feeling the desire to hit him at the base of his skull, but instead he stopped and called out to Robert. "Yo, bitch."

Robert turned around to see the dark figure.

William shoved him with both hands. "Evening," said William, as Robert stumbled several feet backward, feeling the weight of the two hundred and forty-seven-pound angry bull.

Robert quickly pulled off his sport jacket, withdrew his weapon from its holster, wrapped his sport jacket around the weapon and placed it on the ground beside him. "What? You reached down into your wife's panties for some balls, bitch?"

"Shut the fuck up and let's do this," William said.

Robert walked toward William. When he was within reach, the two men swung, both hitting their targets, both realizing the other was brick solid. However, this came a surprise to Robert; he thought William was soft and had no chin. It was then he quickly learned that an angry, six-foot-one-inch-tall, black man who had a fifty-two-pound and four-inch-reach advantage can be quite a favorable opponent.

♦ ♦ ♦

Sergeant Duffy was still feeling suspicious about the phone call. He looked over to Officer Tabbit. "Johnny, do me a favor and step outside and see if you can find the lieutenant jerking off out there. If you do, tell him I need him for a quick minute, alright?"

"Sure," replied Officer Tabbit.

Officer Tabbit came from behind the desk and walked to the front entrance where he saw several officers running. He stepped out looking in their direction, and beyond them, he saw a big, tall black man kicking another black man who was trying to get on his feet. Quickly he realized the man trying to stand was his lieutenant. He yelled, "Sarge!" and joined in the rescue.

William slammed Robert head first into the wall of the precinct. Robert bounced off the wall and back toward William, who then kicked Robert in his mid-section. Robert's body lifted a little over a foot off the ground. The small flock of officers were within a few feet of William when he grabbed Robert's right hand, pulled Robert toward him, twisted the hand, then the arm behind Robert's back, and in one motion, William pushed the arm up and quickly pulled back, breaking Robert's wrist, and his arm in two locations.

"Never touch mine," was the last thing William said before he was pushed and struck from behind with a blunt object.

William stumbled forward, but continued to stand, but was quickly surrounded by a mirage of punches and kicks from his head to his knees.

A car screeched to a stop. Two men jumped out, withdrawing their weapons and wallets, as they ran up to the curb. "Stop! NSA! Back off! Back away from that man!"

"Put the fucking guns down! Now! Put them down!" someone shouted.

"Drop it!" someone else said.

The agents looked about and behind themselves. They were surrounded by police officers with their weapons drawn, aiming at them.

One agent, with his ID held in the air, shouted, "We're NSA and that man is under our jurisdiction!"

"You will drop those weapons and lie face down on the ground, or get blown to hell!" Sergeant Duffy yelled to the two agents.

The two agents quickly yielded and complied. While officers moved in to cuff the two agents, Sergeant Duffy walked over to look at the black man against the wall being handcuffed. He got up to the man and in disgust and great disappointment realized it was William R. Green with blood running from a gash above his left eye, cheek bone and lower lip, in addition to the scrapes and burses on his arms.

"Sarge! It's the lieutenant!" Officer Tabbit announced.

Sergeant Duffy didn't look in Officer Tabbit's direction. He just turned and walked back to the station. "Who gives a fuck?"

Yvonne jumped out of her Lexus, and knew she was too late. Like any concerned wife, she wanted to know the whereabouts of her husband. She saw Sergeant Duffy walking toward the front entrance of the precinct.

"Steve! Steve!"

Steven Duffy stopped, looked in her direction, turned, waved his hand, and walked into the station house.

Yvonne turned her attention toward the ground where she saw two white men in cuffs being escorted inside the precinct, and not too far behind them was William. She approached slowly.

William, holding his head up proudly, looked at her. "Are you here to finish the job? And you asked me to trust you?"

With what little strength she was regaining, Jasmine ran toward her father, calling out to him. Yvonne grabbed her. "Let me go! That's my father!"

"No, baby, there's nothing we can do now. Stop fighting me." Yvonne struggled to contain Jasmine.

"Let go of me! It's your fault! Get off me!" Jasmine pushed Yvonne away, and walked back toward the car, holding her head and slightly bent over.

Officers guarded the entrance. Looking over to her right, Yvonne saw Robert being carried to an awaiting patrol car. She walked over. As she reached the front of the vehicle, she was stopped by a fellow officer. "Was that your husband?"

Yvonne looked the officer in his eyes, straightened her back and shoulders. "Yes. That's my husband we have in custody."

"Well, seek a divorce or something. He won't be getting out for a while. The lieutenant has a broken shoulder, possibly a few broken ribs, and God knows what else…"

"Sounds like he got off easy to me," Yvonne said.

Bewildered by her statement, the officer looked at her and walked over to the driver side of the vehicle.

Yvonne continued her walk on the passenger side of the car. She opened the rear door, and bent down to stare Robert in his eyes. "You wanted a piece of him for so long. So how'd he taste?"

"Come on, close the door!" yelled the officer sitting next to Robert.

Yvonne straightened up, turned and walked toward the station, leaving the door open. She heard the officer's obscene slander and gave it no concern.

Sergeant Duffy exited the building and stood face to face with Yvonne. "Look, the captain is on his way in. I think it would be a good idea if you weren't here. Go home, stay home, and avoid the phone calls. I'll come by later and fill you in."

"Who were those other two men?"

"I don't know. They say they're NSA…"

"NSA?"

"I don't understand the magnitude of this, but it's out of control. It's really a tub of shit! Go home, Yvonne." Steve Duffy turned away from Yvonne and walked to the entrance. "Keep her out of here," he instructed the two officers on guard, before walking inside.

Yvonne turned around and walked toward her Lexus. She noticed Jasmine wasn't there. She looked about, but saw no sign of her.

# After The Storm

*C*overed with one of the four blankets William crocheted for her over the years, Yvonne sat in a chair in the living room. She anxiously waited to hear something from anyone regarding William's situation, but the phone had not rung once all night. She channel-surfed the different news stations for information. She spied the time in the lower right hand side of Channel Seven Eye Witness News broadcast. It was six-twenty in the morning, and she had yet to close her eyes. She's been praying since she left the scene. She was not worried, just uncertain of what was taking place around her, but what piqued her curiosity the most was how the government got factored into this And once again, and all of a sudden? The Heavens will reveal only so much; everyone is on a need-to-know bases. William never privileged her with the details regarding the Filtrex agreement, or how his time devoted to the project. She wondered why, but didn't know why William would leave their home for a couple of days every two months, and would never call home during the time he was gone. She never knew William's little invention had something to do with national security. William wasn't allowed to inform his wife or loved ones that he was flown to some unknown remote location to do test runs on his project and work with other engineers to develop a suitable casing for the Filtrex project. They weren't allowed to contact anyone, not even family.

◆ ◆ ◆

It was eleven-eighteen in the late morning. Agent Donovan found the entire incident of NYPD stonewalling the investigation unnecessary and totally uncooperative for rejecting his 'Get out of jail free card.' He had gotten drug lords and terrorist out of jail faster than this. The situation was wrapped in so much red tape that the Justice Department and FBI had to be called in. They sat in conference with the Chief of Police, their attorneys, and the state prosecutors. NYPD refused to release William and the agents for a multitude of charges ranging from attempted murder on their ranking officer to terrorism since the story went national a little after ten o'clock that morning.

◆ ◆ ◆

There has been no word from Steven Duffy. It was going on eleven-fifty in the morning when she awakened from a short, restless nap. She stood from a place of rest and made her way toward the kitchen. She hadn't eaten since she shopped with the girls yesterday. She heard a vehicle drive onto the property. She looked out the kitchen window to see William's truck driving up the driveway. She looked closely at the driver as the SUV drew nearer. It was Jasmine.

Unknown to Yvonne, Jasmine had spotted the truck double-parked near the corner of corner of Thomas Boyland and Pitkin Avenue. William had left the doors open, engine running to catch up to Robert. Jasmine took the truck to a girlfriend's house and spent the night. Yvonne had been trying several times an hour to reach her, but Jasmine refused to take her calls.

Jasmine entered the living room. The two women looked at each other, not knowing quite what to say. Yvonne broke the silence.

"Your father must still be in lock up. He's not home yet."

"No shit, Mommy. Guess you haven't been watching the news today?"

"I stayed glued to the television until I fell asleep just before eleven. Why? Is it on the news?"

"Duh!" Jasmine replied, turned and headed upstairs.

Yvonne headed to the sofa opposite the seventy-six-inch LED television to search for the remote control. With no luck, she scanned the coffee table, and other two sofas. The doorbell rang, breaking her search. She sprinted to answer the door, hoping it was Steve Duffy, or some official word. It would be even better if it were William.

She opened the door to Jake and Tammy wearing worried faces. A week ago, she would have closed the door in their faces. She had no words for Jake since William sacrificed the family for him, and this chick Tammy, she couldn't stand for multiple reasons. Now she was taken aback by this woman. She was surprised to feel her insides stirring, just as it did last Saturday in the jewelry store when she looked upon another of her kindred. Yvonne stood motionless, and in awe.

"Yvonne!" Jake was taken aback by the appearance of Yvonne. "You're alive!" Jake blurted.

"Yes I'm alive, should I not be?"

"May we come in?" Tammy asked.

"Oh. Sorry. Sure, come in." Yvonne stepped back.

Jake stepped in, stopping in front of Yvonne. "Look, Eve, I know you can't stand me and all, but we're here to do whatever you want. Is there any way we can help?"

"Honey, why don't you go into the kitchen to make us some sandwiches, so we girls can talk for a minute," Tammy said.

Jake knew Yvonne disliked Tammy more than she did him. "Baby, I—"

"Jake, that sounds like a good idea," Yvonne interrupted. "Please, would you make enough for the girls, too? I haven't eaten all day, and the girls are in the pool working up an appetite. I'm sure you know where everything is."

"Well, where is Maria?" Jake asked, not wanting to leave the two women alone.

"She's out back watching the girls in the pool," Yvonne replied.

"Well, yeah, okay." Jake reluctantly agreed, turned and walked toward the kitchen.

"Grace and peace, sister," Tammy greeted Yvonne.

"Grace and peace, my sister," Yvonne replied. The two women walked into the living room area. "I was just about to turn on the television to see what was happening."

"Don't you know?"

"No. I don't know if it reached the news. I was waiting for William to call or for someone from the station to stop by, or something."

They take a seat on each end of the same sofa.

"Well, everyone is meeting with the mayor, as we speak. They're not giving out enough details to the events that took place last night, but they have William's mug shot plastered all over every news station..." While Tammy filled Yvonne in, the phone rang.

"Excuse me." Yvonne stood up to cross the room to answer the phone. "Hello?"

"Eve! It's me," said a woman.

"Vanessa!"

"I can't talk, but I'm over here in Brooklyn—"

"Brooklyn? Why would you be in Brooklyn?"

"They needed extra officers, girl, since they moved William and the other guys to booking central. We trumped NYPD and took custody."

"Say what?"

"Yeah, girl. Once A.D.W. Colon got wind of it being your William causing the buzz, he made some calls, mobilized a small army and we hiked it to Brooklyn."

"You mean little skinny Colon made A.D.W? Damn, I love y'all, girl…"

"Hey, that man done grew, girlfriend, but you know you and William is still family…"

"Have you seen him?"

"Just a glance; he's okay. I don't understand why they said PD fucked him up; ain't a scratch on him."

"Who said that?"

"Don't you watch the news? Look, I can't let them see me on this phone. But he's okay, I'll check in on him, if they let me."

"Thanks, Vee…"

"Don't worry. You know we had to step in and take custody, after hearing PD was kicking ass."

"I know that's right. You be careful. If you see him, tell him just to relax. He's still angry."

"I'll do what I can. Call you later. Bye."

Yvonne hung up.

Tammy scanned Yvonne's face and posture. She could tell that Yvonne was a little worried. "He'll be alright, Eve. No one can harm him."

"It's not him I'm concern about, but what he may do. He's still angry. I can't reach him. He's still so carnal."

"Speaking of which, I see you have come into your own."

"Yes. I'm still transcending…"

"Do you know how long before completion?"

"No I don't. How long have you known about our existence?"

"For a very long time. I was aware of the difference in my being, but it wasn't until I met you and William that I began to examine myself instead of fearing myself. And at some point in time it hit me. I understood things I knew not of, and was able to see truth."

"Did you know of me?"

"I knew there was something special about you. And I felt that there was a link between us, but I couldn't read you. The energy from your anger toward me shrouded you. Was it because I'm white, your reason for disliking me so much?"

"That was the second part."

"And the first part?"

"The first part was you managed to grab a brother from one of my needing black sisters. The only thing that made me feel good about the whole arrangement with you and Jake was you couldn't have children."

"Wow. I see."

"No you don't see. The third part for my dislike with you was my knowing you were fucking my husband."

Shock blanketed her face, her eyes popped, her jaw dropped, her complexion took on every color of the rainbow. "You knew?"

"You damn right I knew! I know about all of you tricks who lay with my man. I felt the insides of each one of you."

Tammy lowered her head in shame, and instinctively for self-preservation, she took several steps away from Yvonne.

"I'm sorry, Eve. I...I couldn't help myself. It felt as if I was compelled—"

"You felt his energy, but you couldn't feel mine? Okay granted, maybe my spirit was weak, broken and torn, but the act of your betrayal was questioned. Now, if you just fucked him one time I might have been able to forgive you, but you fucked him a lot more than once. You went from a need to connect to him to a straight out nasty slut."

Tammy felt the tension in the room growing, along with the heat, which radiated from Yvonne's inner core, and she quickly became frightened. "My sister, please forgive my ignorance, and shallowness. I was not within myself, my Priestess—"

Interrupting her, Yvonne turned her back on Tammy, placed her hands together and stared upon her palms. "For a long time, I hated you, Tammy. I could not find anything good in you to make me like you, let alone forgive you for your treachery, but who was I to throw stones at your glass house? I pushed that man into so many lonely and awaiting arms. All along knowing he was a good-looking black man with a good job, and that alone was enough to keep me on my game, instead of thinking the world revolved around me. Thinking that I was his center, it had to be he who conformed to my expectations and secret desires. When he knew I was doing wrong, he would let me run with it for a minute, but when he grew tired, he would approach me with a line... I came in late one night expecting him to be at work, and when I walked into the bedroom, he was sitting on the bed in the dark. When I turned on the lights, the sight of him scared the living shit out of me. Of course, I had my alibi all setup for such an event, and I fed it to him, but he didn't buy it. The fire in his eyes told me to run, but my knowledge of him knew he would burn me if I did, so I fed him more lies and he looked at me with an expression I'd never seen before. It threw me off. I didn't know if he was hot or cold. His eyes offered no help because they were dark and ominous. So I did what any other smart woman would do, I shut up…"

*He threw all the contents on the dresser onto the floor with the sweep from his long arm. He was pissed. He was angry. He grabbed his head and pulled it downward toward his knees. In an instant, he stood up straight and through clenched teeth, he spoke. "Shut the fuck-up, Eve…"*

*She looked upon him, and what she saw frighten her, so she complied.*

*"Now I'm tired of all the bullshit between us, and I'm no longer pointing fingers, nor will I put any of this shit on you. I'm gonna ride with it, and say forgive me for sending you somewhere else for your needs…" Yvonne's eyes widened. "I guess it's time I step up on my game, because I be damned if I make it easy for any man to walk off with you, knowing that I had the opportunity to make changes and keep what's mine." He reached out for her. "Come. Let's order something to eat. Are you hungry?" She shook her head. "Okay, so I'll order me something to eat and we can sit down, and tell me what clothes and stuff Jasmine and Jermaine need. I'll take Saturday off so we can go shopping, and afterwards we can go hangout at Astroland, Nathan's and walk the boardwalk at Coney Island. Can we do that?"*

*She nodded in agreement while she stained his T-shirt with her tears.*

"This man stood in the devil's playground and did what Adam couldn't do in our Father's garden and accepted complete responsibility and asked for atonement! At the time, I still couldn't understand it. I thought I understood love back then, but I didn't. I saw everything in black, white, and funky colors that bared no truth, as I should have been looking at the aura that shone from their spirit. So instead of forgiving you Tammy, I say to you, I am sorry."

"It's okay, you were…we were in darkness, and we knew not of ourselves. Speaking of which, it was not until last week when you began to transcend that I learned my quest. We are feeding and coming into grace through you, as you know."

"Who is it?"

"The second rider's replacement."

"The second?"

"Yes. I've seen him. He's eight years old now. I should be gifted with him at the age of nine, which draws near."

"Is he of William's seed?"

"I do not know, Eve. If you wish that I release the child unto you—"

"No. Our paths are clear, unless our Father and Lord see change, there will be none."

Jake entered the room, carrying a platter filled with a variety of sandwiches. "Here we are. I made more than enough for everyone, including the kids. They'll be hungry when they get out that water," Jake said.

"Don't you think he'll make a good father?" Tammy said, with a wide smile.

"I think he'll do well," Yvonne endorsed.

"Well, I wish you would just go and have your factory fixed, instead of doing this adoption thing," Jake said, as he placed the platter down on the coffee table.

"The factory is closed for a reason, baby, but I know a beautiful baby boy and girl that will keep you home just the same," Tammy replied.

"Oh, and a girl, too?" Yvonne asked.

"Oh yes, she's the same age and all. She'll watch over him. You know females like us are so much more advanced," Tammy stated.

"Yes, I know," Yvonne agreed.

"I don't know where we're going to find the money for all these raising grown ass children you thinkin' about," Jake said.

"Where there's a will, there's a way," Yvonne replied.

# The Plan

The ocean roared, as it crashed against the rocks, yet it purred when it ran ashore. She could hear the sounds of many ships far out beyond the horizon, blowing their horns rhythmically far off in the distance, all of which took place under the perfect and most beautiful blue sky. The image formed a barrier. One of a few which Mrs. Hartford had successfully used many times in the past to block the inception of her thoughts by her daughter, Andrea.

She needed to get off the phone with her daughter who was carrying on about saving William. Andrea was pleading with her to get him out of jail before any harm came to him, but Mrs. Hartford had already granted William a 'get out of jail free' card.

Andrea knew her mother had put up a wall to block her from reading her mind, but she didn't care about that; what she needed was for her mother to understand the danger her kind will suffer if William's rage was released once more.

"Ma, I know you don't understand what I'm trying to say, but William cannot get himself too upset right now, and he cannot be harmed by the hand of man. We are too close to the end of time for setbacks!"

The waves crashed onto the beach, the seagulls sung in the distance, Mrs. Hartford kept her mind out to sea. "Andrea, I have a meeting which I must attend. I'll see what I can do for William, if anything. Now I have a rapist to catch, and you need to rest. You nearly died in my arms, but all you seem to think about is William, William, William…"

"Okay, okay, I'm off the phone. I'll rest. Please, Ma, don't forget, alright?"

"Yes, dear. I must go now. Bye"

"Yeah, okay. See you when you get home. Oh and don't think that wall you put up can keep me out. I don't push because I respect your right to privacy."

"Andrea, I must go…"

"Bye, Ma." Andrea hung up the phone before Mrs. Hartford had a chance to reply.

Mrs. Hartford let out a huge and long sigh of relief. She didn't know how much longer she could keep up her wall of defense against her daughter, and knowing that her daughter mentioned how she can breakthrough her defenses frightened her, but she had no time to sit back and give worry to a situation she could not control. Besides, she had already set the wheels into motion to take care of her daughter's first love, William, in hope to joy blissfully in the news of his demise.

She sat back and stared and the phone. She remembered picking it up…

*"Hello, officer Jacobs? Yes, this is D.A. Hartford. Do you have a moment to speak? Good. I have been looking over your brother's case, and there might be something I can do for him, but that is only if you can help me out with something. Well first, do you still work in Brooklyn House? Good. There's a problem, which just arrived about a couple of hours ago, and I need that problem to go away. In return for this assistance, I can see that most of the charges your bother has go away. Well, all but the*

*weapon charge and he'll have to give us eighteen months, less*
*than a year if he's a model inmate.*

*"Yes, the problem I'm referring to is the one you have in*
*protective custody. I understand he is heavily guarded... Yes, I*
*do understand the risk involved, trying to convince my superiors*
*to drop these attempted murder, and drug smuggling charges*
*wouldn't be a walk in the park for me either...*

*"No, you don't have time to think about it, Officer Jacobs. I*
*need to know now, if you can erase my problem or can't you?*

*"Thank you. I'll be watching the news. Have a good day*
*Office Jacobs..."*

Not once in her thirty years of service had she ever swayed
from her sworn duties as a lawyer and district attorney. She
stared at the phone knowing that she had just tarnished that thirty
years of service to dispense her own brand of justice to a man
she totally despised. She didn't understand how she came to hate
a man so much, but the thought of him instantly sickened her.

She stepped inside the brightly sun-lit room. She looked upon
the faces of weary men. The small group had poured out countless
hours of their profession and knowledge to learn something of
this killer or to find a break of some kind that would help them
with their investigation.

Mrs. Hartford walked to the center of the large Oak conference
table. Placing her right hand on top of the table and the left upon
her hip, she sighed rather loudly before speaking. "Gentlemen,
before starting, let us pray for a speedy recovery for our friend
and colleague, Detectives Wells, who is not among us for his
run-in with this sub-creature, William R. Green."

"I would love to catch this bastard in a dark alley somewhere,
and give him just what he deserves," Detective Long said.

"Do you know of Mr. Green, detective?" asked Mrs. Hartford.

"Yeah, I know of Mr. Green. I'm not sure of his involvement with the government, but he's connected to some people in pretty high places. I don't know if this will come out in the newspapers, but this was in retaliation against Bobby for knocking boots with his wife," Detective Long stated.

"Ho, Ho, Ho, so his wife's ho! How the hell you like that? This bastard got a bitch in heat and he can't put out the fire, but he beat up on cops who can lay the pipe," remarked Mrs. Hartford who found great pleasure receiving such information. Now she was sure the Great William was just a man, and his spells could be broken.

They all chuckled and laughed.

"Well, gentlemen, let's hope justice is served while he's in lockup and his peers will help save the taxpayers some court expenses. Now let us get down to business. Have we come up with any leads or theories, has the Bureau created a profile on this madman?" Ms. Hartford asked.

"The B.A.U. has not come up with an official profile for this killer, but we believe we have found a common link between all the murders. But the theory behind these links should best be handled by Agent Fox Mulder and Dana Scully," Agent Williams commented.

"What theory, what do you have?" asked Mrs. Hartford.

"Well, actually, we are a little embarrassed to offer you this line of thought, or reasoning because we have no scientific proof or evidence to present..."

Detectives Long and Tait, F.B.I. Agent Williams, and Agent Bradley, looked at each other to speak, but no one wanted to voice this link they uncovered between all the victims. The latest findings shifted the case away from good old-fashion police work to something that was more... supernatural.

"Well? Somebody say something!" Mrs. Hartford raised her voice. "And who the hell are Agents Fox Mulder and Dana Scully?"

The gentlemen chuckled among themselves, yet no one had the courage to voice their latest finding.

"Gentlemen, do I have to remind you that we have an international killer out there, murdering women at what seems to be random, and he's in our neck of the woods, so why don't we place what we have on the table and catch this son-of-a-bitch, place a feather in our hats and laugh all the way to the bank…"

Agent Bradley said, "Forgive me, Ma'am, but I see no glory here…"

"And you're right, Agent Bradley, so stop jerking my chain and tell me what you got…"

"What we have is a collective agreement that we are dealing with something that appears to be beyond our field of expertise. We have found a connection all the victims seem to share, but the connection between them is scientifically immeasurable, which makes it impossible to predict this mad-man's next victim."

"And this connection is?"

"Well, all the victims seem to have a strong psychic ability, which is deeply spiritually rooted."

Mrs. Hartford broke out of character with an ominous laugher. She was so elated; this day could not have unfolded better, even if she had planned it. She lifted her hands toward the ceiling, closed her eyes and thanked her lord for granting this moment of bliss.

"Oh, wow… Gentlemen, we will not be in a better position than this ever again. It seems as if Heaven is smiling upon us. I was contacted last week by a psychic who revealed to me the place, the time, and possible victim…"

The men looked at each other with skepticism. They were not buying into this psychic phenomenon. They believed in good old-fashioned police investigation and solid forensic to make their case.

"I understand you gentlemen may not believe in this sort of stuff, but rest assured we are dealing with something which is abnormal. We are dealing with an international killer that has eluded every form of law enforcement and national and international intelligent agency, globally, so unless anyone here has a solid lead to offer, you might want to hear me out." She paused. "This person assures me that between five and 5:30 p.m., I will come face-to-face with this killer next Friday. I have worked many cases with this person in the past before, and their predictions are quite accurate."

"And why would you be the one to come face-to-face with the person?" Agent Williams questioned.

"'Cause this crazy motherfucker will try to kill me."

"Excuse me, Ma'am, but are you a psychic?" Detective Long asked.

"No, I'm not a psychic."

"How could it be possible you're the target when you don't fit the profile?" Agent Bradley interjected.

"Are you saying the prediction she gave me is wrong?"

"The profile is clear…"

"Now you believe and have faith in the Unofficial profile?"

"Ma'am, all we're saying is this person is targeting—"

"And a very powerful psychic predicted me as a potential target, maybe this is why we'll have the opportunity to capture the bastard because he slipped up…"

"Possible. It does make since," Detective Long agreed.

"Maybe we should keep surveillance on this psychic, just in case—"

"No. She detailed everything to the second, and laid out specifics instructions to follow. The subject will ring my doorbell between the hour of five and 5:30 next Friday. We will place un-mock cars and plain clothed officers on Atlantic and East New York, on Atlantic and Ralph on Ralph and Fulton, on Pleasant Street and Fulton. This way we should have the subject boxed in. Gentlemen, if we do this right, I will recommend accommodations for everyone."

# Gangster Paradise

*2:17 p.m.*

Three correctional officers escorted William to an area where most of the other inmates were out on recreation. William was led into the dorm area with one correctional officer taking point, one at his side and the other in the rear.

"Damn, pop, what you do, where you need three dogs checkin' you?" said a young, fair-skinned man, somewhere in his late teens, about five-eight, and one hundred and seventy pounds. "Shit, I dropped a motherfuckin' fool, and ain't get no service like that, yo."

William didn't respond.

"Clear," the leading officer said.

William entered the showers with his towel, while two officers posted at the entrance leading to the showers.

"Guess I couldn't take a bath right now, if I wanted to, could I?" the young man asked.

"Wish you try," replied one of the officers standing at the entrance to the showers.

Fifteen minutes into William's shower, Officer Jacob walked onto the dorm carrying William's clothes. Another eight minutes passed, and William emerged from the showers, feeling clean and refreshed. He stood before Officer Jacob and inspected the clear plastic bag with his brand new garments. "These aren't mine," William stated.

"What do you mean, they're not yours?" Officer Jacob replied.

William handed the bag back to him. "These are female clothes."

"Shit! My bad." Officer Jacob looked at his fellow officers. "Give me about five minutes, and I'll be back with the right clothes."

"Damn! Brother you're going home? Yo, let me get those digits. I wanna hook up with your crew when I get out. You gotta put a nigger down," the young man said.

"I don't deal with niggers," William replied.

"Say what? Look. man—"

"You know your time might go faster, if you shut the fuck up."

"Let it go, brother. Mr. Green why don't you continue with your shower, until we get the right package?" an officer said.

"You know, fuck you, pop. I would drop yo' fuckin' ass if you didn't have the police guarding ya."

"Officer, please, let me drop some science on this fool." The officer nodded and William faced the young man. "It appears to me that your momma never taught you anything about respecting your elders, did she?"

"You don't know my momma, fool."

"No, I guess she didn't. What, she's in her mid to late-thirties, eighteen, nineteen, years older than you? She was part of that baby-having-baby era, right? Just another half-raised chicken head who thought she knew everything. Hung out in the streets trying to find someone to love her, but she fucked up, and got knocked up, and gave birth to a pissy-tail, no raised, *nigger*. A bastard child who has no respect for nothing, no one, not even for himself…"

"Who the fuck is you? You don't know me. Don't talk about my momma, my momma is twice my age, with a good job, fool. And—"

"And this is how you honor her? Why should I or anyone else think your mother is worth more than the shit she produced? You young, fucking assholes have no concept of life at all. Who don't know you? I know you. You're the worthless piece of shit that shot that two-year-old girl who lay asleep in her stroller! You the bitch-motherfucker, who squeezed off shots, hit that old man in the thigh and shattered his femur bone, and he bled to death alone in his half-empty studio apartment. I know you, boy! You the snake that showed the fourteen-year-old tenderoni what being a real woman was all about! But what you don't know, bitch, is that you're a daddy for the third time. Oh, I know you. I know your kind. You, and those like you, are the illness of life. You're a nigger! You're like a gnat, a blowfly, a fuckin' maggot; you're shit that got spawn from shit. An Incubus, a Succubus is the breed of your kind.

"Instead of you honoring and enjoying the freedom other blacks have died to see you have, you give it back to the people they fraught against. So in my mind, you are a nigger, and I can't stand niggers, regardless of their race." William turned away, and shook his head. "Why are my brothers steady placing their dick in the dust, uncaringly bringing genocide to his people. Nigger's are designed to act like crabs in a basket, stepping on the backs of others while pulling down the one before you…"

"Go shower man." An officer pushed William toward the showers.

The young ran toward William. "Fuck you, motherfucker. Don't let me see you walkin' in the city. You better breathe deep, 'cause your days are numbered, you bitch ass…" The young man was tackled by the officers.

"Fuck you, too, Po-Po. Get the fuck off me. You're a dead man, motherfucker! I'll be out this motherfucker in two days, and I'm gonna kill you on sight. I swear on my kids… "

"Don't you mean your bastard babies, *nigger*…" William shouted from the shower.

"Take this guy out of here. I'll watch this one," offered Officer Jacob.

The three officers lifted the outraged young man into the air, one on each arm, and one restringing the legs as they carried him down the corridor.

◆ ◆ ◆

Vanessa entered the control room with her belly filled and satisfied. "Okay where my boyfriend at? He needs to get his recreation in," she asked while she'd reached for two clipboards at the far end of a counter.

"He's over in E, captain…"

"In E! Why?"

"He needed to shower…"

"What's wrong with the showers in P.C.?"

"The drains started backing in the showers…"

"Under whose authority was he moved?

"Captain Johnson…"

"Have two escort officers and Johnson meet me there."

"Yes captain."

"You people better hope all is well. Didn't anyone find it strange that we have a plumbing problem in P.C. when we have a high profile individual in custody there?" Vanessa turned and headed for the doors. "Also, page the ADW and patch the call to my phone."

"Yes, ma'am."

A chocolate woman stood and called out to Vanessa. "Ma'am!" She alerted.

"What is it?"

"Ummm… for whatever reason, inmate Green's escort team is escorting an unruly inmate to E."

"Okay, give me an alert in E, and dispatch a team, tell them to secure the entire section, and secure all personal, including any officers…"

"Officers, Ma'am?"

"Did I stutter?"

"No, Ma'am."

Vanessa powerwalked as fast as she could to E section, worried about what she would find once she arrived, and if the situation would turn out to be grim. Her stomach flipped at the mental images of the blood stained cell or would she find William's nude and molested body hanging from a showerhead. She feared to think any further so she focused on how many heads was going to roll on this caper.

The voices were cloudy and congested; the scene was surreal, like an addict tripping off acid. "The colors man, the colors."

Vanessa couldn't believe her eyes. Everything, everyone moving in slow motion, everything but her heart, which was racing like a heart on steroids just beats away from A-fib.

Her stomach turned from that familiar smell of sulfur and copper. The bloodstained walls shook the foundation of her nerves, and she prayed, feared and fought to maintain her stone-faced look, as she strode closer to the showers. Stopping at the sight of blood that streamed with the water from the showers, rushing toward the drains.

An officer stepped out from the shower to brace Vanessa. "Captain, we were too late."

Those words ran circles around her mind, before crashing upon her heart, causing a sudden loss of breath. How the hell was she going to explain this to Yvonne? Speaking of which, her cell phone began to vibrate. She knew it was Yvonne because she had been blowing her up for the last eighteen minutes, but she didn't possess the courage to speak such words like, "I'm so sorry, Eve, but William died on my watch."

She swallowed hard and continued taking in the gruesome details of carnage and mayhem. She laid eyes on one shank, which looked like a triangular piece of scrap metal with a sharpened point on one end, and cloth wrapped around the object that acted as a handle. A few steps further her eyes laid upon a second shank, then her bottom lip quivered, her breath shortened, her feet became weighted from the load upon her shoulders. It was there she spotted William's nude body lying face down on the bloodstained ceramic tiles, with multiple stabs wounds and lacerations on his back, arms and legs. She looked further up, on the far side of the room to behold the corpse of two large naked black men, and Officer Jacobs giving his statements on the event that unfolded.

"Lieutenant," she bellowed.

"Yes, Captain."

"Take that officer into custody; get a forensic team down here stat…"

"Yes, Ma'am."

Her cell phone vibrated once again. "Oh my Father in Heaven, how bad have we fucked up now?"

# The Aftermath

**3:19 p.m.**

"What the fuck is this shit! I can move mountains, find human slaves, and make a billion dollars faster than getting this man out of jail!" Agent Donovan yelled into the telephone receiver. "It took me twenty-eight hours to get my two agents released from NYPS, so what's the hold up with William? Bullshit! Have you seen the news? Dead, dead, dead! I'm not going down for this one; no way will I take the fall for this shit. If the powers of Washington couldn't get him released, what the fuck am I supposed do? How do we pick up the pieces and move on from here?"

Agent Donovan took his seat behind his desk, sat back and prepared himself to listen to the voice on the other end.

**3:21 p.m.**

*What the fuck happen? What a mess of things. Jesus, I just hope none of this shit makes its way back to me.* Mrs. Hartford paced in front of her desk. *How could Officer Jacob fuck up a task that was so simple? Inmates get killed daily, but this one was a high profile arrest from the very start. Maybe I should have thought better. Use better judgment, but all that's too late now. Who the fuck is William that he complexes everyone's life so severely? Nothing left for me to do other than pray this Officer Jacob keeps his mouth shut.*

**3:25 p.m.**

*"Vanessa, answer the damn phone!"* Yvonne yelled at her cell phone. Her ranting was interrupted by the chimes of an incoming call. She viewed the caller information and switched over to the incoming caller. "Of One."

"Of One, Ona. We suffered many losses last night, which could have been avoided. It is understandable you're still in transition and not yet totally within your own, but we cannot afford any other mishaps like last night. We nearly lost all four riders, along with Momma Green…"

"Everything started spiraling out of control. William is no easy measure."

"No he isn't, nor was he design to be. Your error to remove him was flawed."

"I received the word, but he…he—"

"He was still protected. The work you were preforming was not totally the will of our Father. Jealousy crept into your subconscious and changed the purity of our Father's will to your will for revenge, which made your entire act sinful."

"I see."

"Go, turn on your television and turn to CNN. They are about to announce a late breaking update." Mrs. Simons concluded the call.

While the television booted up, Yvonne wondered what had she done to displease her Father in Heaven. She remembered the crackling of thunder in the clear sky above her, and a soft whisper within that thunder saying, "Return him unto me."

Their eyes met. The stare caused them to look deep into each other's entity, which revealed their truth, honesty, and love. A pure form of love that is unknown and unfelt by mankind. She felt the yearn to connect to him, to be a part of him, to stay with him forever, but how could she disobey the directive which was just given to her, for it was not her will, nor was it in her heart to comply with her Father. She knew this being; she had loved this being for a very long, long, long time. Even though he is not her kind, he had chosen her, and bonded within many worlds for many missions. She could not pull that trigger, she could not follow the commandment given to her by her Father, for the love and the bond she had for this being before her was stronger than the word of her God, yet her will not to pull the trigger could not withstand the corruption of sin.

She pulled the trigger for the jealousy and content she held for Joann and William's relationship. She pulled that trigger from the split second of feeling the bitterness, which clouded her reasoning and the link she had with her Heavenly father, Eloheim.

"…in recent turn of events involving William Green, the man who severely beat a New York police detective, was attacked by two inmates and is now fighting for his life. When we arrived on the scene this afternoon, we heard rumors there was a plot, better yet there was an attempt to assassinate William Green while he was in the custody of New York City Corrections Department. Mr. Green is about to be rushed to Long Island Collage Hospital for multiple stab wounds. Although he is not expected to live, no one is allowed near him or the Brooklyn Correction Facility. It's reported that the two inmates who tried to assassinate William Green was killed during the process. It is still unclear how these inmates died, whether they were killed by correctional officers, or William Green. To take this case to another level, we hear reports stating that the Mrs. Green has asked for…the department of Justice to get involve and oversee this case…"

*What! When did I do that? I can still remember the last time the feds came into my life they were trying to lock me up for life. What plans do they have for William and me now?*

**3:26 p.m.**

"Jerome is this the same guy you were telling me about?"

Jerome walked into the living room to view the CNN news coverage. "Yeah, yeah. That's the dude, man."

"Damn, from the sound of this, you might be wasting your time. This motherfucker is up against the worst odds of surviving the fucking week, than getting shot by you."

"I really don't care how or who take him out, but he has got to be put down. The fate of this entire planet, all of man hangs in the balance of his death. "

"Are you serious, Jerome? I know you made everything about you, about God, but really? Really? How could one man be the link between life and death of mankind? That bullshit ain't in my Bible—"

"Don't be so damn sure, because the entire Bible is all about one man who is the link to every man, woman, and child…life and death. His name is Jesus!"

"Yeah, well he ain't Jesus. This cat is just a nigger you need to deal with to fix your home."

**4:11 p.m.**

The five-foot-five, fair-skinned woman had been sitting in the hospital waiting for more than an hour since her arrival. It had been over thirty minutes since she was last told her sister's operation went well and she was resting in her room, but she would have to wait an hour more before she could be allowed to go upstairs. The woman was relieved by the doctor's brief visit, but not enough to take away that edgy feeling.

Thirteen more minutes passed before she was standing in front of her battered and missed understood sister. "Hey, how are you doing?"

Her entire body hurt, she felt as if her insides were somewhat misaligned. "How the hell do I look?" Joann replied, as she tried to focus in on her sister's face.

It was four-forty-three by the time Mary made it up to Joann's room. Joann was showing remarkable signs of recovering from her injuries. She was healing so wonderfully they brought her down from ICU a couple of hours ago.

"Well…you don't look so hot," Mary replied.

"Yeah, well I feel fucked up."

"And you look it, babe," Mary finally admitted, as she surveyed the bruises, which were exposed on Joann's forehead, face, and arms.

"Why does it feel like someone shoveled out my insides?"

"Because they did. The doctor had to remove a few things from you."

"What? What are talking about, Mary?" Joann stared at the blurred image standing before her.

"Don't you remember the doctor talking to you?"

"No. I don't remember anything. The last picture in my head was when your mother came into the hall and started kicking the shit out of me. She was screaming on me something bad, and she even pissed on me, calling me a whore and everything in the neighborhood of hell's demon child. That's it, nothing else. What happen? What did they do to me, Mary?"

"They gave you a hysterectomy. Don't you remember signing the paper?"

"Mary, I don't remember shit. I'm telling you. Ah, man. Why? What the fuck for? What? What the fuck did they do to me?"

"Well, you went into some kind of a diabetic shock during your ride to the hospital. X-rays showed you were bleeding internally, but once they opened you, they saw you were bleeding everywhere down there, so they had to operate. They gave you a hysterectomy; you also have a fractured pelvis, and a collapsed uterus."

"So she really tried to kill me? My mother tried to put an end to me." She put on a fake smile. "I guess there'll be no more sex for me. No more having babies for me. I guess it was for the best. I don't need any more kids, anyhow. I've fucked up with the ones I have. So what of it? I'm better off, right?"

Mary had been waiting to see her sister for hours, but she could see that visit taking a turn for the worse, and her end wasn't the favorable side. "Hey, look, I'm kinda tired and I got to get home to start dinner. The doctor said he'd stop by before leaving tonight. You going to be okay?"

"Mary, I don't know anymore. I'm just all fucked up right now. I don't know what I'm feeling. Humph, I don't think I can make three days, let alone talking three months or years," Joann declared.

"What you talking about?"

"I don't know. Some shit William told me. He said if I don't change my ways, I only have three years or something to live…"

"Well, William isn't much of a smart dog, and I don't think he's sanctified enough to prophesize—"

"I don't know anymore, Mary. This motherfucker ain't human. There's too much going on inside of him. I feel it…"

"Yeah, you're right. He's a super dog. I'm sorry, but I have no respect for any man who cheats on his wife and family."

"And me, Mary?"

"What about you?"

"Do you have any respect for me, with all the shit I've done? You side with Mommy don't you?"

"Aww, Joann, we ain't talking about you—"

"Answer me!" Joann was seeing Mary clearly now.

"Joann, Aww! I knew this shit was coming. Look, no I don't respect the things you've done with your life, but that has nothing to do with my love for you as a sister…"

"I see…"

"Have I ever abandoned you? Have I?"

"I don't know, Mary. You never believed in me. In fact, for years you wouldn't really have anything to do with me until you started going to church." Joann turned her head away from her sister and looked out the window at nothing. "And you never called me while living with Mommy. You didn't start calling until you got a place of your own."

"Joann, this shit is not fair. I've always stood by you…"

"Yeah, but you never stood up to Mommy for me. You felt the same way she did. And to this day you don't believe I'm a victim of all this bullshit your mother has done to me."

"You ain't right. All the things I've done for you and you throw this shit in my face?"

"You just said you have no respect for the things I've done in my life." Joann tried to move her arms unsuccessfully. "You must be thinking I'm just some whore bitch who's on hard times and deserves every bit of the struggle—"

"Joann…"

"Admit it, Mary!"

"Yeah, okay. I don't have any respect for shit you've done with your life. You fucked up people's lives. You broke up marriages and families. You sent people to jail, you sent people to hospitals, and you sent people to their graves. My sister, the fuckin' whore. My sister, the fuckin' drug dealer. My sister, the home wrecker! I'm a wife, for goodness sake; I hate your kind. Do you know how hard it is to keep a man, and remain disease free? For years, I've blamed you for destroying our little family. For taking away the one man I knew as a father, and for making my mother such a bitter bitch. And I blamed you for not being there for me! You ran away from me! You left me there to get raped night after night after night. Where were you when I needed you? You was too busy fuckin' this one, that one, and the other to give me any thought. You weren't the only victim, Joann!"

Silence.

Mary sniffled as she fought back tears.

Joann swallowed and took a deep breath. "I'm sorry. Forget what I said. I'm just trying to find someone to blame for my shortcomings, but let the truth be told, you're the only one standing here with me. You're right!" she squeaked. "I have destroyed many lives, including my own, and my children's. My whole life I've been looking for someone to say "I love you," yet I never gave anyone love in return, just the wrong motherfuckers who had nothing for me. I have spread myself so thin that now there's nothing left to me." She buried her teary face into her hands. "I'm sorry! Mary, I am so sorry! I never bothered to think about you, or the love you have for me.

"You're right; it was selfish of me to leave you there. I was wrong for not calling you; to make sure you, my baby sister was okay. I never gave it a thought you needed me to help you out. For so many years, it seemed as if you was my big sister. I only call you when I need something, but you call me to see how I am, and to make sure I'm okay. You have always been the only one here for me. You're the only one standing here. There will be nobody else coming to visit. If I died today, you would be the only one at my funeral; you, my son and the preacher. I'm so sorry." She lifted her head to face Mary, crying. "I would hug you, but I can't move." Choked by her tears, she managed to say, "I...I'm...I'm sorry..."

Mary could no longer hold back her tears. She joined her sister in a good, soulful cry as she gently wrapped her arms around Joann.

"Stop it; you're making me cry, too..."

"I love you, Mary," Joann squeaked. "You're all I have. I'm sorry. Please don't hate me, too."

"I don't hate you. I can never hate you. You're my big sister, and I love you."

"I love you, too."

The two women braced each other until they both recognized a very familiar name broadcast over the CNN news program showing on the television hanging on the wall opposite Joann's bed.

"*...Dave that's right, four, not one, but four ambulances left out from this Brooklyn Corrections Facility at the same time, but in four different directions, which one carrying William Green is not known at this time, or the reason for the deception. Also, Dave, sources have confirmed that those two deceased inmates was part of a hit squad trying to cash in on a hit that was placed on William Green's head. This case keeps taking these unsuspected turns, one has to wonder, who is William R. Green?*"

"Joann, I'm not one to gossip, but I think your superman is in some serious shit..."

"What hospital is this?"

"Kings County."

"Do you think they will bring him here?"

"I don't know, Joann. Even if they did, I don't think they will let you anywhere near him."

"Someone is trying to kill my man, he needs my help..."

"Joann, you can barely help yourself..."

"I bet you it's that bitchy wife of his..."

"Joann..."

"Where's my bag? Mary, where is my bag?"

"Joann! Mind yourself. Calm down, damn."

Joann caught herself and out of fear of her sister leaving her angry, she focused in on her baby sister. "I'm sorry for running off, and getting crazy..."

"It's okay, it's okay..." She walked over to the closet next to Joann's bed to retrieve Joann's pocketbook. "I just want you to take it easy and relax yourself. There's nothing you can do for William right now and you need to heal. Your body has gone through a lot of trauma, and you're too weak to fuck with

William right now. I'm just asking you to think about you for now, okay?" She handed the bag to Joann.

"You're right. It is time I start thinking about myself, and a brighter future."

Mary gave her a big smile. "Look, I need to get home and get dinner started. Are you going to be okay?"

"I think so. If not, can I call you?"

"You can call me anytime." She leaned in to plant a kiss on her sister's cheek. "I love you."

"I love you, too. Kiss my nephew for me…"

"I will. Bye."

"Bye, Mary."

Before Mary could reach the elevators, Joann was rumbling through her bag in search of her cell phone. By the time Mary pressed the button to call the elevator, Joann had speed dialed William.

*Hello, I'm sorry I missed your call. Please leave a message and I will return this call as soon as possible.* Beep.

"William, baby, call me as soon as you get this message to let me know you're alright. I am so worried about you. Baby, please call me. I don't know what that wife of yours tried to do to you, but if you need somewhere to stay you know my place is your place. You're always welcome. Bye. Love you."

She hung up the phone, placed it on her night table, and then slowly returned the articles in her bag. In went a scarf, eye shadow compacts, lipsticks, and a pack of Double Mint gum. She stopped again when she came across her box-cutter. She stared at it for a moment then wondered where her money was. The last thing she remembered was stuffing $172.00 into her panties. Her head started to pound. Tension and stress increased in her temples, as she feared she had lost the last bit of change to her name.

She looked at her closet, and tried to will the strength she needed to get out of bed to search through her clothing, but that will was only wishful thinking; she was too weak and sore to accomplish such a task.

She pressed her head deeper into her pillow, sounding a low whimper. Pain shot through her forehead. She swallowed hard, trying to force her ache down. After no such luck, she opened her eyes to look for the nurse's alert button, but once again, she had lost her ability to see clearly.

"Look, you should have been here twenty minutes ago to pick me up! I don't understand this shit; they wouldn't let you go until now. You were supposed to get up and walk the fuck out. Your husband comes first before that nickel and dime joint you call a job. I don't give a shit! I'll see you when I get home. Yeah, that mean don't pick me up. I'll catch a cab. Bitch, I said I'll catch a fuckin' cab from here. Take your boney ass home and make sure I got something to eat when I get there…" He glanced to his right to see Mary coming out from the hospital's exit. "Look, I gotta go. Do what the fuck I told you and I'll see you when I get in."

He waited until Mary walked into the parking lot before he went back inside the hospital to the security desk. "Yes I'm here to see, Ms. Joann Garcia…"

**4:34 p.m.**

*E*leven stitches pulled at her scalp, closing the wound, which will serve as a visual reminder of the events that caused her current condition. When she awakened, she will not remember the fall that gave her the painful concussion that pounded at her skull, nor will she remember the images of William that blinded her from seeing the stairs she tumbled down, but she will remember her reason for trying to leave her apartment in the haste in which she did. Him, the one she called her 'other half,' with whom she hoped to spend the rest of her life.

He sat next to her bed. He held a small digital recorder/player near her ear. It was in play mode. His voice echoed in her head. Repeating the same theme: *It's him or me. It's him or me. He doesn't love you, as much as I love you. Come be my wife.*

She might be unconscious, but her mind was active and coherent. She couldn't believe he was trying to take advantage of her while she was unconscious and in a state of rest, healing. She thought he was a better man than this. Besides, didn't he know forcing her to make a decision meant she had to make a comparison and judge the better differences of the two! Did he consider the option that he might lose?

She loved this man's strength, his mastery in the art of sexual pleasure, and his confidence. The man was fire and ice. No other man had ever been able to set her ablaze and cool her down like him. She would often dream about the first time they made love…

*"I never had an orgasm; at least I don't think I have…"*

*"You don't know?"*

*"Truthfully, no I don't. I know when I'm making love I come to a point where it feels like I'm floating down a warm stream, and the flow of the water is rushing quickly to the edge of the waterfall, and just before I go over, I snap out of it…"*

*"Why do you snap out of it?"*

*"I don't know. I'm afraid to go over the fall. I…I don't know what's on the other side."*

*"You're big damn O is on the other side, that's all."*

*"What do you think it is? I mean, I always seem to wear out the guy while I'm chasing this climax."*

*"I think you're afraid…"*

*"What am I afraid of?" She spoke in a semi-seductive voice.*

*"Many women have trouble reaching this point of climax, but you don't share the same problem they do. You're getting there, but you fear that big bang. You fear that bang because you know it will conquer you. You know it will leave you venerable. You're afraid that while you're in your free-fall your partner will not be there to catch you, to help you plant your feet back on solid ground, to let you know it's okay to enjoy your venerability without fear of losing your self-respect."*

*"Hmmm. So I guess if I let you spend the night, you will respect me in the morning?"*

*"You already know I have mad respect for you."*

*"Well that leaves my venerability. Can I trust you not to break my heart into a thousand pieces? Never make me cry? Or leave me lonely in the heat of the night?"*

*"No."*

*"No? No you won't do any of the above, or—"*

*"No, as in I make you no such promises. The truth is that I will stress your heart, your patience, and your forgiveness. You will shed tears of joy, madness, and sorrow. I will be with you in heart and soul, but it will not take away the loneliness you'll feel. I won't make senseless promises I can't keep."*

*"Woo!" She thought for a moment. "Will you lie to me?"*

*"If it will keep you from kicking my ass..."*

*"Mister William Green, you got a lot of shit with you."*

*"I promise to keep it real with you. I promise what we share together will be real and meaningful. I promise to catch you and place you on your feet when we go over the edge."*

*"My sisters tell me I should leave you alone."*

*"Your sisters are right. I'm Mr. Wrong. The price for me is extremely high."*

*"How high?"*

*"Your soul."*

*"You're sick."*

*"Just a little, but that changes nothing I said."*

*"Kiss me before you say something that changes my mood."*

*He leaned in, and she planted a kiss upon his lips. He placed his right hand behind her head and tongued her deeper. She accommodated him. Their breathing became heavier. Their hands began to roam. They couldn't care less about being located on the first floor, the lifted shades, or the shear curtains which offered them no privacy, but that was cool for the onlookers who sat on the stoop across the street.*

*He sucked upon her lower neck, while her hands worked at his belt, then his button of his jeans. Once she had it undone, he stood to step out of his sneakers; she slipped her hand into his boxers to explore his manhood, and massaged his balls, as he pulled his shirt over his head. She slid off the sofa, placing her knees on the floor, but he reached for her hands, and pulled her up to her feet. "Let's play in the water."*

*They disrobed, giving the small group of onlookers a delightful striptease show. Their clothes led a trail from the living room to the bathroom. Their playtime consisted of them leathering each other, gently washing each other and kissing upon each other. They admired each other's body, and she was mesmerized by his patience, tenderness, and attentive care he afforded her. When they finished their shower, he helped her out from the tub, looked her in her eyes and said, "Let's go over that waterfall together."*

*She nervously smiled, then led him into her bedroom. She asked him to lie on the bed. He obeyed while she lit the scented candles, which she had placed about the room.*

*She slid herself on the bed to join him. On knees, elbows and forearm she maneuvered between his legs, softly kissing the inner part of his thighs.*

*She slowly moved toward his stiffness, finding pleasure in seeing, hearing, feeling his body quiver from her touching, her kissing, her licking, but the moans he released when she placed a testicle in her mouth, crowned her. She felt empowered, in control until that moment when she found both her hands wrapped around his erection and there was still more of him seeking attention.*

*She wondered if she could accommodate the fullness of him. It had been awhile for her. Shit, it hurt sometimes when she placed a finger or a tampon up there.*

*During all of their conversations, he never mentioned he had a foot fetish. This man did things to her feet she didn't know a tongue and lips could do.*

*He was so attentive to her entire body. He licked and sucked her fingers, her palms, up her arm to her elbow, up to the pit of her underarms, where she felt unknown pleasures. He was a true to life freak, and he was hers.*

*She used to be very self-conscious about her little treasure chest between her thighs because she would get so excited her river would overflow, and worse, she was the not-so-proud owner of two very large labia's. Her outer lips were thick and deep, while her inner lips protruded and hung past the outer ones. To put icing on the cake, her clitoris had a long hood, which was why she called her vagina a treasure chest. One would have to go deep to find her pleasures treasures.*

*However, William enjoyed what he was doing, loving her. He sucked and licked each lip, then rolled back her hoodie and sent her over the waterfall.*

"It's him or me, it's him or me. He doesn't love you as much as I love you. Come be my wife."

*Why is he trying to convince me I need to be with him? What bullshit is he trying to pull? Or does he really love me enough to go this far? Does he really love me this much he would do some dumb shit like this? It would be nice to love and live normal. But is he only marring me because he found William to be a threat, or because he loves me enough to spend the rest of his life with me?*

Her head slowly turned in his direction. He stopped the little machine, and watched her eyes slowly open. Neither one of them said a word. Their eyes fixated on the other.

# Promises Kept

*H*e stepped off the elevator, looked left, right, then at the plaque on the wall. Room 539 was to his left. He wondered why she was there, then he thought about it again, and he didn't care why she was there. It was just a good thing that she was, so he wouldn't have to hunt the bitch down.

When he came up on Room 539, he could feel his heart banging against his ribcage. He looked around. The nurses' station was back where the elevators were, out of view. Several patients had their televisions blaring. He closed his eyes and wondered why he feared going in, as something told him to turn and walk away.

He poked his head inside the room for a visual. He spotted Joann sleeping. If he was going to do this, the time was now. He stealthily moved closer to her bed. His eyes fixated on her face, watching for movement of any kind.

He moved closer, silently and with precision, like a thief in the night. Within striking distance, he moved in. He stopped suddenly when he noticed the nurse's call button was on the other side of the bed.

Joann inhaled deeply, her nose twitched. She caught the scent of his cologne. She knew that cologne. She used to like it until it was worn by him. Her eyes opened.

She startled him. For that brief moment, they stared into each other's eyes.

"Get thhh…" Joann managed to speak before his left hook connected with her jaw, dazing her. She grabbed and clawed at his hands to fight for air.

She extended her right hand to feel for the nurse's call button.

His left hand released her neck to deliver two blows to the right side of her breast.

She managed to fill her lungs with air before he commenced to choking her.

Through her tear-soaked eyes, she felt darkness creeping slowly toward her, and death was not far behind.

"Yeah, bitch, can you feel it? Can you feel death? Can cha bitch? Do ya feel the pain, like I felt it? Your boys tried to kill me, but I held on. I fought death and won. I held on and won because I promised to lead death to you…"

She had no fight left within her.

He leaned in closer. "I told you I was going to kill you, bitch."

His eyes bulged. He quickly released the grip he held on her, only to grab hold of his own neck, while stumbling backward and falling to the floor.

Blood oozed from his wound with every beat of his heart. Through clenched teeth, he watched Joann struggle to breathe.

She'd dropped the box-cutter and pressed the nurse's call button, then looked at him. With what strength he had left within him, he threw his right bloody hand outward toward her, in a last attempt to chock the living shit out of her.

The blood splattered on her face, snapping her out of her daze. She leaned forward slightly.

"I told you if you ever put your hands on me again, I will end you. From here to your fourth generation shall I see the death of all your man-child before the age of eight, for the sins of the father shall be placed upon thy sons. I shall see the womb of every other of your daughters, and I will empty them until your bloodline lives no more. Now die, you bitch motherfucker."

A scream came from a woman out in the corridor.

Joann exhaled, then all faded to black.

# My Husband

"*V*anessa, where is my husband?"

The dark-skinned woman's voice cracked when she tried to explain. "E…Eve, I am so sorry, but I…I don't have any answers for you."

"What!"

"Eve, the feds came in here and locked this facility down. They have taken charge of everything."

"Vanessa, you were my eyes and ears—"

"I know, I know. I am so sorry, Eve. I fucked up. I fucked up big time."

"So who's in charge? Which agency? They can't take over a NYC Correctional facility."

"These mother-jokers had papers signed by the U.S. Attorney General, and people I ain't heard of. They could and they did. The National Guard standing our post, we are under martial law. NYPD is not allowed a half mile with in this place…"

"But what about William?"

"Eve, I don't know about William. They took all of the bodies, and split them between three ambulances and ran decoys separate from William's departure."

"Is William going to live? How bad is he?"

"William is going to live, Eve. At first it was life-threatening, although he was cut up bad, but his rate of healing is remarkable. Then the Fed's came in here, snatched him up, and they're not letting anyone near him."

"Oh, thank God!"

"Hold on… I hear them calling my name. It's my turn for interrogation. Eve, why is all of this happening? Who is William and how heavy is the shit you guys are into?"

"I can't tell you, Vanessa. I don't know, but apparently this shit can get you killed."

The call was abruptly disconnected. Yvonne pulled the phone from her ear, looked at the screen and saw that the phone was still connected.

"I know you can hear me. Where is my husband? I want to see my husband!"

"Mrs. Green, my name is Agent Donovan. Agents are about to knock on your door. You and your family have been placed under my care."

"Excuse me?"

"Please, listen to what I'm about to tell you. You and your family are under protective custody. Agents will be placed outside your residence until further notice. You and your family will be somewhat restricted and you will be escorted to and from your daily activities."

"Now just wait a minute—"

"I'm sorry for the inconvenience and having to take such actions, but I must maintain the safety of your husband and your family."

"Where is my husband?"

"Two agents will escort you to my office at 26 Federal Plaza. I will explain everything to you face-to-face."

The line went silent, and then the doorbell rang.

### 26 Federal Plaza

"Mrs. Green, I'm Agent Donovan. I wish it was a pleasure to meet with you face-to-face again, but it's not. Would you please accompany me to my office?"

Yvonne ejected herself from her seat, stunned by the appearance of the six-foot-three-inch, broad-chested, dark–olive skinned white man who terrorized her life, her marriage, and her family over six years ago.

Agent Donovan damn near destroyed her law enforcement career by calling her and William murdering drug dealers. A charge, which still keeps her under watchful eyes whenever William financed their parties, or outreach programs. He said they murdered three drug dealers up in the Bronx, but William and she were never charged. Just as fast as it stared, it ended.

Now this agent has popped up again with her man who supposed to be behind bars for trying to beat a cop to death, but who had once again become the target of someone's madness.

She wondered what she should expect once they reached their destination. With this character, she expected the worst, like her captain and Internal Affairs waiting in his office, probably for some shit William was suspected of doing. She hoped it had nothing to do with murder. Ironically, William confessed to her he'd killed people. She was a little taken aback, but that confession held no weight in her making her decision to kill her husband or not.

Once they reached his office, he opened the door and offered her a seat. Yvonne looked about the room and quickly decided the office was bland and boring.

Degrees, accommodations, bookcases, and three, large-framed portraits of his favorite democratic presidents: Obama,

Clinton, and Carter hanging against the dark-tan colored walls. To complete his boring office were two file cabinets, two chairs, a long brown desk with a computer monitor, keyboard, and papers scattered about, all sitting on top of brown carpet, which has seen its days.

Agent Donovan walked behind his desk and sat down.

"Where is my husband?" Yvonne inquired.

"Before we get to that, I must make sure your husband is absolutely safe."

"What is this about, Agent Donovan?"

"On the night before your husband's altercation with Lieutenant Well, there were gunshots heard at your residences at the time William was driving off. Do you have an explanation for those shots fired, Mrs. Green?"

"What are you saying?"

"Look, Officer Green, you're a cop, so let's not play games. Did you try to kill your husband?"

"Excuse me?"

In a raised voice, demanded, "Answer the damn question!"

"No! Why would you think something like that?"

Agent Donovan turned to type something into the computer, followed by a few clicks on the mouse. What came next surprised Yvonne.


*"Mommy, no," Jasmine screamed.*

*"Eve!" Jenny said.*

*"Mommy, what's wrong with you? Have you lost your damn mind?"*

*"Better me taking him, then them killing him." A brief moment of silence. "Jasmine, get my keys off the table and bring the car around while I go back upstairs to get dressed."*

*"Why, you're going after him?"*

*"We have to."*

*"We? I'm not going anywhere with a mad woman who's trying to kill my father!"*

*"You have to. He's not going to listen to me, and I'm going to need all the help I can get."*

*"He's not going to listen to you? Hell, you're trying to kill him! What's wrong with y'all, he almost ran me over and you, and you... Aww!"* A moment of silence. *"My head is killing me!"*

*"I know it is, baby, it's your father's rage. That's why we must stop him before he hurts or kills all of us."*

*"What are you talking about, crazy lady?"*

"You have my home bugged?" Yvonne was appalled.

"Yes, Mrs. Green, your home is bugged, you have been followed, and photographed, and videoed, but the only thing we haven't done was step in and shut your reckless behind down before all of this had gotten out of control."

"How deeply involved is my husband in this?"

"Mrs. Green, I will ask you once more. Did you attempt to kill your husband?"

"He's my husband for goodness sake! Why would I try to kill him?"

"Did you fire those shots or not?"

"Yes I did. I fired at his tires, Agent Donovan. I was trying to keep my husband from getting himself killed."

Agent Donovan sat back in his black, hi-back, leather chair to evaluate Yvonne's response. He inhaled deeply, released that breath loudly, and looked Yvonne in the face. "Keeping your husband alive and from harm over the years has not been easy,

Mrs. Green, and this last week has been the most difficult period since taking over this assignment…"

"Years? Years as in over the last six years?"

"Yes."

"Agent Donovan, what kind of work is my husband doing for his country, if I may ask?"

"His invention, our involvement with your husband, is his invention…"

"The Filtrex?"

"Yes."

"I thought we settled that years ago?"

"We went into an agreement years ago. We purchased your husband's invention and he's been on our payroll ever since to prefect the Filtrex to our standards, ever since our misguided beginnings."

"I guess that would explain all the secrecy and his weekends out with no contacts."

"Yes, Mrs. Green, that would explain it."

"And here I thought he was up to his old tricks, and making a fool of me."

"I'm sorry, but the secrecy was an essential part of protecting your family."

Silent reigned for a moment.

Like two worlds colliding together, the devastation from this vile truth and revelation numbed her spirit. As she would have only trusted her husband just a little more than she had, their lives would have been a little different from where they were. Was it possible she could have had that happy little family she had always dreamed of? A church going family, which was led by a God-fearing man who was faithful to his Lord, his family, and wife.

Her numbness disappeared; her face smirked to the left with a slight grin. *Oh please*, she thought.

"What about my husband, Agent Donovan?"

"Your husband is undergoing surgery as we speak at an undisclosed hospital here in the city—"

"What hospital?"

Agent Donovan hesitated.

"I want to be with my husband."

"I have one more issue to clear up before I get to that. Did you have, or do you know of who, and why someone, or group of people would want to bring harm to your husband, and his former mistress, Joann Garcia?"

Yvonne's jaw dropped.

Her mind raced, but settled on a single thought: *The devil is busy and I am barely keeping up.*

### One Week Later, Thursday, 9:32 a.m.

*T*he flight to Augusta, Georgia had been a bumpy one. Wind turbulence bounced the Boeing 757 up and down, side to side, rather moderately, scaring its passengers nearly half to death, and more than William would have liked. His body was still sore. It had been a week since his surgery. He wasn't expected to make it out of the operating room, let alone survive the week. He lost a lot of blood before and during the surgery. If it weren't from his blood type being AB+, making him an universal recipient, his speedy recovery would have been hampered by a shortage of blood.

He walked off the plane with two escorts—one in the front of him, the other behind him. Once they reached the front of the terminal, he was greeted by Agent Donovan and their driver. The five men made their way to the waiting black SUV. They were noticed by everyone, the oddity of the small group of men was they looked as if they were going to a Men in Black convention.

"How was your flight?" Agent Donovan asked William.

They stepped out into the hot Georgia heat. The early morning sun had the temperature at ninety-three degrees, well on its way of being another three-digit day. The men placed their dark sunglasses on their faces, and loaded themselves into the SUV.

"Bumpy," William replied.

Agent Donovan handed William a large brown envelope. William took hold of the package and opened it. He reached in and pulled out a sheet, which listed the contents within the envelope—his cell phone, wallet, wedding band, pinky ring, wrist watch, three-hundred and twenty-seven dollars in cash, a set of keys and two dollars and forty-three cents in pocket change. William recalled the items being listed when he was arrested and transported to Brooklyn's Booking Central, where he was then whisked away by D.O.C. and transported to Brooklyn House Detention Center.

"We'll be arriving a little after services have started. We'll take seats in the rear of the church while you sit with your family. You can ride the limo with your family to the burial site, and back to the house for the repast for two hours, then we all—your family included—will head back to New York."

"Sounds good," William replied while he enjoyed the circulation of cool air on his face, and neck.

William and his posse reached their destination about 11:20 a.m. and were surprised to see so many people attending his grandmother's funeral. The overwhelming number of people should have been sent home, but the family decided to have them partake in the services. They found seats wherever they could, like from other nearby churches and community centers, but the small crowd were forced to listen at the mercy of the heat.

Warmth, joy, cheerfulness, sorrow is all William felt when he was greeted by his two little girls who ran up to him when he stepped out of the vehicle. His older children stood alongside their mother. Though happy to see him, they were already beaten by the sizzling Georgia heat. William scooped his two daughters into his weak and battered arms, where they were all hugs and kisses all the way inside of the church, and out of the heat. Handshakes, hugs and kisses came from the rest of the family of aunts, uncles, cousins, and long missed friends he hadn't seen or heard from in a long time.

The children missed their father dearly and likewise he missed them just as much, but when it came to Yvonne, his wife of twenty-five years, he had mixed feelings. He loved her to no end, but she tried to kill him. He could not erase the vision of those bullets chasing after him and exploding just outside of his vehicle.

When William and Yvonne faced each other, the tension grew thick quickly. They exchanged kisses, but it was for show. Agent Donovan picked up on their tension and became uneasy. This was not the place to exchange gunfire and put down whoever appeared to be a threat, which included Yvonne. Fortunately, William and Yvonne acted the way a husband and wife should. They were smart and kept the peace.

Reverend Green, one of William's many first cousins, started the service. "Brothers and sisters, we are gathered here on this day to say our final goodbyes to one of God's chosen."

"Yes, Lord" and "Hallelujah, sweet Jesus" came from the attendees.

"Those of us who were close to Mrs. Green know exactly what I'm talking about."

"That's right, Pastor."

"I know. Keep talkin'."

"Yes, Lord."

"For those who don't know what I'm talking about, let me be plain. We had an angel in our midst. I'm talking about a true live angel. And now she has been called back to a place where most of us pray we will get to one day."

And a true angel she was. If anyone knew William well, it was his grandmother. If there was anyone who could keep William grounded, it was his grandmother. She knew him, and he knew her. Her job was to guide him through his darkest periods. She provided him the pathways, prayers, and, sometimes, personal sacrifice when they came for him—the dead ones who served the other—and the fact that she's gone, scared him, and even worse, the guilt weighed heavy on him, knowing he was the one who killed her.

She told him time and time again, "Boy, how many times do I have to tell ya? When you fail the spirit and give into the flesh, you become a tool to be wheeled against your very own."

William finally realized he'd been played. He now knew his content for Robert, and blinded rage for revenge, caused a backlash against his order, leaving him to contemplate on his own question he would ask the bewildered, *How deep is deep?*

After the service, William and his family were escorted to their limo, and the black SUV followed closely behind. They made it to the cemetery and back to his grandmother's home where they held the repast, without incident.

William, Yvonne, and the children mingled among family, friends and those gracious to attend. Afterwards, Yvonne and William found themselves meeting in the center of the room, facing each other.

"I'm going back to New York alone," William announced.

"Why aren't we all going back together? Agent Donovan said—"

"It's not his call."

"Well then who called it?"

"It's my call. I'm going back to New York alone and I will be staying in Brooklyn—"

"You're staying with your mother?"

"No."

"Wh… wh…with my father and sister?"

"No. I'll be staying anywhere, some place where it is that you can't get to me."

"William, you're making a big mistake."

"Eve, I know you've changed, but I can't tell if it's for the good of the Heavens, or some bent up payback from days gone past. But whichever one it is, it means the death of me."

"I shot at you because you were killing all the others who were here for you and of your order. Many had died because of your rage, just like your grandmother."

"You're just as much the blame for that rage as the motherfucker who pissed me off. So step back, Jacky, before you get jacked. Respect my decision. As I said before, I need time and a place from you to think."

"What about the children?"

"I'll see them when I am at the house working."

"You can't leave my counsel. Many others will die, William. You need me."

"At the moment, I don't need a fucking thing you're offering."

William turned and nodded at Agent Donovan who followed him outside. Shortly after, William and his crew were gone.

*Friday, 8:24 a.m.*

*H*e inspected the twenty-four-inch blade in the shape of a surgeon's scalpel. He kept all his swords and daggers extremely sharp. He needed them that way. Sharp. Each pass of the blade must have an positive effect on his subjects. Like the shock upon their faces to see a limb drop. Oh, what joy he found it that.

He kneeled down abruptly, showing his respect and legend to his master. "Yes, my Lord, I'm here for you always. I am always ready to serve you, my Lord. Who is she my Lord? Show her to me. Yes, my Lord, I will seek her out. Yes, my Lord, I will take care of her. Leave it to me, she will pay dearly."

*9:21 a.m.*

She stood over her desk, organizing her case files that were on the day's docket. Her first case was due to start at 10:00 a.m. This gave her time to sit and enjoy her breakfast in peace, so she thought until her cell phone rung.

She picked up her cell phone from her desk and spied the screen for the caller's info. It was one of her son-n-laws. She hadn't heard from this one in quite a while, but she knew he would check in soon, being that she had his wife.

"Jerome, how are you?"

"I'm fine, ma'am. How you been?"

"I've been better."

"I hear that, I did. How is Andrea?"

"She's fine. Why would you be asking me that question, haven't you called her?"

"You mean you don't know?"

"Don't know what, Jerome?"

"That we're separated..."

She placed her hand to mouth and gasped. "No. Please, Jerome, don't play with me like this, say it isn't so."

"I wish I could, but Andrea asked for a divorce."

"That damn, William!"

"I can't believe she hasn't said anything to you."

"She has been as tight as a virgin living with two gay parents."

"How you know that William was behind her madness?"

"Because he always has been the reason for her madness."

"I'm sorry I failed you, Rhonda..."

"Jerome, never. This problem existed long before your time. There's always one person in all our lives, which we will never get out of our system. Most of the time we have the strength to fight the urges. Others are helpless against their spell."

"I see."

"What I don't understand is why he isn't dead?"

"I don't know either, but I'm here to see it gets done."

"You're here? In New York?"

"Yes, ma'am."

"What do you intend to do, Jerome?"

"I come with the spirit of the Lord, and I'm here to strike the beast straight in its heart, and put this evil one to rest."

"You be careful, Jerome. This man is like a leprechaun, magically lucky."

**2:43 p.m.**

She stood silently at his bedside and watched him sleep. He looked so peaceful. What a fucking deception. This man was the spawn from the devil's ass himself. She wondered how he managed to deceive her for as long as he had. She wondered how she was able to fuck this man, and place him above her husband. Damn, living wickedly was so damn deceiving.

Her stare must have weighed heavy upon his body, as he started to stir. His eyelids opened slowly. He knew there was a person standing before him, but he couldn't tell who it was. He blinked a few times and forced his eyes to clear and focus quickly, and then he saw the woman before him. He knew her, and she frightened him.

"Well, he awakened from the dead."

Through his dry raspy voice, he spoke. "What are you doing here, Eve? Shouldn't you be home with your champion?"

"Oh, are we salty? Come on now, you finally got what you asked for. You been egging him on for years, and now that you got what you been asking for you wanna call foul?"

"I'm not calling anything. What I'm saying is you got your nerve showing up here."

"Damn, you're not happy to see me. So there really is a thin line between love and hate."

"What do you want, Yvonne?"

"I want your job."

"I might be broken, but I can be fixed, and come back to the job in about a year."

"I don't think so, Robert. You're bad for the department..."

"What..." He coughed. "What are you talking about?"

"I'm talking about the assassinations of eight drug dealers, two women, a two-year-old child, one unborn, and for the attempted assassination on my husband, William. Need I go further?"

"I don't know what you're talking about…"

"Let's not play stupid, stupid. You know exactly what I'm talking about. Killing all those people was how you made lieutenant. Trying to kill William was how you tried to get me.

I always knew you wanted me, but I didn't know how low you would sink. The details for that night were sealed by the feds, so no one really knew exactly what happened except them.

There were two shooters that night: one sent by you and another sent by an overly-concerned mother."

"Look, I told you I don't know what you're talking about."

"Here are your options: take an early retirement, live large and long."

"Or?"

"Or, keep that foolish idea you have spinning your head of coming after me, and you will die early."

"I think we're going to have to play this one out, because you have no proof to these allegations, or you would have gone straight to Internal Affairs. So I warn you, stay out of my yard."

"And you've been warned. Good-bye, Robert."

*3:32 p.m.*

She caressed his erection as she sucked hard on his nipples, causing him to moan from the painful pleasure she offered him. His fingers pulled at her hair, danced upon her scalp, and pushed her head deeper into his flush.

Moments later she sat up on her knees, he slid himself underneath her. She allowed her hands to stop massaging her breast to slide down the contour of her body and around her big ass cheeks, to part them as much as she could to give him access to her tender, moist, and awaiting underside.

His wet tongue slid up her thigh and into her thick forest. She was always self-conscious about her bush. In spite of all the methods she tried, she finally accepted the fact that she would have to shave her little Geo-puss every other day. She would sculpt her muffin with a fade, having the single band of fuzz looking much like an explanation point, which sat above her enormous clit, which embarrassed her more than the scrub she grew down there.

William eased her mind, he accepted her for her uniqueness, and by loving her, and all she had to offer him. William wasn't fond of a shaved or hairless pussy. Bald pussies were mounted on babies, while women managed their main. As he would often say, "There is nothing cute about a hairless cat."

She released her butt cheeks for a more pleasurable spread of her moist, tender lips, which exposed her large swollen peal. He shoved his tongue inside her, in search of her thick, sweet nectar. He threw his hands around her to take hold of her big round butterscotch ass, then he spread her fat, soft, jelly cheeks, which permitted him to rim her, giving her pleasure she hadn't felt in a long, long time.

She inhaled deeply, clenched her teeth, and exhaled with a loud huff. His warm tongue probed inside her while his hot breath provided smoothing warmth to her throbbing kitty, which craved for his personal attention.

"Fuck me, William. Fuck me, baby." She grabbed a breast with one hand and William's stiff erection with the other. "I want it." She kissed the head. "I want it; I want it now, baby."

She nibbled on him. He felt her teeth bite into him, and felt pleasure from the pain, and then he felt the warmth of her tongue and the saliva that ran down his shaft when she gagged from trying to swallow more of him than she could.

She coughed several times, inhaled deeply to fill her lungs with some air, followed by more coughing.

William placed his hand on her head. "Joann. You okay? Joann…"

Her eyes opened slowly, forcing her dream to fade into nothingness. She looked into the face of the man that called out her name, and the temporary fear and confusion was quickly replaced by a warm, tingling feeling.

"Are you okay?"

"Yea… Yes, I'm okay. Why you ask?"

"You were moaning."

She smiled. "Yeah, baby, I'm good. Thank you for bring me home." She looked underneath her sheet to find she was dressed in her nightgown.

"That's okay. No need to thank me, I'm happy I could help."

"Did you undress me?"

"Yeah."

"You didn't try to take advantage of me did you?"

"Nope."

She felt between her legs. "Did you put a pad on me?"

"Yes I did, you were spotting."

"Thank you. You're so sweet."

"You don't have to thank me."

"Yeah, I do. Come here."

He sat on the bed next to her. She threw her arms around his neck, and pressed her lips against his.

He held on to her, squeezing her when he sucked her tongue. She inhaled his breath and became one with him. He felt her. He hadn't felt her in a very long time. Her energy was getting stronger, her spirit was getting stronger, and she was slowly becoming the being she needed to be. That inner being sparked a flame within him. They stopped their kiss to gaze into each other's eyes. They each saw the blue flame burning deep within their inner-core. They both felt the bond, the heat, and the love they had for each other.

"Wow, you really know how to kiss a woman."

"Was it a kiss, or something else?"

She placed her head on his shoulder. "I don't care what it was, I liked it."

"Yeah, me, too."

"Are you going to spend the night with me?"

He held her close to him; he wrapped her within one arm, while his hand from the other rubbed her back. "No. I need to stop by my mom's apartment and straighten out a few things before she gets in tomorrow from Augusta. Then meet up with my brother before getting back to the hotel."

"What hotel you staying at?"

"I'm at the Marriott Hotel on Adam Street, downtown…"

"Are you sure you want Jonathan to meet you there?"

"Yes, I'm sure. Have him come by about noon on Sunday, and we'll leave from there to go shopping up on Fulton Street, then onto King Plaza. I have a suite on the twentieth floor. Tell him to ask for me at the front desk, plus I'll inform them of his visit."

"Thank you for looking out for him…"

"Yo, you don't have to thank me for anything. In fact, I'm sorry it took me this long to handle my responsibility."

"So… Why? Why did you leave us?"

"I left…I left you, him, I left everything. My world was crumbling round me. The feds was trying to lock me up for those bodies up in the Bronx."

"Are you serious?"

"Yeah, I'm serious. They thought I was some Kingpin drug lord and shit. So I stayed away from you, Jonathan, and everybody else."

"Why you never told me?"

"Because they knew something, but they didn't have all the pieces to the puzzles, and I wasn't giving them you, so you didn't exist, and I stayed away."

"Wow, all this time I was thinking you abandoned Jonathan and me, but you was actually protecting us."

"Yeah kind of, but I still feel bad because you had a rough time surviving, and I had the ability to make things easier for you." There was a moment of silence. "You won't have to struggle anymore. I've opened a bank account for you where you can draw a thousand dollars a week. I've set aside a five-million-dollar trust account for Jonathan that's his on his twenty-fifth birthday, another trust account that will take care of his education…"

She lifted her head from his shoulder, and he saw the tears rolling down her face. He cupped her face and wiped away her tears with his thumbs.

"…and when you're feeling better, and back on your feet, I want you to go find yourself a small home for you and Jonathan."

"Why are you doing all of this?"

"Because I owe you, and you have suffered enough. You have always been a part of me."

"What about your wife? This is all wonderful, but you don't need the drama that will—"

"I have to do what's right. It took a dead woman to teach me that I can't fuck them and leave them. So call your friend and have her send Jonathan home."

### 5:16 p.m.

"I'm sorry to disturb you, Eve, but I received some disturbing news."

"What is it, Tammy?"

"My friend, Anna, who works at ACS, just informed me that the woman Joann has taken Jonathan back."

"What do you mean taken him back?"

"I mean, she will no longer be giving him up for adoption."

"Why not?"

"She said Joann told her that his father has stepped up to do the right thing and will be taking care of her son and her—"

"And that father was, William, wasn't it?"

"I'm sorry, but yes she did mention William as to being the father."

"Thank you, Tammy. Maybe it will be easier to obtain the child this way, through William."

"Sounds like a plan."

"Thank you, Tammy. Have a good evening. Of One."

"On One, Ona."

Yvonne placed the phone back onto its base. She picked up the novel she was reading before the phone call. She tried to continue from where she left off, but her mind was no longer on the book, but back in time when William's pager was sounding off, and she respond to it, and caught Joann trying to play it off acting as if she'd called the wrong number or something, but Yvonne didn't entertain it, not for one minute…

*"I think you have the wrong number, or something, your man ain't here. But I do suggest you get some skills if you want to keep him home."*

*"Bitch, I will fuck you up!" Yvonne screamed.*

*"No, bitch, you better fuck your man up. A'ight? 'Cause this way he won't be sniffing around other women's crotches."*

*"Yeah, talk that shit over the phone..." Yvonne said.*

*"What! You wanna step to this, bitch?"*

*"Yeah, where you at, ain't no fear in my heart, bitch. I got some skills for that ass, a'ight." "You wanna know where I'm at? You better ask somebody."*

*"Yeah, well, just for you to know, when you go down on him tonight keep this in mind, I just got off of it, you nasty, tricky ass, ho!"*

*A piercing thud was the sound of the phone in Joann's ear before the silence.*

*"Oh no! Oh, fuck no. She didn't call me a ho. I'll kill her. I'd pull the hairs off her pussy, and shove my baby's bottle up her ass..." Then it hit her. "Oh I got some payback for you, bitch. Oh, you just got off it, huh? I'm gonna see you never get on it again." She'd dialed star-six-nine. The phone rang twice. "Com'on pick up, bitch. Come get some of this—"*

*"What you want, ho," Yvonne answered.*

*"The name is Holly, so get used to it, 'cause it's going to be a household name round there..."*

*"No your name is low life, bitch. What you call for, this shit is tired?"*

*"Fuck you, I don't need this, where is my baby's daddy, is he home?"*

*"You fuckin' ho bitch, don't fuck with me..."*

*"I ain't fuckin' you, and don't see how he can, but my son needs some Pampers, and milk..."*

*"You want Pampers and milk? Meet me at the Lindenwood Diner on Linden Boulevard, bitch, and bring that bastard baby with you," Yvonne demanded.*

*"You see, you gotta be a rude bitch, so now you get nothing but baby's mama drama from here on—"*

There never was that much baby-mama-drama. However, the seed was already planted. The thought of William having another child outside their home was always there. She would search his pockets for receipts, read his emails, and check his phone records just to see if he was communicating, or supporting the child. She never thought William would be the type of man not to support, or provide support for any of his children. She figured he was a responsible man in that respect, but when she wasn't able to find any evidence of him supporting a child outside their home, she relaxed just a little.

She knew now that if she had a stomach it would be twisted in knots. He didn't come to work today, and now she knew why, this *mofo* done left home to go move in with this woman, and start a new family.

She's been trying to reach him, but he turned off his phone. She's been leaving messages, but he hasn't returned any of them. Now it all became clear.

## *10:33 p.m.*

William walked through the lobby of the hotel to the front desk where he was greeted by a short, dark-skinned woman who reminded him of Yvonne.

"Good evening, Sir, how may I assist you this evening?"

"Good evening. I'm expecting a couple of packages."

"I'll be happy to assist you with that. May I have your name, please?"

"William R. Green."

She copied his name on a small sheet of paper. "Thank you. I'll be right back." She walked down to the end of the long counter, looked through a few cubicles, retrieved three packages, and brought them back to the counter where William stood.

She handed William a clipboard to sign for the three packages. While doing so, he asked the receptionist, "Can you inform me where I can find a nearby car rental location?"

"Yes. You have several car rentals along Livingston Street, which is a few blocks up if you walk—"

"I know where, thank you."

Once William reached the comfort of his suite, he opened the two boxes most important to him—the one containing his new HTC cell phone, which he needed to replace because his former Blackberry was used as someone's toilet and the box containing a sim-card, and Bluetooth headset. He loaded the sim-card into his new phone, then plugged the two items into an outlet, and made his way to take a shower.

He took an extremely long shower, much longer than usual. He wrestled with his thoughts on how to move forward. He wondered if he was betraying Yvonne by assisting Joann and Jonathan, but knew deep down inside he owed them. He had been blessed in many areas of his life, especially monetarily. He knew his Father blessed him so he could bless others. He knew with his death drawing closer, if he failed to right his wrongs, he could fail his purpose to exist.

He also gave great consideration to Yvonne and her latest tactics. She tried to kill him. He tried to put that thought to the side and focus on the larger picture, but he couldn't. The woman he placed above all women, the only woman he allowed himself to feed off of, was the woman who tried to kill him. He can't see himself harming her, but he knows if they were to go head-to-head, his very nature would destroy her.

All this thinking gave him a headache.

He stepped out from his shower, grabbed a towel, dried his face, hands, feet, and then tossed the towel onto the vanity. He strutted into the bedroom, over to the desk, picked up the hotel's menu, made his selection, and called room service where he ordered two tuna fish on rye bread sandwiches.

He walked into the living room, retrieved his headset and cell phone, which were charged more than halfway. He dialed the 800 number he received with his sim-card, and followed the instructions as directed to activate his new sim-card and phone, downloaded and updated his address book, and then he called into his voice mail account to listen to the thirty-eight new voice messages.

The first six calls were from Yvonne. Most of them were just checking to see how he was doing and where he was staying, but the one he paid attention to was her very first call.

"Hi, William. I guess you really can't stand the sight of me, but believe me I mean you no harm, but I must do what I am commanded to do."

*So you're trying to tell me God put you up to that fowl shit?*

"I know you don't believe me, but I have no reason to lie to you. You must come to terms, and complete your task before it all becomes too late.

"I need you to meet me in the parking lot of the Christian Cultural Center on Flatlands Avenue on Saturday at twelve noon. Please, William, I employ you to meet me there…"

*Why? I if don't, God is going to order you to shoot at me again?*

He gave that outburst some thought, and concluded if she was told by his Heavenly Father to kill him, then yes, it would be more than likely, God would order another hit on him.

He saved Yvonne's message and continued listening to his missed calls. A few of the missed calls he returned, others he listened to and updated his calendar, task, and to do list, but out of the thirty-eight calls, none bothered him more than that of Dana's voice mail. "Hi, William. I do hope you're okay. I've been seeing some stuff on the news about you, but I have no doubt that you will straighten out the chaos…" Dana paused, and then William overheard a noise in the background. "So look the reason why I'm calling is do you remember when you told me you would step back if I needed you to so I can move on to develop my relationship with Kevin? Well I need you to do that." Her voice cracked.

"You see Kevin and I… We're, we're getting married soon, and it's not fair to him that I keep such a close relationship with you. I know you'll understand and would agree with this decision. Please don't call, stop by, don't text me, don't I/M me, or try to reach out to my family and friends concerning me. I'll be changing my number. So I guess this is good-bye. Good-bye, William."

William felt a pain in his chest, and his breathing became shallow. He wasn't having trouble breathing. He didn't want to breathe. He didn't see this coming. He wasn't sure how to react, or how he should feel. She was no longer his lover, but she was still his friend, a close friend he shared his heart with, yes, but still, just a friend.

He disconnected the call, closed his eyes, and whispered, "Good-bye, Dana."

# The Prophecy

The phone rung four times before William answered. It was the front desk, informing him that his car had arrived from Carefree Lifestyles, a family-owned business that catered to those who had a desire and money to pay for their wants and obsessions. From cars to jets to yachts, and executive private security, one just needed to place a call, and have a high credit card limit, or the ability to wire funds anywhere in the world.

He grabbed his cell phone, Bluetooth headset, iPad, which was the third package he'd picked up from the front desk last night, and his suit jacket.

When William reached the lobby, he was pointed to a gentleman who was awaiting him. The man handed William some papers. William looked over the papers, signed several of them, handed them back to the gentleman, and then he was handed a set of keys, and given directions to his rental.

William took the elevator several levels down of the underground parking lot, walked several yards in the direction he was told and found the 2013, cream-colored Rolls Royce Phantom, which matched his light brown suit, cream silk crewneck T-shirt, and cream-colored penny loafers.

When he unlocked the door, his cell phone rung, playing Beyoncé's, "Me, Myself, and I," which was the ringtone he assigned to his daughter, Jasmine.

"Yel-low?" William answered.

"Daddy?"

"Yes, Jasmine?"

"How you been, and when are you coming home?"

"Well, I'll be at work all this week…"

"Yeah, but when are you coming home?"

"I gotta work a few things out before I can deal with your mom…"

"I know, but Dad, you were causing us a lot of pain. I thought my body was going to explode."

"You felt it, too, huh?"

"Boy, did I."

"I'm sorry, baby-girl, I didn't mean to cause anyone any pain, and I know I hurt you, your brother and sisters, and I may have even killed a few people like my grandmother. Look I'm on my way to meet up with your mother to work this out. So hopefully if our talk goes well, I'll be back home Monday."

"Monday? Why not today?"

"Because there are some things I gotta do here in the city before I come home."

"Daddy…" she whined.

"Look, don't push it."

"Alright. Oh, yo da, you need to talk to your son."

"What's up with him?"

"He's been mad disrespectful to Mommy. He's not listening to her when she speaks to him; he's yelling at her, he's just off the chain. Him and I almost went to blows this morning because he was yelling at Mommy. Telling her, she's not allowed in his room—"

"Okay, okay, I'll talk with him when I get home. I gotta go, it's getting late."

"Alright. I love you."

"Love you, too, baby-girl. Later."

"Bye, Daddy."

William stopped at the red light on the corner of Pennsylvania and Flatlands Avenue, preparing to make a right turn onto Flatlands Avenue when the light turned green. The stares he received while behind the wheel of that car made him feel a little awkward. He knew he looked good in the vehicle, but it made him feel a little pretentious.

He drove slowly toward Louisiana Avenue, looking across the street into the large vacant lots of Christian Cultural Center, for a visual of his wife. He's amazed to see the church owned the entire property, which was damn near four and a half city blocks long. He remembered this church used to be a little place located at 1400 Linden Boulevard, a couple blocks across from Brookdale Hospital.

He spotted her car in the field, which appeared to have the appearance of a parking lot. He saw the opened gate, drove up a block to make a U-turn.

As he pulled into the lot, Yvonne stepped out from her car as a security guard approached her from a distance. Yvonne removed her sunglasses, looked at him, and he stopped dead in his tracks, as if he was frozen for a moment. He turned around and went back to wherever he came from.

William witnessed the entire event, and smiled to himself. "So the girl got skills. This visit is going to be interesting."

Yvonne was somewhat impressed as she eyeballed the Rolls, and when William stepped out from the vehicle, she looked him over and was pleased. She loved him in bright color clothing, because they softened his features, and complimented his darkness.

"How did it feel to alter someone's thoughts?"

"It felt like playing with a human doll. You look good."

"You look better."

"Where you get the car?"

"It's a rental…"

"You look good behind the wheel. It shows off your classy side."

"Yeah? You don't think it's a bit over the top?"

"Who cares, it fits you."

"I'll keep that under advisement."

"Oh, I like the sound of that, does that mean we're back on our original agreement, and—"

"We ain't on anything. I'm here to hear what it is you got to say."

"I see…"

"And I don't. Why have you invited me here if you don't have—"

"Because we are running out of time. You're dying and the devil is hot on your tail."

Realization forced him to look at the situation objectively. "Meaning that if I don't do what it is you need me to do, you're going to have to try and kill me once again?"

"I like to refer to that line of action as, *sending home.*"

"Whatever. What is it I'm supposed to do?"

"Believe it or not, there are only a few things you need to do."

"Oh?"

"Yes. The first thing you need to do is to release those you've damned and hold captive."

William swallowed hard, and looked away from Yvonne. He was not ready to have this conversation with Yvonne, or anyone else for that fact. He knew where she was about to go, and this was a topic he had prepared himself to discuss with God personally on his day of judgment, and not one of his representatives. "Why are we here in this parking lot instead of a restaurant, or somewhere—"

Yvonne hesitated to answer his question, but that didn't stop William from listening to her inner thoughts.

"Holy ground?" William inquired.

"Stop reading me…"

"You ain't talking…"

"It's for my safety…"

"'Cause you're stronger on Holy ground… You…You're afraid of me?"

"Don't flatter yourself, and let's not change the subject. We're here because this is where you need to leave your burdens and for you to leave the things that belong to our Lord here with the Lord."

"I have nothing that belongs to God."

"Vengeances is mine, oh say the Lord."

"What he said was, *'Dearly beloved, avenge not yourselves, but rather give place unto wrath: for it is written, Vengeance is mine; I will repay, saith the Lord.'* Romans 12:19."

"Yes, that's correct."

"But I am not of man. I am a spirit, am I not?"

"Half-truths, William. You are a spirit within the vessel of man. When you shed this vessel of a man, your spirit must be free of the things that are bond to you while you were of man."

"But what is of man should remain of man, for he was born condemned out of the sinful dust that bears his brother's blood. So what does it matter?"

"Because the ground cannot indulge a spiritual sin from a spiritual being like yourself…"

"Bullshit. Was not Adam a spiritual being who sinned, and was he not cursed—"

"No. That's a misconception. Adam was a man, which means, Red, because he was created from the red clay of the earth. Mankind was condemned because of the nature of man, which was deemed sinful. In First Corinthians, 15:45 says, '*And so it is written, The first man Adam was made a living soul; the last Adam was made a quickening spirit.*' King James Version."

"There was no last Adam…"

"You are correct, but we'll speak about that at another time. Your sin is spiritual, and the ground cannot absorb that of the Heavens…"

"Not forgiving is not a spiritual sin."

"No it isn't, but to damn one's soul is. You have cursed those who crossed you. They cannot be judged, nor can they be given a chance to atone for their doings. You must release them."

"I don't need to do no such thing…"

Yvonne exhaled deeply, while asking the Heavens for guidance, or an idea of how she should reason with William. The Heaven's offered her nothing.

"When was the last time you attended a service, other than funerals?" Yvonne asked.

"I haven't."

"It's time to close the circle. If you can still love me after all the misguided things I've done, surely you have enough love to forgive them." William turned away from Yvonne and lit a cigarette. He really was not feeling the conversation.

"That's just it, Yvonne, I don't love them. Why don't you just leave all this up to God to take care of?"

"But He can't take care of what you won't release. Follow the ways of our true being, release the flesh."

William turned to face her. Yvonne looked into his eyes. She saw the straggle between his spirit and the soul of his flesh. She felt William's left arm tighten and the palm become moist just as it did last Sunday. Yvonne looked deeper, further back into his eyes, she saw a little boy, about eleven years old, in the clutches of a pastor. Little William was trying to break away, but he could not, little William didn't have the strength to repel the man, and the little he did have was fading away quickly as the pastor forced his tongue into William's mouth.

The little, skinny, sixty-six-pound William felt the hairs of his thick mustache stinging against his soft tender lips. He could smell the breath of the hot heavy breathing pastor, which nearly cause little William to pass out as he forced William's tiny left hand up and down his erection. William balled his hand into a small knot, and tried to pull away from the man's grip. With no success, the pastor gyrated against William's tight little fist, and shoved his tongue deeper into William's month, which caused William's head to bend backwards in search for air. The minutes passed. They felt unusually long. Kind of like being in a dimension void of time, where only forever existed, so it seemed to little William.

Relief came after the pastor's semen exploded, and erupted onto William's fist, which the pastor had moved down into his trousers. He released William, and he fell backward onto the floor. The pastor began apologizing and tried to offer little William money, giving no concern to the coughing and the horrible sounds he made as he tried to pull air into his lungs.

Through the tears that distorted his vision, William got up and ran out the pastor's office, and passed the piano. That damn piano, the piano that William would practice on every Tuesday and Sunday after services.

William broke through the doors onto Nostrand Avenue, running as fast as he could toward home, but he didn't go there. He stopped running when he reached the handball court only to walk quickly through the park and playground of Marcy Houses, where he tried to erase the memory of that event, and lose the dirty, smelling stench of the pastor that stained the insides of his nostrils. He tried to make sense of the attack, but the more he gave it thought, the faster his head would spin.

He jumped the turnstile of the Marcy and Myrtle Avenue G line and walked toward the front. As the train came rolling in, he walked to the edge of the platform and stared into the lights of the oncoming train, and leaned forward as the deadlights came upon him.

"Get out the way, you damn fool!" the motorman shouted as he applied the brakes. His heart tried to beat through his chest because he knew the train was not going to stop in time, and he closed his eyes, so he wouldn't witness the decapitation of this young boy's head.

At the last possible moment, William blinked, breaking the spell of the deadlights, and leaned backward, leaving him to fight the air-current, which tried to suck him back into the speeding train. A hand pulled him back when the tip of his nose brushed against the iron horse.

"What are you trying to do? Kill yourself?" the middle-aged woman said.

William turned away from her without saying a word, ran out of the station, and home where he never uttered a word to his parents, but received a beating for coming in late.

"William, let it go," the teary eyed Yvonne said while she continued to peer into his pain, and watched a skinny, four-foot William poring detergent and bleach into his bath water, attempting to scrub that man's body odor off him.

"At least release him from damnation. You must leave this to our Father."

"Frankly, Yvonne, I feel to release him is to forgive him, and…and I'm afraid if I do that, God's punishment would not meet my satisfaction for retribution."

"William, do you understand what it is you're saying?"

"Eve, let's cut the shit. As long as I bind him, he can't repent, and he can't mend his soul. If I release him, what satisfaction will I have received? Even Satan can give up his quest right this minute, repent and in time, his grace will be restored. We both know that."

"Yes, this is true. And as you already know your curse has prevented that for this man. Hasn't he suffered long enough? It's been more than thirty years."

"And for what? The shit he did to me and the other twenty-eight boys should weigh heavy on his soul for him to feel remorse. The shit he did to me could have had a real negative affect on me. How many kids recovered from this type of violence? Were you and I spared from the lingering tremors because of who we are, or what we are? How many nights did you wake up in a cold sweat? You were a flat-chested, thirteen-year-old girl, but eight months later after that night when your friend's father lift your T-shirt and sucked on your tiny nipples, you grew into B-cups. Have you forgiven him?"

"I…I—"

"I'm not finished. What about the time you were raped by those dikes in the girl's bathroom of Maxwell High School, when it was an all-girls school? To this day, you refuse to believe that anything happened because you blacked out. Remember? Or how about the time when you was sixteen and Bobby raped you—"

"Stop It!"

"He was a grown ass man, approaching thirty! Did all that have an effect on you in some way? Just because you didn't turn to prostitution doesn't mean it didn't suppress a part of you, or killed a part of you. I think that's why you hide your sexuality, your freaky side. I was molested by both sexes several times before I was ten. I'm lucky I'm not gay, but did it have an effect on me? Who knows, maybe that's the reason why I fucked every slit that looked moist and wet? Maybe I've been trying to convince myself of something."

"Are you finished?"

"No. Answer the question. Have you forgiven them?"

"Yes."

"You're a bigger man than I am, because all those motherfuckers who crossed me, and who crossed you, and that piss-ass preacher, will suffer my wrath, which hell cannot match, till I see it fit to release them, and that's never."

"Feel better now?" She felt the tension ease. She knew William had never mentioned his molestations to anyone but her. She knew he was never given the chance to express his anger, or to vent so he could release those demons that held him captive.

"Yes. Yes I do."

"Good. That's good. Sometimes we have to let the madness out to make room for all that our Father has made *good*."

William looked at her, grinned, and shook his head. "You know, you are becoming a pain in my ass."

Yvonne smiled. "Oh? Although I'm a bigger man than you, I have such a little thing." She walked up to him. "Maybe you should listen to that tape you have about bitterness. I think you may truly begin to understand and live for the answers to your questions."

"And which questions might they be? The ones you keep dangling over my head to make me submit to you?"

"How deep is deep, William? We're here for a purpose, not for our convenience."

"Yeah, I know, to save mankind."

"No, William. That's not our purpose, and it's not yours. You've mistranslated your visions, but it is my purpose to teach and to prepare you and the others to come into your own, or send you home."

"Prepare me? Prepare me for what?"

"I have to prepare you, and the others to fulfill our Lord's prophecy."

"What prophecy, Yvonne?"

"Soon, William. Not now, not today, and not tomorrow, but soon."

"And you want me to forgive, and I don't get to know why?"

"I'll tell you this much. You have to forgive so you can get to 'Go', and be eligible to start the next round."

"Damn! You sound just like me."

"Yeah, well we've been together a long time."

"Yeah, you're right. A quarter century."

"You didn't have to put it that way." They laughed. "Once you do this, forgiving the others will come much easier."

"Ah! Shit! Don't you give up?"

"I'm here as a woman. Am I supposed to?"

# Daddy's Kind of Love

## Sunday

The morning started off like all the others for the last couple of months, hot and hazy. The heat wave refused to break. The summer had already been marked the hottest recorded summer ever.

It was 8:20 a.m., Maria prepared breakfast for the family that would be raising from rest hungry in about another hour, but Yvonne was already up and pacing on the baloney outside her bedroom.

The air was thick, full of tension, and just felt damn creepy. She knew this was a day where accounts was going to be settled, and the devil would be coming for those he laid claim to, Jehovah could come pick up the pieces of the innocent ones if he liked.

She tried to reach out to William, to feel him in any capacity possible, but she could not, so she reached out to those of her kind. Many of them were still recovering from William's night of blinded rage.

She called upon them to be vigilant of William and Joann's comings and goings. They must be protected at all cost.

## 8:43 a.m.

"Have you located him yet?" the raspy voice bellowed.

"I'm sitting on top of him now. I'm just waiting for the right moment to close the deal."

"Wonderful. How did you find him?"

"I staked out the wife, and she led me to him. They met in some church parking lot and chatted for a while. I followed him back to the Marriott Hotel, downtown on Jay Street…"

"I wished you would have called me, I would have told you to take them both out."

"You know how I feel about taking down women…"

"I don't give a damn how you feel, but this one is mine. We shared too much together for me to cheat her out a proper disposal."

"I'll do it for another five stacks, but it's your dime…"

"I said she's mine, you just get the job done today."

"I got this, boss."

### 8:52 a.m.

"You shouldn't have followed me here, Jerome."

"Don't be so self-absorbed. I'm not here for you, Andrea. I come to accept the fact that I've been no more than a pawn in your little game. There are more important things that need attending to then just our marriage…"

"Jerome, stay away from, William. He's dangerous…"

"I'm dangerous, Andrea, and it's about time you recognized that."

"I'm in no condition to argue with you, Jerome. Please, I beg of you to walk away."

Jerome doesn't feel like walking away. As much as he blames her for their failed marriage, he can't help but blame himself for letting it get to where it was. He loved his wife and only wanted the best for her, but he couldn't compete with her powers, and he couldn't erase the memory of William.

He understood the moment he left Texas he would not be returning. He figured he'd end up locked behind bars for ridding the Earth of William, the anti-Christ.

"I know you love him, Drea, and now I understand that when you enlisted into the service that you was running from something, or someone, but my love for you blinded me from first helping you resolve your issues, before marring you... I was full of sinful lust and all I wanted was you. I didn't care if you had unresolved issues..."

"Jerome, I've been so unfair to you. I never gave you any children. I've always opposed you, and criticize your faith. I feel I have cheated you out of so much, that it would be best to let you go and find someone more deserving and willing to fulfill your needs."

"Like I said, you were all I ever wanted, and for that sin, I am paying the price. Good-bye, Drea..." He stood, walked to the door, paused, and without looking back, he walked through it.

### 8:58 a.m.

"Okay, Hun, I'll meet you at services..." She leaned down to kiss her husband.

"I don't understand why you have to run over to your sister's now, and again after services?"

"Because she needs the help..."

"I thought you said Jonathan was home with her?"

"Yes, but he's leaving to go see, William..."

"William? Why she messing with that guy again?"

She kissed him on the forehead. "I don't know, babe. Some people just have to get it out of their system, like I could never let you go. I would be your stalker..."

"Oh? I would hire security to handle that little problem..."

"I don't think so, babe."

"And why not?"

"You stay broke too much to afford security."

"Oh, you got jokes..."

She kissed him once more, this time upon his lips. "I'll see you at eleven. Make sure the kids put on what I've left them, and don't buy them anything to eat."

"Yeah, yeah. Go."

Mary made her way to her car only to find two flat tires on the driver's side, which made her furious. "Damn kids got too much time on their hands, the little vandals."

She reached into her purse, searched for her cell phone, which took a minute to locate, then called her husband.

"Hello..."

"Yeah, Hun, you won't believe this, but I got two flat tires..."

"Two? So what you wanna do, take my car and come back for us?"

She spotted a livery cab slowly approaching her. "No. I'll take a cab there and catch up with you at church... Taxi!" She haled the livery cab.

"Okay do that and I'll get someone to come fix the flats. Everything else is good, no broken windows?"

"No just the tires. Okay, I'm getting in a cab now. Love you, Hun."

"Love you, too, bye."

**9:12 a.m.**

Three young men entered the library of the Green Hill Correctional Facility. They walked over to a table where a young man sat alone, studying geometry from an old and half-adequate G.E.D manual.

One of the men tossed a book titled *The Book of Lilith* authored by Barbara Black Koltuv. The young man stared at the book in bewilderment. The three men took seats around him. The black man sat across from him, while the white man sat on his right side, and the oriental man sat on his left. The young man never saw these characters before, and he didn't feel easy about their presence, nor the reason for the book.

"Did you know that your very first grandmother was famous, and one hellish bitch?" said the black man.

The young man did not respond. He didn't know what to say, nor did he understand the question.

"In fact, most of the first born women in your bloodline are some wicket little bitches. But your mother, she is a very special bitch, much like your very first grandmamma. You probably don't know this, but that bitch is so old, she was here long before time recorded—"

"Look, I don' t know what all this is about, but I—"

"This is about your whore mother. She'd chose to follow him and give you up to be adopted. But don't feel any despair, your new mommy, Keisha will take damn good care of your ass, and I mean that literally, Raymond Garcia."

The black man let out a wicked laugh, and then the other two men began hacking at his body with their shanks.

Blood splattered and splotched in a twenty-foot radius, sending everyone out into the corridor, while the alarms blasted throughout that wing.

They ripped pieces of fabric from his blood-soaked clothing, which was riddled with holes, just like his body. They soaked the fabric pieces in his blood and began to write, "William, William,

William," about the library walls before being overpowered by a rush of correctional officers.

### 9:23 a.m.

The livery cab came to a halt outside of Joann's building. "How much would that be?" Mary asked, knowing it should cost her no more than twenty dollars.

"You're receiving the special today, ma'am. It's gonna cost you, your life..."

Their eyes met in the rear view mirror. Fear numbed her body. Surly she didn't hear what she thought she heard.

"I'm sorry, how much did you say?"

The sound of the door locks clicking t was the only reply.

Her eyes widened, followed by her scream as she saw the blade of the hatchet come over the front seat, toward her.

Blood splatted across the back windows and spilled onto the seat. A puddle of blood began to form on the rear seat where her head rested.

The driver got out the car, opened the backdoor, laid the body down on the backseat, climbed in, undressed the corpse, pulled out his penis, and fucked it up the rectum until he nearly drained the body of all its blood. Once he was satisfied, he pushed a piece of paper—with the letter F written on it—into her rectum.

He finalized his presence by stepping outside and walking to the rear of the car with her bra and head in hand, using her head as an inkwell, and with her blood, he wrote the word—WILLIAM—on the hood of the trunk, and used the head as an ornament.

**11:34 a.m.**

Jonathan arrived earlier than expected. William was on the phone with Jenney. He cut the call short and attended to the young man he fathered the first two years of his life.

William took hold of him moments after he passed through Joann's birth canal and into the world. William fed him and changed his pampers, and played with him in the parks. He bought him baby formula, toys, a baseball glove, and clothes. Taught him how to throw a ball, helped him walk, and say his ABCs and 123s. He was called Daddy and he called the boy son.

"How was this week in day camp?"

"It was fine. We went to the Bronx Zoo, and the Natural Museum of Art, this week."

"Wow, sounds like you had a busy week. Was it fun?" William asked while putting on his shoes.

"It was okay. I have been to the Bronx Zoo a few times already."

"Has it become boring to you?"

"No. I just don't get excited anymore, that's all."

"So what excites you these days? What do you wanna be when you grow up?"

"I want to become a doctor. I want to find a cure for cancer, so all the pain and suffering will end."

"Wow. Are you up for the challenge?"

"I'm ready. I know the cure is out there. God has provided us everything we need to fix and repair our earthly bodies. The secret is in the ground, somewhere…"

"In the ground, why in the ground?"

"Because everything originated from the ground; it contains everything to create, build, and destroy."

"You're too smart to be so young; I have no doubt that you will find the secrets that have eluded us for so long. Come on, let's go."

"Can I get some Jordan's?"

"Well, I actually think the man has enough money, and he can do without mine, but it's your day, whatever you want."

"Yes!"

They made their way down to the lobby and out onto the busy street, and were quickly spotted by Robert's hit man, who screwed a silencer onto his 9mm Glock, and hopped out the car, placing the weapon in his waistband behind his back under his shirt.

He kept a good distance behind them to avoid being noticed. He had been in this position once before. He had William dead in his sight, but something went wrong. William was shot a slit second before him when he pulled the trigger. The paper offered up little information about that event that night, but he was determined to complete his objective this time. He wasn't sure how many lives William had, but he planned to put enough bullets into him to kill them all.

Fifty minutes and eight hundred and sixty dollars into the shopping spree, they stopped at a frank cart for a quick meal of hot dogs outside of Macy's on Fulton Street, and as faith would have it, they were spotted by Jerome and his Army buddy, Roe, from across the street.

"Is that your pigeon down the street there, standing at that frank cart with that little boy, at two o'clock?"

Jerome turned and looked in the direction his friend indicated. "I think so… Yeah, yeah that's him. You got that piece?"

"Yeah, but I can't hand it to you out here in the open."

"Slip it into that bag with your wife's dress and hand it to me."

"Not my wife's dress…"

"I don't want your wife's dress, I just want the piece."

He placed the weapon in the bag and extended it. "You gonna shoot this guy in broad daylight? This place is laced with cops everywhere, you'll never get away with it, and they will shoot you dead—"

"None of that matters now." He grabbed the bag, withdrew the dress and handed it to his friend.

"Let me get the receipt, just in case it doesn't fit."

Jerome reached into the bag and fumbled for the receipt, and handed it to his friend.

"You sure about this, Jerome?"

"It's not my choice, but it is my destiny. It's been an honor." They embraced each other for what seemed to be there last few moments together.

William and Jonathan left the frank car and walked in the direction of Vim's.

"Can I ask you a question?"

"Yes, future doctor, you can ask me anything."

"Promise not to get angry."

They stopped. "Whoa, is it that serious?"

"Yes. And you have to promise not to tell Ma."

"Okay, it's a deal. Speak what's on your mind?"

"I know you're my dad and everything, but do you know where my real father is? Ma said he's with his real family and don't care about us, but if you know where he is can you take me to see him?"

The question left William speechless. He was not prepared for this. He never, ever gave thought to Jonathan's biological father, until this moment, which was a mistake.

They made eye contact. Jonathan locked in on the blue flame he saw deep in the center of William's eyes, then he saw his father chasing behind his mother in a rage.

She jumped into an awaiting car, and William jumped out pointing a gun. His father stopped in his tracks, but told William he was a dead man, and he stepped backwards, promising to repay William for interfering and for being a part of Joann's little plan to disfigure his wife.

Then he watched some men telling William that a man in a dark, navy blue Buick was driving around Pink Houses looking for him. William knew who this was, and made the decision to fix this problem.

Jonathan saw his father begging for his life. "Come on, Will, please, you don't have to do this…"

"No! Motherfucker you came looking for me. You got this thirty-two in your pocket, and you're trying to tell me what?"

"It's not what you think, man. I would never do that to you, William. Honest, my brother, I wouldn't do that…"

"So what's the gun for? Tell me why the fuck you carrying a piece and looking for me?"

"I just wanted to scare you, man, that's all, that's all…"

"And that was a mistake…" William pulled the trigger twice. The man fell flat with blood oozing from the two bullet holes in his head. William stood over him and released one more for good measure.

Jonathan dropped his can of soda and frank while backing away from William.

"Jonathan let me explain…"

Jerome withdrew the weapon from the plastic bag, and moved quickly toward William and Jonathan.

Jonathan took off running down Albee Square. As William dropped his soda and sausage to give chase, he heard a shot ring out, and felt the heat of the bullet as it passed by him. He looked in the direction from where the shot came from and recognized the man holding the nine-millimeter.

"Don't run now, motherfucker. Talk about my mama now, bitch," said the young man from Brooklyn's lockup, who William had an argument with, then he squeezed off two more shots.

William raced down the street after Jonathan. "Jonathan, get behind the cars! Jonathan!"

Jerome raised his gun and took aim at William's back.

For three seconds the frightful sound of gunfire filled the air. Women, children, and men were running and screaming during the moment of pandemonium.

William's bodyguards who were shadowing him had neutralized all threats, but not before the damage was done. Agents secured the inmate's lifeless body. Other agents secured the wounded Jerome, while others raced to the wounded William, who was crawling to his wounded stepchild, Jonathan.

"Call for a wagon for the injured!" the agent shouted to his partner just before briefing agent Donovan. "Yeah, Donny, it's bad. We have two suspects down, one wounded and the other dead. We have multiple injured in crossfire, and William and the child's been hit, also. I'm not sure if they will survive..."

# Through the Fire

*D*ressed in black attire, she wept in the front pew. Her pain was unbearable, her tears burned the sides of her face, and her spirit was numb. The loss of life was so depressing, incomprehensible, and was not consoling for all those who attended the services. If this was someone's evil plan to tear her to pieces, then they succeeded in breaking her. No one knew if she would ever recover; she felt there was no reason to carry on. How could God have forsaken her? How could he allow such wickedness to come and devastate an entire family—two generations wiped out in one day? But let it be known, Hell will have no fury, like this woman scorned. The world will pay for this; everyone who breathes will pay and suffer her pain. Even with all the love she has for William, not even his darling little angels will be spared from her quench for vengeance, for the bitterness that churned in the pit of her stomach will sour and cause a hatred unbelievable toward mankind, even though she knew the reason for her loss was for her love and her choice to remain in alliance with William.

The church was filled beyond its capacity with family, friends, and well-wishers. The atmosphere was filled with sadness and the sounds of sobbing, but time seemed to have stopped and all went silent when William walked down the center aisle. He was unknown to most, and unwanted by those who knew little of him.

Mrs. Garcia, the woman who nearly killed her firstborn weeks ago was allowed to grieve with her family, shouted slurs, insults, and demanded that he leave. Joann stood up and shouted back at her mother, and all those who sided with her, in William's defense.

Men jumped from their seats and out into the aisle to block William's path, but with a gesture of his hand he parted them and held them in their places. He reached the front. Joann stepped up from her seat.

"Stop, William."

He complied.

"Please leave us. You are not welcome here..."

"Joann, I—"

"No, William. No more. No more pain, William. I can't take any more pain. The cost for loving you is just too high. It's too painful. I have nothing else to sacrifice. It hurts to love you and I'm so tired of the pain. Go! Just go away."

William stood his ground.

"I said leave!" She pointed to the doors in the rear.

William turned to leave the church.

In agony, Joann watched, but stood firm. "You cost me everything I love, and all those who loved me, for me. Why does it have to hurt to love you?"

With his eyes staring forward, and pride in his voice, he answered. "Because pain just seems to embrace me and everyone who's a part of me. There can be no love, if there is no pain."

Moments after William exited the church, a loud grunt filled the sanctuary, which caused the church to rumble, and was followed by a burst of wind, which tossed flowers, Bibles, and children about the church, throwing the three caskets onto the floor, and caused all three bodies to spill before Joann's feet.

William walked away from the church, hurt, ashamed and disappointed. He didn't understand why these people or his loved ones had to die for him. Who the fuck was he, what was he, and why did he have to forgive a fucking child molesting preacher? God was asking for too much.

◆ ◆ ◆

Agent Donovan reclined in the leather chair, as he spoke into the phone's receiver. "I can't explain all the shit that's going on with this man. It's not the Chinese, or the Russians, or the Iranians; it's his fucking past finally catching up with him. There's no other way to explain it…" He listened. "And how do you suggest we eliminate this problem? I see… The entire family? I see… I'll get back to you when I've put something together." He placed the receiver back on its base, swiveled his chair around to look out the window into the night and the city lights. "And may Gods help us all, because I have a bad feeling about this one."

◆ ◆ ◆

William sat behind the steering wheel of his rented Rolls Royce, hurt and confused.

"Did you think showing up here was going to turn out any other way?" Yvonne asked.

"I don't know what I expected, and I don't blame her for hating me…"

"She will never hate you. She loves you more than she loves our Father."

"Eve, those people died in my name. I wanna know what the fuck is going on?"

"What's going on? You were told what was going on. You were told this would happen. Tuatara nearly explained everything to you before I forced her to return home."

"Tuatara? You mean Grace!" He thought back to that afternoon he sat on the grass in a cemetery talking to a dark-skinned, naked dead woman...

*"We are in flesh, and that has become a serious problem."*
*"How?"*
*"It's not how, when, or why, it's from whom."*
*William looked at her puzzled. "Who?"*
*"Currently, it's you."*
*"Me? How? Why me? I love life. I love to see what man can become. I love the glory, the grace, and the spirit. How can I be the problem?"*

*"You are not our only concern as we await the opening of the book, but you have become a serious issue. You know and do not see. You speak but do not listen. As a healer, you have wounded, and as a leader, you have forsaken.*

*"Others, besides myself, have died for you, but sadly there will be more whom will die for you in order to keep you along the path. We are here to fulfill the prophecy and keep you from harm and from an untimely death..."*

"So you wanna know what's going on?"

"I asked you a fucking question."

"Can you handle the truth?"

"Speak, Eve."

"You are the Dark-One, *six-six-six and two;* you are the beginning of and the end of man."

Of One.

http://lordwilliams.net

http://www.goodreads.com/author/fans/1220402.Lord_Williams

Look for the chilling sequel:

*Petals in the Sand*

Also, look for the soon-to-be release:

*The Consequences*

A story of love, innocence, betrayal, and murder. Find out why girl loves boy, then girl finds new boy and leaves old. Old boy falls in love with new girl. New girl finally gets over her ex-boy and gives new love a try. All is well until first girl comes back to reclaim old boy and all hell breaks loose.